RAISING MYSELF:
A TEENAGER'S ODYSSEY

I0527669

Raising Myself is the memoir of a young girl who was, for the most part, her own parent. Her adolescence is molded by circumstance, class expectations, and a stubborn insistence that she can succeed. She believes in taking initiative, in pursuing answers to important questions, and in accomplishing something "worthwhile." At the age of thirteen she is out in the world, alone, and, in order to survive, she must raise herself.

It's a story of the birth of women's liberation. It's the eternal struggle between genes and environment, between what one learns as a young child, what one experiences as an adolescent and what one hears in the heartbeat propelling the directions of one's own life.

It's a twenty-first century female Tom Sawyer!

By

Carla Brooks Johnston

ISBN: 0984248927
ISBN-13: 9780984248926

Published by

PARLANCE

P.O. 39114
Cambridge, MA 02139

For

Jesse, Kelsea and Tenzin

Eric, Debbi, Elise and Keri

And for

Those with Hopes and Dreams

Also by Carla Brooks Johnston

- "Kids: do we really mean that they are precious?," <u>Island Reporter</u>, Breeze Corp., Cape Coral, FL, August 21, 2008

- <u>Screened Out: How theMedia Control Us and What We Can Do About It</u>, Armonk, N.Y.: M.E. Sharpe, 2000.

- <u>Global News Access: Impact of New Communications Technologies</u>, Westport, CT & London: Praeger, 1998.

- <u>Winning the Global TV News Game</u>, Boston and London: Butterworth-Heinemann/Focal & <u>Broadcasting & Cable</u>, 1995. (The '90s revolution in global access to news)

- "China to Korea by Ferry," <u>The New York Times</u>, New York, June 6, 1993.

- "The Press and The Electoral Process," <u>The Radcliffe Quarterly</u>, Cambridge, MA: Radcliffe College, Vol. 78 No. 2, June 1992. (Visit to Moscow: Observer at Russia's first Presidential election in 1991.)

- <u>Election Coverage: Blueprint for Broadcasters</u>, Boston and London: Butterworth-Heinemann/Focal Press, 1991.

- <u>Local Initiatives for Affordable Housing</u>, Boston: New Century Policics, 1989. (Local government's options)

- <u>Reversing the Nuclear Arms Race.</u> Cambridge, MA: Schenkman Books, 1986. Forward by Gene R. LaRocque, Rear Admiral USN (Ret.) (Influences on policy making)

- <u>Under the Interstate.</u> Boston, MA: MA Department of Community Affairs and the National Endowment for the Arts, 1975. Editor. Winner of NEA Nationwide City Options Competition. Focus: Ethnic Heritage in Immigrant City.

Table of Contents

Chapter One

Dealing with an Adult's Decisions

FOURTEEN AND GROWING UP FAST

"Keep your mouth shut!" I am given this order as an arm reaches around my neck in a stranglehold. It's dark. I'm walking home from a high school church youth group's play rehearsal.

My instinct was right; someone *is* following me.

It's not even 9 PM. Car headlights flash by on this main thoroughfare into downtown Syracuse. But the cars can't see anyone on the sidewalks. I left the rehearsal as I always do—quickly. I can't let the others know that I don't have a ride home. Everyone else has a ride. They will insist on giving me one. Actually, it's nice to be by myself sometimes. Clear air. Stars. Usually, there's no problem walking home.

But, I guess this time there is a problem. The footsteps are getting closer. Oh, God! What do I do?

"Heeeeeeeeeeeeeeeeeeelllllllllllllllllllllpppppppppppp!!!!" I scream at the top of my lungs. I'm discovering that to survive I must stand firm and speak up.

But, what if this isn't a good time to do that? Then again, maybe 'shutting up is worse?

I think to myself, that it's a good thing I'm stubborn. I screamed again!

I feel a dull thrust into my right side. I see my assailant's face. I see his hunting knife. That's all.

My scream scares him. He flees around a corner.

For a minute I'm not sure what happened. I just stand there—alone. It seems even darker now. Then I feel it—the gush of wet from my side. I'm getting woozy. I look at the wet on my hand. A dark liquid. Lots of it. It's all over—all over. "It's blood. I've been stabbed! Oh, God! I've been *stabbed*!"

That was last night. Those moments, frozen in time, run through my head again and again and again—like a broken record. I still can't quite believe it.

It's March, 1955. I'm lying in the hospital room. I can't move. It hurts too much if I try to lie on my side. My arm has tubes stuck into it. I sleep—sort of. I can't eat. But, it doesn't matter because all I got last night was Jello.

Only my eyes have legs. They move from the white walls to the white ceiling to the white bed covers to the stainless bed frame to the stainless chair to the stainless cart. There's no color here! Life needs color! The nurses and doctors come and go—all white, all muttering to each other. When they come near my bed, they switch on their fake smiles and say something dumb.

"How do you feel?"

"Awful. I want to get out of here!"

There's nothing to look at. There's nothing to read. There's no one to talk with. There's not much to do but think.

The doctor says I'm lucky to be alive. But, how did I get into this mess?

This sort of thing doesn't happen to little girls from upscale white American families. Does it?

Will I be O.K. enough to get out of here? What happens next?

Most kids have parents to ask questions to. But, I can do this. It's O.K. to figure these things out on my own; I like puzzles. How do I figure out what's best to do next?

I do have a step-father. Sort of. I wonder if he will come to visit me. It's really alright if he doesn't. He's never been helpful.

I slipped back under my covers and started trying to figure out how I could have ended up in this predicament.

A WEDDING

Probably a stranger on the street would be a better step-father than Don. How did Don, this handsome tennis player and stock broker, come into my life? Did his bachelor eyes ever look beyond my sparkling widow Mother's smile and figure to see that she had a daughter—me? Why is *he* the so-called "relative" to take care of me now?

I remembered the day that sealed the agreement to add Don to my life. It was in August 1949. Mother and Don were getting married. Grass-hoppers were jumping. One landed on my shoe. How long would it stay there? We were in a beautiful garden.

I was supposed to stand very still. Watching the grasshopper was one of the few things that were possible to do while standing very still. Those extra long legs were amazing. Sometimes I stalked grasshoppers in my yard. I'd take an open bottle, quietly slip up on one, quickly plunk the bottle down on top if it. If I caught one, I'd put some grass in the bottle, a bit of water, and put on a lid—with holes of course. I watch it eat a leaf through the bottle wall. At the end of the day, I let it go.

Unfortunately I couldn't catch this grasshopper—not with white gloves. I was very dressed up, even new shoes. I was nine and one-half. I stood next to my Mother in the Close's back yard. Charlie Close is a Judge and he performed the wedding ceremony. He and Mother had been friends since they were in college. He used to take her ice skating. That was nearly twenty years ago. They'd have been a dashing couple on an ice rink. Mother was a good figure skater, agile, petit and graceful. On this day, Charlie's wife, Gladys, had prepared a table of refreshments for us to eat—if we ever got to move around. I learned much later that Charlie was the person Mother trusted—more than Don, fortunately for me.

For the onlooker, the wedding was a quiet garden party of about twenty upper middle class professionals and their friends. The groom, also a widower, once had a lovely home across from the Country Club where he'd been tennis coach since returning from his duties as an Air Force Major sitting out World War II in the Pentagon. The bride—my Mother—was an artist, a university professor, a widow. Both were in their 40s.

That wedding scene six years ago wasn't all that it appeared to be. Perhaps that was the source of my problems?

A sad story lay beneath the visible image of happiness, affluence and well-being.

Mother had been a single parent for eight years. During this time, it had been a constant struggle to hold on to her self-respect, her career, her family's status, and—mostly—to keep the family viable. The family? That was Mother and me. Now Don is here. He and Mother enjoyed each other's company.

They even had the same birthday. But I sensed that it wasn't just about love. I can't explain it—even now. Mother had always been so independent, so much the artist, such a careful planner of every essential. In contrast, Don seems not to take anything very seriously.

An attractive woman would catch his eye. He takes that very seriously! It gives him much pleasure. He likes his pleasure. As near as I can tell, that's all he likes.

Mother looked stunning on her wedding day. She was a petit 5'2" tall; her widow's peak punctuated the wavy brown hair. Her broad brimmed straw hat framed her face. I'll not forget her clear blue eyes and the smile that—when flashed—could melt anyone in sight. Her blue silk dress with the flowing calf length skirt shimmered in the breeze. The dress was the same color blue as her eyes. She wore a string of real pearls and matching pearl earrings. Her white gloves matched mine.

It was a good day for costumes.

That day I imagined that I was at one of the gala events in the Renaissance paintings that Mother and I saw when we went to the Syracuse Art Museum. These paintings were part of my diet—every Saturday. The only difference between our event and the paintings was that our party was now and I knew more about the people's feelings than I could tell from an artist's brush stroke. I like the idea of knowing more than the artist's canvas can tell.

Aside from a few relatives who drove from Rochester to Syracuse for the wedding, most of the other guests were Mother's friends from the Daubers Club—the local artist's organization. Everyone wore lovely late summer outfits.

I liked the women's hats best. Before the grasshopper landed on my shoe, I studied all the hats. Some had small half veils that just covered the top of one's face, others with full face veils. They were the fine net veils that match the color of the hat. Other women had hats with wonderful feathers. One had a pheasant feather—dark multi-colors. Another had two white lacey feathers—maybe egret feathers. I loved feathers—such spectacular plumes.

Mother's artist friends had such 'pizzaz' in how they dressed. The women from Rochester were stylish too—but with less flair. I liked the flair—the dashing angle of a hat, the splash of color, or the long silk scarf draped around a neck and hanging all the way down to that woman's ankles. The men—well they all look alike in their dark suits. Thank heavens they got to wear different color neckties.

Grandma was crying. She had said something about my real dad as we were coming in. She seemed upset. Why? Maybe it's nothing. In the movies Mothers always cry at weddings.

"Do you, Helen, take Donald to be your husband," Charlie Close said.

Mother and Don kissed. Charlie Close shook hands with them. Relatives and friends started mingling.

I was near Mother's friends. I knew most of them. On Saturdays, at the museum classes, I loved to show Mother's friends my art work. They showed me how my picture would change if I used chalk, or charcoal, rather than water colors. They described how I could emphasize what I wanted something to mean just by switching from color to no color, or by switching from one medium or another. The other nice thing about the museum was the smell of turpentine.

"Look, Carla Lee, I brought you something special," Ruth Lee called. "You should have a wedding present too," she said.

I opened the wrap and found a yellow and blue pin-wheel. It turned green when I blew it. "Wow, thank you," I said.

"Whoosh," I blew again. "Look. It changes colors when it turns. It's amazing."

I was still standing with the group of artists, but already, their conversation had moved on—on to adult things.

"Did you see the Picasso exhibit in New York?" Jack asked Ruth Lee.

"Not yet, I'll go down after I return from the autumn leaf photography trip to Quebec."

Jim was talking to Ann, both professors at Syracuse University. "I really enjoyed Helen's recent exhibit of the water-colors that she painted in Nassau and Key West."

"So did I" replied Ann.

It was time for me to go. Clearly I had become invisible. Kids are invisible a lot of the time.

I slipped momentarily out of my reminiscing to open my eyes and realize that I'm trapped in this white metal hospital bed. That's a scary thought. Best to continue reconstructing what happened. Am I in this dilemma because the wedding changed everything? There's no way to know.

Back at the wedding, I wandered around the garden waiting for refreshment time. As an only child, I had a lot of practice at finding creatures other than people to communicate with. Birds played in the nearby bushes. They chattered, flew, and hid—blue jays. They're beautiful birds sitting on a branch in front of the blue sky and white puffy clouds. The clouds were fun to watch too. They just floated into the shape of one animal, then another. Too bad I couldn't lie on the grass and just look straight up at the clouds on that wedding day. Mother would not have approved. I'd have gotten grass stains on my dress. All these rules!

"Come, Carla Lee," Mother called. "Come have some cake with us."

Finally!

Mother had been busy introducing her new husband to all her friends, and posing for pictures. But she always had an eye out for me. Every little while there was a glance, a smile, a wave. She' inherited her Mother's (my grandmother's) propensity for worrying and coupled it with the double vigilance required of a single parent. A single mom could easily do three things simultaneously—watching me, earning a living, and trying to live her own life.

Charlie Close greeted me: "Nice to see you Carla Lee. You look all grown-up today. I bet you'll be a wonderful figure skater, just like your Mother."

"Thank you," I said. "I took skating lessons last winter, and this year I really hope I can skate a lot. I've learned to do a triple twirl on one foot, and to skate backwards on one foot."

"What an exciting time for you, Carla Lee," Gladys Close chimed in. "At long last you have a father—well, a step-father."

I didn't reply. I just smiled politely, and fortunately one of the adults said something to Gladys. It was not noticed that I didn't reply. I had become invisible again.

Charlie and Gladys Close were good hearted, albeit very proper. Their house was full of antiques and oriental rugs gracefully placed on perfect hard wood floors. There was lovely art on the walls. The food on the table was properly displayed on silver trays and a center piece of beautiful fresh flowers—zinnias of many colors.

I loved zinnias. I liked the strong colors. The goodies tasted wonderful. I had an extra scoop of ice cream!

I bet Charlie and Gladys Close would come to visit now if they knew that I was lying here in this hospital bed. They're only a half hour away. He'd know what I should do, too. He's a Judge. But I don't know how to find him.

Mother and Don moved away from the food table to talk with friends. I took my cake and ice cream to the yard to eat. It's always a treat to find kids at these adult gatherings. Here there were only two—the Close's boys. They were proper too—just like a judge's children should be. They were dressed in suits, and looked like they hated it.

"Hi. Want to play ball or hide-and-seek or something?" I asked.

They ignored me. So I tried again. Maybe they didn't hear.

"Hi. Want to play ball or hide-and-seek or something?"

"Well, we're busy," one of them said while sitting with his brother eating ice cream.

"I can wait. I'm not quite done with my cake either." I said.

"Oh, don't bother, we'll probably be busy all afternoon."

Boys!! I thought to myself. They were older than me, just enough older not to want to be seen playing with a girl. Someone might call them sissies.

I hated it when boys acted like this. They thought they're more important than girls were. That was dumb!! Get over it!

"Mother," I called.

"Yes?"

"Can you come over here, just for a minute?" I asked.

"I'll be right there," she said. "We're getting ready to leave now. Do you have your suitcase in the car for your weekend trip to Grandma's in Rochester?" She walked over to me.

"Yes. I'm ready. But, can I ask a question before we go? Will everything with us still be the same now? Will Don be nice to me? Will I be in his way? When we live at the new apartment, can I ride my bike? Can we still do things together?"

"Yes. Yes. Yes. You'll be fine, Carla Lee. Come along, now," Mother said. "It was nearly dark and the party was over."

I was hustled off to a cousin's car. "We'll pick you up at Grandma's on Sunday afternoon. It's a three hour drive back to Syracuse and Monday morning we move out of our apartment and into Don's apartment," Mother said. I sat in the back seat. Grandma was in the front seat with Alton, the cousin who was driving.

"Bye," I waved to Mother.

"I love you," she called to me.

"Love you too," I replied. "See you Sunday."

As I recall the weekend at grandma's passed quickly. Grandma crocheted, and talked on the phone. She and I made cookies together. We always made cookies. I spent a lot of the time in the wonderful big rocker on her splendid big front porch—eating the cookies. I loved that porch. I just love porches.

A nurse comes to my hospital bed. No time to think about grandma's cookies. She takes my pulse and writes something on the chart at the foot of my bed.

"Feeling O.K.," she asks.

"No!" I reply.

"You'll be better soon," she smiles and walks away.

"I'll see you tomorrow." The door to my room closes.

What a useless conversation, I think to myself. Why can't people really care about people and think about what helps? It's better to return to my past. And, maybe I'll get some clues about what my future might be.

FROM THE BEGINNING–NO CHANCE FOR NORMAL

"You were tiny then—just sixteen months old when your Mother's life—and yours–suddenly turned in a whole new direction," Grandma said.

When we got back to Rochester, she wanted to be sure that I knew what happened to my real daddy. It was unusual for her to talk about serious things to me. None of her (my) relatives had adult discussions around children. As the nine year old who had just been to my Mother's wedding, I knew that I was not a child. Grandma never knew that, but on this day she needed to tell me something.

"Your daddy died that day."

"He was working in the garden of your new home. You were out there with him–crawling in the grass. Your Mother was in the house. He had a heart attack and fell, right there. What a shock! I still can't get over it."

Grandma put down her dish towel and wiped her eyes. Then she continued.

"You probably won't understand, but I'm thinking about your Mother and daddy too, because of your Mother's marriage to Don. Let me tell you the rest." Grandma was breaking her usual code of silence.

Grandma had made meatloaf for dinner—the kind with onions and white bread crumbs in it. She'd fixed mashed potatoes and beans—bean's from her neighbor's garden. I snapped the ends off the beans for her. We're sitting at the kitchen table and eating. There's homemade apple pie for dessert! Grandma's house was always stocked with homemade baked goods.

"The pie is yummy, Grandma," I interrupted.

"It was in 1941. Your daddy was a young man, just 40." She reminisced.

"Those were turbulent times. World War II was coming. The Depression was barely over. Your daddy died just three months before the Japanese military attacked Pearl Harbor. The War was about to change American life. The hilarious flapper memories of your Mother's college days in the 1920s had slipped into the scrapbooks when the depression began. Soup lines throughout the 1930s were center stage for many Americans."

Grandma poured me some more milk.

"Our Rochester family was very lucky to avoid those soup lines. So when beggars came to our back doors every night, we'd give them the left-overs from dinner, or make them some new dinner."

Grandma was thin. She wore her hair in a row of turned up tight curls that ring her face and neck. It was the style for older women in the 1940s. She was intense, and always eager to help. She cared a lot and worried even more. Every dress in her wardrobe had a tailored top, a full skirt, and thousands of tiny flowers all over it. It was as if she wore her wonderful flower garden wherever she went.

"For your Mother," Grandma noted, "your daddy's death changed everything. In one second, she shifted from having been spared the depression's economic hardship to needing to find a job to pay her bills. Jobs were hard to find—especially for women."

Grandma continued. "After your daddy died, his business partner, due to the absence of legal papers defining the partnership, totally took ownership of the insurance agency that the two men had founded together. Your Mother inherited nothing but the feeling that a trusted friend had put greed before friendship. She had no income. She had to make some quick decisions."

"She dismissed your nanny, closed her art business because it didn't make enough money, sold your new house, packed up the antiques, the silver and Wedgwood china in hopes that one day she could use them again. She started sewing all the clothes to save money. Finally she found a job as a professor at her alma mater, Syracuse University. Syracuse had given her that scholarship to study in Paris and now Syracuse needed faculty because the boys were all going to war."

"Just one of the many sad pieces of this story," Grandma continued, "was that your Mother needed to move to Syracuse and could not take you with her. So she brought you to live with me until you were old enough to not need a babysitter."

"I remember the day she left you here. She was in tears. You kept asking for her every day for weeks. You lived with me for nearly five years."

"Your Mother drove a half day every Saturday from Syracuse to Rochester to see you, –every weekend during those five years. Then she drove a half day back on Sunday. When she had a holiday, she'd stay here for a few days. It was war time. Gasoline was rationed. Getting the gas to travel 100 miles each way took careful planning."

"Do you know what rationing was, Carla Lee?"

"It was when the government needed the gasoline for the war and people could only buy a very small amount each week."

I remembered riding in Mother's 1940 Chrysler. She'd always shut off the car when we could coast down hill. I never before understood why.

"That's why she shut off the car. She was saving gas." I noted.

"Sure. I remember living with you Grandma. I remember when the ice man delivered that big block of ice for your ice box every week. I wish you still had that ice box. It looked much nicer than a refrigerator does."

My mouth waters for the taste of fresh ice—fresh chips—sometimes with a little sand on them.

"Don't get so close to the truck," the ice man told us back then. "You could get hurt."

We didn't pay too much attention to him. Our objective was to scurry for the chips that came off the ice block when he pulled it from the truck. His big tongs usually would cause a few more chips to fall. The chips landed on the back floor of the truck. They landed on the back bumper and on the ground. He'd sling the ice block over his shoulder and head toward grandma's kitchen. We'd follow because more ice chips usually fell in the sand on the way up the driveway. We didn't mind the sand.

"Just use the tail of your shirt to wipe it off—quickly," my playmate said.

"Ice melts."

It was fun the day the ice man came. It was fun to see how much you could hold in your mouth at one time—fun to try to chew it without breaking a tooth.

Grandma replied to my comment about her old ice box. "I like my refrigerator. It doesn't make the mess that the ice box did."

I return from my daydream to my hospital room. You'd think I could at least get some ice here in this hospital room. They don't need to wait for an ice man anymore. I'm thirsty. It takes so long to get someone to come to my room. The present is too hard to deal with. I might as well return to sorting out how I ended up in this hospital and to figuring out what happens next.

Meanwhile, I ring the call button—again.

COMSTOCK AVENUE IS HOME–BRIEFLY

I was really excited when I was old enough to move from Grandma's to Syracuse to live with my Mother. I was 6½ in 1946 and Mother thought that I was old enough not to need a baby-sitter after school. I became a 'latch-key kid.' I wore the key to our Comstock Avenue apartment on a string around my neck. Only very big kids and very trustworthy kids got to let themselves in and out of their apartments when no adult was home. I looked forward to the responsibility.

One of the first days after I joined Mother, we went to visit Professor Ford, one of the other faculty members in the Art Department at Syracuse University.

I thought everything is perfect about my new home. But he sounded worried. I didn't understand why. I was sitting on the floor next to Mother, eating a cookie, looking at a book—and listening to the adults.

I listened much more than adults thought I did. How else could I make sense of what they said and did? Besides, there wasn't much else to do when sitting in a room with adults.

"Helen, do you really think it's all right for Carla Lee to grow up in that tough neighborhood?" That part of Comstock Avenue just isn't a good place for a proper middle class family."

Mother answered him. "I'm a widow and I have to work to pay my bills. This is the only job that lets me do what I love to do—what I am trained to do—teach art at the university. I can't afford to live anywhere else. It's been dreadful having Carla Lee not live with me for the last five years. I've missed her so. Now, she's old enough to be with me. I've looked and looked for apartments that I can afford—something with a yard and near the university. It took me a long time to find this place. I can't afford a babysitter so I need to be as close to work as possible. I don't have any relatives in Syracuse who can watch her while I work and I can't get a university teaching job in Rochester. We just have to make it work. Carla Lee's a good girl and she has a lot of common sense."

"Well, surely, you aren't going to send her to Madison School?" Professor Ford continued. "I know it's only a block from your apartment, but it's such a poor school—all those children from poor families, colored families too."

"I'm not worried about who lives there and who attends the school. I don't care how rich they are, or what color their skin is," Mother replied. "But I am worried about the academics. Madison School isn't well cared for. The teachers lack supplies, and some of the teachers aren't the best. I have petitioned the School Department to allow her to go to Thornton School. It is a good twenty-five minute walk across the park, but she can do that."

I tucked these comments away. If our neighborhood was exciting enough to make it worth talking about, it probably was a fun place to live. I'd have adventures! I liked that. And I liked that Mother thought I was big enough and trustworthy enough to live here and go to a school that is far away. Besides, I needed to figure out why Professor Ford was so critical?

Our neighborhood was also a place where there were other families like mine—families with just one parent. That was really nice; most families had two parents and I wondered if anybody else was like us. The skin color thing made no sense to me; just because the kids I played with were both colored and white, I didn't see why Professor Ford called it tough. It was just normal people doing normal things. He was right though that most of the families that had some money lived up hill. Does that matter? Why?

I did go to Thornton School. It was a long walk. There was nobody to walk with because all the kids I played with went to Madison School at the bottom of the hill. But I liked walking across the park. I watched squirrels chasing each other. I collected acorns—only the ones with perfect hats that came on and off. I painted faces on them and they had tea parties with me. These toys were better than the store toys because I could use my imagination and make them as I wished.

One day the walk across the park wasn't so nice. I learned then that bad things do happen.

I was skipping on the path through the park, stopping to pick up red maple leaves. School was out and I was on the way home.

"Got her. I'm Captain Hook," yelled a red headed boy about 11 or so as he tackled me.

"Here, Let me help," a freckled faced kid told Captain Hook.

"Leave me alone! I'm not bothering you!" I yelled at them.

I struggled to get free, but there were three of them. They tied me to a tree with a heavy piece of rope.

"You stay put," ordered Captain Hook. "We need to go back to get our pirate ship." The boys ran off.

O.K, I thought to myself. What do I do now? There's got to be a way to get out of this.

I tried to wriggle—not much wriggle room. Captain Hook and his friends tied good knots.

Maybe someone will come down the path? Maybe they'll come back, or maybe they are playing with Peter Pan. Peter Pan would rescue me. I was sure of that.

Forget the fantasy. I'd just have to get out using my own wits. A big black ant just walked from the tree inside my collar. Ugghhh, This could get scary. When I tried to move my arms the rope scratched, but—if I really pushed—I could almost get my one hand back to where the rope was tied.

Finally, my hand had the knot. Now, could one hand undo it?

It was getting dark. Mother would wonder where I was. I had at least another five to ten minutes of park to cross before I got to the real street. My fingers maneuvered through the rope until I felt it move, just tiny bit. Ah, I thought to myself. I'd figured it out. I just needed to keep working this spot until I could really loosen it.

At last! I could wiggle down under the rope. I set myself free! I brushed myself off, and shook to get the ants off. It was really dark now. I hoped those boys wouldn't come again. I ran. Fast. There was my street. I was home.

"Hi, you're late," Mother said. She was surprised to be home before I am, and not pleased. "Where were you?"

"Nowhere," I said. I kept my adventure to myself. Mother would only worry if I told her. What good would that do anyway? Besides, I was pleased that I was actually able to get out of that mess—all by myself. Yep—soon I'd be nine and nearly grown.

Except for that day, the park was O.K.

My books at school told me the same sort of thing Professor Ford told Mother when we first moved to Comstock Avenue. We read about Dick and Jane. We were told that that's what 'good' families were like. Good families had two children and two parents. And everyone in a 'good' Dick and Jane family had white skin and lived in a whole house, not an apartment.

Why does everyone say that ideal families aren't like mine? My 'family' is just fine! Mother and I are a family. We were happy.

Did I get stabbed because I'm not part of a Dick and Jane family?

Did I get stabbed because I lived with my grandma when I was little? Because I lived in an apartment rather than a house?

Well, you know, I don't care what people say, I liked living on Comstock Avenue. I liked my family. And it's wrong to say that some people aren't as good as others!

"Here's some crushed ice for you," a nurse says. "I can't give you more liquid than that just yet."

"My side really hurts. And I can't turn over," I tell the nurse.

"You just try to get some rest now. The doctor will come tomorrow morning." She left.

Chapter Two

What If There Is No Dick and Jane Family?

MOVING AWAY

It's dark. There are muffled noises down the hall. Nothing is audible here. That strong antiseptic hospital smell is inescapable. It could make a person even sicker than they already are. All I can do is scrunch into the pillow and make my mind return to thinking through this story. Mother had a new husband and we had to move into his apartment. That was in 1949, a whole six years ago now. But it must have mattered, because I remember all the details—clearly.

"Mother, I don't want to move," I said the day that we moved. "I like it here. I like going to campus with you. I like my school."

"Are you sure things will be the same?" I asked her. The stories I read and movies I saw, all had "Dick and Jane families" doing only what the husband wanted to do. Wives and children didn't seem have any opinions of their own. I knew that Mother and I both had opinions!

"Maybe your career won't matter to Don. Maybe you'll stop being happy. Maybe I won't grow up to have a career. Maybe….."

Mother interrupted. "You'll be fine at Don's apartment. You'll have a whole bedroom all to yourself for the first time."

I wonder if she believed what she was saying? She stayed focused on moving. Maybe she didn't see how anxious I really was. Once again, nobody listens to little kids. I should know that by now. But, then, sometimes it didn't seem like I should really tell her my thoughts.

"Come now, we have to get the last of these boxes down stairs."

Our big corner house, 116 Comstock Avenue, was like a mansion in a haunted house movie. It was very tall, and had a round cupola on the top front corner. Lots of starlings flew around the cupola. Once it was a real mansion—not a house with lots of little apartments like it is now. Now, it is old.

I guess old isn't supposed to be as good as new. The houses at the top of the hill are all newer. That's where we go when we visit university friends.

I like old. Old has lots of stories that can't be found in places that are new.

Mother and I lived in a two-room apartment on the top floor of this old Victorian house.

"Here, you put your violin in the car," Mother said to me. "I've arranged to bring you back to the university from our new apartment to continue your lessons with Professor Zazorsky. Isn't that wonderful?"

"Sure, Mother." I picked up the violin—secretly wishing it would fall down the stairs and break so I wouldn't have to practice any more. When will she understand that I just can't play it. I've tried. It's been three years of weekly lessons and a teeth-clenching half hour a day of hearing the awful noise that I make. I simply don't know how some people make beautiful music from this instrument. I wish I could. But I can't. All I get are sore wrists from twisting them into proper position. I know Mother's disappointed, but I just can't learn to play the violin!

"I can take this box, too," I told her as I picked up a second parcel. I started down the three flights of stairs to the curb. This time I walked. Usually I slid down the banister. The great wide banister that curved was great for sliding down. Down was fast! Do you know what fun that was? And each of the landings had beautiful stained glass windows—just like the one in our apartment! When sliding the banister I passed spots of light made by reflections of the sunshine coming through these windows. It was spectacular. There'd never be another house like this one.

I took the box and the violin to the curb and put them in Mother's 1948 Plymouth.

Slowly, I started back into the house and up for the next load. Our house had a huge round porch. Porches were wonderful. I liked playing on the porch—out of the rain, yet outside. What could replace the fresh smell of rain mingled with the smell of grass and mock orange or lilacs. The front door was massive—heavy dark wood. In the main vestibule before climbing the stairs, I ran my fingers through the crevices of the carvings in the fancy woodwork. I liked the feel of it. I liked the idea that people long ago cared enough to make all those special things to look at and to feel—beautiful decorations.

This moving day, I took one last look at the big chandelier in the front hall. It was huge. It was also very dusty and not all the bulbs lit up. I always liked to imagine who had walked on these highly polished oak floors in earlier years. Who put the chandelier up? How long ago did people stop dusting it? I climbed up, and up, back to our apartment.

"Just one more load," Mother said. "Then this chapter is history." I couldn't tell if she was sad like I was. Mother always put on a smiley face when she talked with me.

I walked through the apartment—one last time. There were only two rooms with a bathroom in between. So many memories. I slept on a pull-out day bed at one end of the big kitchen. Mother slept on a sofa bed in the living room. Mother baked a lot, and my bed was delightfully close to the stove and the wonderful smells of newly baked cakes and cookies! I liked being there, because after I went to bed, I could still watch what was going on—and maybe get one more cookie.

Mother's bedroom doubled as living room, and art studio. She kept a big easel at one end. The center window over the front of the house was a beautiful stained glass window. It was unique. Most windows weren't round. All the other windows were big and let in lots of light, (and cold wind). Living here was like living in the treetops. We were eye level with the birds!

The bathroom had a crack under the door. During the War, when the sirens called for a black-out, Mother and I went into the bathroom. People were afraid the Nazis would bomb American cities. Mother tried to pretend it wasn't scary. She would put a rug over the crack at the bottom of the door so no light could escape. I guess that rug kept Hitler out of our bathroom. We sat there—on the toilet lid, or on the floor. Mother read me stories. Sometimes we were in the bathroom for hours before they sounded an 'all-clear.' Local air raid wardens kept a watch on all this—to make sure that no one had lights on in their apartment. They called this civil defense.

I didn't know much about Nazis; but I knew that they were very bad. I could tell from the expression on Mother's face when she huddled by the radio to hear what Walter Winchell and Edward R. Murrow had to report. I could tell from the terrible pictures in the newspapers, and the newsreels in the movie theater before a movie would start. I wanted everybody to be safe from Nazis—safe from war. In the movie theater news reels, war looked like people shooting each other, people slogging through mud dripping in blood and carrying dead people. But in our bathroom, we were safe!

"Mother, how can we leave such a nice apartment? How can we leave all the things we remember?"

"It's OK. You'll bring the memories with you. And, you never know—you might find a new place nicer than the old one."

"That can't be," I said as I slowly trooped downstairs with the last box. Mother stayed behind to sweep up.

GIRL WINS SCHOLARSHIP

I wish Mother were here now—visiting me in this hospital room! Maybe, if she were here I wouldn't be in this mess.

My Mother was special. I loved her being a professor. It was uncommon in 1949 and it's still uncommon. Here in this hospital, some of the nurses are probably Mothers. But even now, in 1955, not too many Mothers are professors. Most Mothers just stay home, do dishes, mop floors, and mix the margarine from that orange pill in the center of the plastic package of white stuff. My bed is in the hospital that is part of Syracuse University, Mother's school.

I smiled as I remembered one visit to the university. It was the day Mother took me to see her painting hanging in the lobby of one of the lecture halls.

"See, Carla Lee. It's that big oil painting straight ahead. It's *Monsieur Seriziat*—a copy of the original by Jacques-Louis David. The university sent me to Paris to paint it in 1926."

"You painted that?"

The 4' by 6' oil painting seemed huge, and commanding. *Monsieur Seriziat* looked down on us from his place way up there on the wall.

She nodded.

"And it's hanging here in this big building? A person can just do something that important—just by deciding to do it?" I was impressed—not so much by the painting, but by the idea that one person could do something that made a difference— something a whole university decided was important enough to hang in one of their main buildings. I hope I can do things that are worthwhile.

"I'll tell you all about it later when you are older," Mother said. Neither of us had any idea then that 'later' would never come.

Mother had taken me there because, while packing to move, she had found the newspaper article about when she went to Paris. The article in the Syracuse newspaper in 1926 was headed with — "Girl Also Wins Scholarship." The 'girl' was my Mother.

I asked her about it. "Why isn't your name on the headline, like the man's name is? You both won scholarships."

"That's just not the way they did it, Carla Lee."

"And why did they call him a 'man' and you a 'girl'? You're both the same age. Yesterday, in English class, the teacher said that boys and girls complement each other, but that when talking about people over eighteen, we should call them men or women. The English isn't right in the newspaper. Can a newspaper make a mistake?" I asked.

"You're right that the correct English would have been to call him a man and me a woman. But it's hard to change the way people do these things. I'm glad you see what's correct, Carla Lee. Maybe one day things will be fair." Mother had decided to move on to things that she might be able to influence—like completing the packing of our belongings.

Mother told me what happened after her year in Paris. She lived in New York City where she met my daddy. He had moved to New York City from Miami where the hurricane of 1926 had destroyed everything. They later moved to Mother's home in Rochester and got married. From the pictures I'd seen, daddy was tall, handsome and well dressed. He always wore those wide-brimmed 1930's panama straw hats. People who knew him tell me that he was very kind hearted and thoughtful.

"Look, there's your picture in another newspaper in that box on your desk," I called to Mother.

"What is it?"

"You're all dressed up in a long skirt and a very big hat and you're in a chorus line of five dancers." I was amazed.

"That picture was in the campus newspaper when I was a student. That was before I went to Europe and before I married your daddy. Those were exciting times—the mid-1920s. We were flappers. It was the first time it was considered acceptable for women to cut their hair short. And, in 1920 women got to vote for the first time. By 1924, I was old enough to vote for president. It was wonderful to feel that I mattered when important things were decided," Mother said. "This picture was taken about the same time. We were dancing the Charleston."

"Show me how to do the Charleston," I had asked.

I laugh to myself as I remember how we stumbled around the living room floor stopping to sit on packing boxes. It's fun to remember the good times.

"You'll get better at this," Mother told me.

REMEMBERING THAT "ALL THE WORLD'S A STAGE"

One more thing I would miss when we moved to Don's apartment was living near the university's winter snow sculpture. Every year they had a competition. It lasted for a wonderful week—and I could walk to the sororities and fraternities from our apartment. The best year for the snow festival was the last year we lived on Comstock Avenue.

There was the sculpture portraying Shakespeare's *As You Like It*. The students made a snow globe sliced to have a stage in it. They posted above it the Shakespeare quote: "All the world's a stage, and all the men and women merely players; they have their exits and their entrances And one man in his time plays many parts."

"Look, it's an invitation," I said to my playmates.

We climbed onto this giant snow stage. We just knew that it was our moment to set the direction for the world! That was a wonderful feeling.

We took turns acting out different skits of ourselves on the world's stage.

"Look, everyone in the whole world has TV," shouted one of our group of kids. "We can see what's going on everywhere. We can hear everybody's music. They can hear our music. Everybody can see us too."

"Hey, everyone," another girl says. "Let's dance and sing."

We did.

"I'm in India. I think I'll turn my big scarf into one of those beautiful saris that Indian ladies wear," another kid fantasized. "Carla Lee, show us how your Mother's student from India wears her sari."

I used my winter scarf to demonstrate. I liked the fact that someone I know is from India, from the total other side of the globe. Indians have dark skin. They are Hindus, sometimes Muslims. They wear beautiful clothes.

"I'm in Lapland. We studied that in school last week," another kid proclaimed. "Let's all pretend we have reindeer." We galloped around the ice stage riding on or herding our pretend reindeer.

"Let's go to China," I said. Do you think if I don't eat my dinner, I can really send it straight through the earth to starving people in China?" I asked. "That's what my grandma said will happen.

If they really are starving, I'll send the food. That's fine with me. Besides, then I won't have to clean my plate. Let's dig to China." We all pretended to dig a hole through to China for the left over food we don't like—especially brussel sprouts.

"Good deal. That helps both the Chinese and me," I said.

"Hey—isn't this fantastic—we're in charge of today. We're in charge of the world today," my friend Kenny proclaimed. Nine was a wonderful age!

For about five minutes, the world was ours on that day. We didn't have to wait to be grown-ups to matter. All of us were important—now. This included girls, boys, white kids, black kids, poor ones and rich ones, kids from Christian families and from Jewish ones. We never noticed who was what. We just played together because we lived in the same neighborhood.

"You kids get off of there." Someone came out of the sorority house and yelled at us.

"Get out of here!"

"We worked hard to build this stage, and you're ruining it." College students rushed toward us. We were chased away.

We ran before they could catch us.

PRETENDING TO BE A DICK AND JANE FAMILY

Now that I had a step-father I guessed that I was supposed to be part of a Dick and Jane family.

Somehow that seemed like another pretend game on a different sort of stage. Maybe there are more games in the world than the ones they sell in stores and the ones like hopscotch?

A year had passed since the wedding. We settled in to the new living arrangement—Mother and me in Don's apartment—a new 'family.'

Don's apartment was on the first floor in this apartment building. I did have my own room. That was nice, but it looked out on a dark ally.

"Mother, I have to keep the shade pulled all the time. All I can see is trash cans and the next building." I complained.

She just hugged me and said it was nice that I had my own room at last.

The apartment was full of Don's stuff. Don's furniture was all blonde. There is pretty blonde wood. But this isn't that. Don's

stuff looked fake. I preferred Mother's antiques, her bright paintings and vases of fresh flowers.

Don, apparently had a wonderful home before he met Mother.
I saw it one day; really nice with a huge yard. After his first wife
died of cancer, he sold that home and moved into this apartment.
He'd been here for a few years. So, I guess he must be happy. He
never talked about his past, or what he felt—not to me anyway.

Since we moved, I had finished fifth grade at my new school
and was starting sixth grade. Mother was no longer a professor.
She was just a wife and a Mother now. She lost her teaching job
in 1949. They didn't give her tenure. The War was over. The
boys were home again and they returned to their jobs. So there
was no job for Mother.

Mother was bored staying home. I could tell. She was always
good to Don and me, and our apartment was nice. Dinner was
always on the table at the appointed time. That's what the school
books said is supposed to happen in Dick and Jane families.

She just seemed to have lost her sparkle. I saw it whenever
she and I went out to the countryside to sit in a field and paint.
Those days were like the old days. I loved it. I loved watching her
with her water colors and palette. She was alive again.

"Here, you try, Carla Lee." Mother handed me a piece of wet
water color paper. "See, this is how you blend colors. And this is
how you can make the white clouds melt into the blue sky."

"Look, I did it." I showed her. "What fun!" (Now, if I had s
set of water colors in this hospital and if I was able to get out of
bed, just think about how I could improve the walls here!)

I finished my water color landscape and showed Mother.
Somehow, I always finished before she did. That's OK. I like
what I'd painted. I set it aside to dry. Then I would run.

I loved running through the country fields—leaping over the
rocks, hiding among dried out corn stalks. I loved lying in the
tall grass. The grass was taller than me. I could see each detailed
blade, the multiple colors of green and yellow, the wild flowers—
and the clouds. No one could see me in the field, but I could see
the whole world.

I love wondering what it would be like when I grew up. I hoped that I would go to Paris, like Mother did. Will I ever be so lucky? It doesn't look like it.

Even though I'd lived for more than a year with my step-father, I hardly knew him. And he didn't know much about me. Don stayed on the sidelines. He let Mother and me work things out. He never seemed to want to know what I cared about. On rare occasions he'd try to do something together with me—sort of.

"Carla Lee, come help me polish the Nash," Don said one day. We are in front of the apartment. I am playing hopscotch on the sidewalk. I had carefully marked off the squares and numbered them so my new friend Nancy and I could count the score when we each bounced the ball and hopped from square to square. Sometimes when we finish cycling we played hopscotch.

"O.K," I replied.

Don's green 1950 Nash is longer than Mother's old car. I liked the idea that a Nash car could also turn into a big bed when you put the back seat down. Don spent a lot of time polishing his car.

Don also spent a lot of time taking care of his body. He was always sun tanned, and always wore carefully pressed clothes, and always made sure that he played tennis several times a week. And he took care of his stock portfolio—at least he frequently headed off to Loeb Rhodes where he worked as a broker.

"Here, Carla Lee. Take this soft cloth and put some of the simonize wax on it and rub it into the hood until it's gone and the hood shines."

I polished.

Cars and tennis balls just aren't as interesting as going places, or creating things, or wondering about what one sees, or talking about fixing things that are important. I thought to myself as I endured the polishing. Why do people waste time like this?

"Atta girl," Don said as I polish his Nash. "All that exercise and pretty soon you'll have a body just like the movie stars in your paper doll books. Won't that be wonderful?"

I just looked at him. I wasn't quite sure where he was going with this—or if I wanted to go there. Is this how dads acted in Dick and Jane families? How was I to know? I'm certainly no expert on dads. I guess this is how Don thought he should act toward girl kids. He didn't even notice my stare. I polished.

"I think I'll take my bike and go to the park," I said to Don when the hood was finished. "Nancy is going to meet me there in a while."

"O.K.," Don replied. "Don't forget that by 6:00 you need to come in. We'll have supper. And tomorrow is a school day."

ONONDAGA PARK

"Sure," I called as I ran to the back cellar stairway to get my bike. I rode off down the street. It was three blocks to Onondaga Park and the big elm tree where I'd wait for Nancy.

I loved sitting under that tree in the park. Onondaga Park was big and had lots of paths. It was fun to ride on those paths. There was a big lake in the center of the park. That's where Charlie Close took my Mother ice skating when they were in college. It's also where we kids longingly wish to go swimming during the summer months.

Some kids did go swimming. But any parent who knew what was going on didn't let their kid swim here now. Swimming in the lake was one way, they said, that polio was transmitted. Every summer, the whole community lived in fear of polio. It is a dreadful disease. My friend Adrian had polio. Adrian had been a perfectly normal boy. Then he was paralyzed. He was in the hospital for months.

For a moment I think about my own hospital dilemma. Will I ever get out? Will my life be changed the way Adrian's was? Or will it change some other way?

Adrian never was well again. He couldn't come back to school. He was in his bed most of the time, except when his parents lift him into a wheel chair for a short time. He had trouble eating by himself, and writing, and—for a while—he had trouble speaking. He'd spend hours on end in a thing called an iron lung. Adrian was lucky; he lived. Other kids just died. We'd hear about that when school started every September. They'd tell us who was not coming back. Scary stuff. You wouldn't think a person could get polio just from swimming.

The day I met Nancy was a fine crisp late October day. It was one of those wonderful Indian summer days when the sky is deep blue and the trees have changed the color of their leaves. It was too cold to swim, but perfect for cycling. I loved cycling.

Nancy was my new best friend. It was 1950 and we'd gone to school together for a year now and we loved the same things—even home made oatmeal raisin cookies. Her last name is Owen so she would not have sat near me in school, except that our teacher went up one row and down the next when she assigned seats. It just turned out that B for Brooks ended up in a front row seat and O for Owen had the front seat in the next row over. That's how we met. I was the new kid, as usual. She'd been at Bellevue all five years and she came from a real Dick and Jane family. She was really friendly and we spent a lot of time together.

"Hey, whatcha looking at," Nancy called as she wheeled to a stop next to me.

"Do you know this ant is carrying a crumb or something that is about three times bigger than he is? See." I pointed.

Nancy looked for a minute. "Wow! I wonder if a person can do that? I don't think so."

"I'm not sure I want to do that," I replied.

"Let's cycle around the lake."

"I'm ready," Nancy said. "I had gym class today. You did too, right? What do you think about those stupid new gym suits? We have to wear them for another whole year."

"Who would ever choose blue bloomers with snaps down the front? You have to take the whole thing off to go to the bathroom. I don't know why we can't just wear shorts and a T-shirt like the boys do," I complained.

"Let's go around the lake again," Nancy shouted as she headed off on the lake path. Neither of our bikes had gear shifts, but we went fast!

"Sure." I replied. "Nancy, what's your dad like?"

"Oh, he's just a normal dad. He takes us places on weekends. And he fixes things around the house, and he wrestles with my brother."

"Does he ever tell you that you'll have a sexy body in a few years?" I asked.

"No. Why would he do that?" Nancy replied.

We kept cycling. End of conversation. "Hmmm," I said.

We cycled around the residential streets near the park and finally came back to Bellevue Avenue—where I lived.

"Come in now. It's time for dinner. Put your bike away, Carla Lee." Mother called me.

I heard her, but I rode on for another five minutes in the neighborhood of Don's apartment. Nancy's Mother would be calling her soon, too. We always hated to have the day end. Cycling was the best fun. I felt so free with the breeze rushing through my hair. Nancy showed me all the places to go from this apartment. I liked having a friend to play with. It must be a little bit like having a brother or a sister. People with brothers or sisters are really lucky! They have somebody to talk with who knows what they are talking about, someone who understands where they are coming from. They have somebody they can count on.

I cycled past the big Catholic Church across the street from my apartment. I liked to watch the sky glow with the evening sunset. Then the light grew dim and I watched the silhouette of the birds circling the church belfry. The bells rung at 6:00, and every half hour. When they start to ring, the birds always flew away until it was quiet again.

"Good-night, Nancy," I shouted.

"Same time tomorrow?" she asked.

"Yes!" I responded. "Meet you by the same tree at 4:30."

Maybe having a good friend makes up for not having a real Dick and Jane family? Maybe a Dick and Jane family isn't all it's supposed to be anyway.

Chapter Three

What A Latch Key Kid Learns

Soon it will be breakfast time. The hospital will bustle again with white robots who glide in and out of the room. One takes my temperature. Another reads my chart. Another brings a tray. Another gives me a shot. Later today there will be 'visiting hours.' So far my only visitors have been two city cops who came to ask me a lot of questions about the identity of the person who stabbed me. One of the nurses told me that my step-father left a message saying that he and his new girlfriend decided they needed to 'get away.' They went to Florida. He'd call when he got back, I was told.

Maybe the reason I'm at this dead end in a hospital bed is because Professor Ford was right about the neighborhood my Mother had brought me to. But, I don't think so. We kids just had adventures. Kids need to have adventures in order to grow up! Could it be that it doesn't matter why I'm here, that what I end up doing next is what matters? But since there's nothing to do other than lie here, I might as well see what happens when I put the pieces of all these adventures together.

THE GARAGE KIDS

I liked being a "latch-key-kid."

I was really responsible. And I did a pretty good job at doing that right. But, I also got to see things that I might not have seen if I hadn't been a "latch-key kid."

I remembered the garage kids. Now there was adventure! I never was really part of that set, but I did get to watch. And that itself was an experience.

The last time I saw the garage kids was the day we moved to Don's apartment.

"Mother, I've got to go say good-bye to the kids down the street," I called up the stairs. "I'll meet you at the car in a few minutes."

"Don't go into that old garage," she shouted after me.

I ran off through our yard and behind the house.

Beside our house was the brick sidewalk that took one down to the bottom of the hill—or up to the university. Downhill, you'd find buildings where the paint was peeling. The garage kids hung out in one of those buildings. Down hill was preferred by all the kids because it was a place where a whole mix of kids could have some privacy. It would be really difficult to find a place like our hang-out if you went up hill.

I think Mother didn't want me to go down there because of what happened to her last year. It was winter and there had been a really heavy snow storm the night before.

We got almost to where Mother parked her car, another old garage. Mother had forgotten her umbrella. We went back to get it.

A huge crash and the thick cloud of snow startled us as we rounded the corner to return to Mother's car. "Look at that," I screamed. The roof of her garage came down under the weight of the snow. All of it. It was concrete—thick concrete. Mother's car was totaled!! Had she not gone back for the umbrella, we might have been inside the car when the roof came down. We might have been killed.

Anyway, Mother's garage catastrophe had nothing to do with the garage where the kids hang out. Kids went to this garage after school. Not every day. Just a couple times a week. It was a little scary, but no one ever got hurt. There were no gangs or crime.

This garage sat between two houses. The front of it was even with the front of the houses on each side. Everything was near the sidewalk, not way back in a yard. It's the way things were built in the city. The garage was one story high with a flat roof. The floor was dirt over old thick concrete and rusty metal mesh. The walls were concrete blocks. The doors were like ones on an old carriage house—two green doors for each garage. They should pull open. I don't think these doors had been opened for years. There was a broken panel on the bottom part of one door. That's how we got in. I waited until no one was in sight. Then I quickly ducked through the broken panel.

It was pretty dark inside. And it smelled really musty. A hole in the roof let in a little light. It also let in water, bugs and who knows what else.

"Hi there," Jonas said. "Ya movin' away today, huh?"

"Yep," I replied.

"Shhh, don't interrupt," someone in a corner called. It was so dark that it was hard to see much.

"John's showin' us some pictures he got from a sexy magazine he found in the trash. The boys in the corner—six or so—huddle in a circle with a flashlight giggling over John's magazine.

"OK, OK, you show me yours and I'll show you mine," a boy and a girl were negotiating in the dark in another corner.

They were older—maybe eleven. They were two white kids. I didn't know either of them very well. They lived up the hill from me a block or so. I think the boy's dad works in a bank downtown. He always wore a suit to work. The girl's dad taught at the university. I don't know where their moms thought they were. I also don't know what they're getting so excited about. What' the point of showing each other private body parts? Maybe I'll want to do that when I am eleven. I guessed that eleven must be different from nine.

My eyes adjusted to the light. I saw the circle of boys in the back corner. The girls were closer to the hole in the garage door. Nadine, Melissa, Alice, and Mary Anne. I walked over to them.

"Just wanted to say good-bye. We're movin' today. I got a new step-father. We're going to his place."

"Yeah, I had a step-father too, for a little while," said Alice, my friend from the bottom of the hill.

"I never knew that white kids had step-fathers." Alice muttered, almost to herself.

"Wonder if there'll be any cute boys near your new apartment?" Nadine asked. "Did you know Mary Anne is starting to get tits?"

"That's pretty strange," I replied. "Wonder what that feels like?"

"Are they big enough for a bra?" One of the other girls asked. I didn't wait for the answer.

"Gotta go, my Mother is gonna be angry. She doesn't know I'm here."

"So? Nobody's Mother knows they are here," Melissa added. "But we'll never find out about sex if we just hang around our Mothers."

The garage was the perfect hide-out. I never told Mother I went there. I thought about telling her; but it just didn't seem worth an argument. I was, however, in deference to her, always aware of how to get quickly to the door panel so that I had a way to get out fast. And I always made sure I was with the group of girls. Mother may have been worried about more than the roof falling in. I usually listened to Mother, but I am, after all, starting to grow up. I am entitled to my own view about the garage—if I'm really careful, like she's told me to be, at the same time.

On the way back from the garage, I cut through our yard. My Comstock Avenue house had a big yard—well big for the city. It was full of wonderful flowers, and huge shrubs. In late spring the peonies are in full bloom. They are shiny, smooth, either pink or white, and with an incredible fragrance. My favorites. Then the tantalizing fragrance of mock orange floats across the garden in early summer. Just now, only the chrysanthemums were blooming. We played house under the cavernous forsythia bush in the back. And we had a fort under a giant spyrea bush beside the house. In the summer, Mother put a sprinkler in the yard and we'd run through it and get all wet. In the evening, at dusk, we had wonderful games of hide-and-seek. Sometimes we played sardines where everyone crawls in with the person who is hiding—often in a hole that led to under the porch. It's the same kids who played in the garage. Just a different day. A different place. All routine play, as far as I knew.

I wondered then if there would be garage kids in my new neighborhood. My new neighborhood, at Don's apartment, had no old garages. The kids would hang-out in the park or by the side corners of the big Catholic Church. But they had to go to the side where there were no doors. Otherwise the sisters, human sized penguins in long black robes with white yokes in front, might come out to chase them away.

CROUSE COLLEGE

Another aspect of being a "latch-key kid" was what happened on Saturdays and school vacations. On those days Mother took me with her to where she taught—in a spooky old castle called Crouse College. If there'd been someone to stay with at home, I might never have been lucky enough to go to Crouse College.

These trips also ended when Mother married Don and we moved.

Crouse College was a mysterious brownstone castle with a sharp spire on the very top rising from the top of the highest hill on campus up to touch the sky. It was a very long climb up the steps on the hillside to get to the giant front doors—just to get to the bottom floor of this awe inspiring building. The huge heavy front door opened into a cavernous, sort of dark, front hall. The ceiling was very high. Whenever someone made a noise, it echoed.

"Don't go in any classrooms," Mother said. "And don't go outside the building."

She went into her studio. She said, "Be back here by 12:00."

I could explore the whole building—except where there were classes. There was a massive and ornate central staircase. The climb to the top took a really long time. Then I slid down the entire curving banister!

I liked to imagine that the steeple of Crouse was haunted.

I told Mother that one evening. "Watch the bats circling round and round at dusk. I'm sure the spire is haunted."

"And, I think the basement may be haunted too." I declared.

"Probably not," she said walking on without even looking up.

Adults can be so boring, I thought.

Take the Crouse College basement for example. If I were lucky, when I went to campus with Mother, she'd take me into the basement to look for some supply item that she needed upstairs in the art studios. While she was looking through the canvasses and easels, I'd locate imaginary secret caverns and places to store treasure. I imagined the people who lived there—people who come out late at night and wore long gowns or suits of armor. After they dined on the best of foods, the men—and some of the women would go riding on splendid horses. Others stayed in the castle, painted beautiful pictures and talked—until dawn, when they their entire world turned from real to fantasy. They disappeared. The daytime people came. I wondered if other people ever imagined nighttime worlds anywhere. I wondered if watching a night-time world ever gave people ideas that altered daytime decisions?

I went to Crouse College with Mother whenever she had an appointment with a student and I had vacation. Otherwise, I'd be home a really long time by myself. If I wasn't sliding down the magnificent spiral banister, I'd be discovering parts of the building where other nighttime adventures might occur. For example, under the base of the stairway was a small unfurnished chamber that could, if one wished to create the idea, become a secret door to an exotic garden—the garden of the night people.

It was hard to share imagination games with the kids in the neighborhood or those at school. Most of them just played with brothers or sisters. None of them had Mothers at Crouse College—or Mothers who worked. It seemed that so often the Dick and Jane kids had other people creating their games; they didn't do the choosing. Their games were just 'there.' They wouldn't ever have had the need to consider how to make waiting for their Mother into an interesting game. How can people really have fun, or really use their brains, or really be creative if they don't get to use their imaginations?

I remember wondering, when Mother and I moved in with Don, what we would do without being able to go to Crouse College. She won't be teaching anymore.

DOREEN

Doreen lived across the street from Mother and me on Comstock Avenue. She and I were best friends.

She was the closest neighbor who was my age, and a girl. We visited each other's home and played board games. Parchesi was a favorite. We played that at Doreen's house. She had one little brother—too little to play with. Her parents were around a lot. Her father was an accountant and her Mother was a housewife. They kept to themselves and I rarely talked with them. Their apartment was also in an old house, but just a normal old two family house—not one with a cupola. Doreen's family is Jewish. Some people say Jews are different from Christians or other people. I hear adults talk about this stuff. I guess it was a big deal for the Nazis to hate Jews.—the same Nazis who wanted to get past Mother's bathroom rug on the 'blackout' nights.

Doreen's uncle and aunt had just moved in with them. He, his wife, and a son escaped from the Nazis and came to America. Doreen and I were playing Parchesi when they came in.

"Hello," Doreen said. "This is my friend Carla Lee."

"How are you?" I asked.

I think I startled them. They looked at me—didn't answer our greeting. They had been talking when they came in. It was another language—made no sense to me. Doreen told me later that it was Yiddish. I'd never heard of that before. It might be fun to see if I could understand it—that is if I ever hear them talking again. I'd like to speak another language. Why not?

"Are you leaving?" Doreen called after them.

They were gone. They left the room as soon as they saw me. Doreen's Mother had watched this from the kitchen doorway.

"Mother, they just left. I wanted them to meet Carla Lee. Why did they do that?"

"They've had a really hard time," Doreen's Mother said. "They don't trust anyone who's not Jewish."

"But how can they tell?" I asked.

"Doreen and Carla Lee," her Mother started. "Here's what happened."

"Things in their town in Holland had been fine. Everyone got along. Then, the War came. The word spread that the Jews were being forced into trains and taken far away. The only option was to hide. They barely had time to hide in the hay in a nearby barn."

By this time, Doreen and I were sitting at the kitchen table eating cookies and milk and fascinated with the story.

"The Nazis came with bayonets poking through the hay. A bayonet almost poked their son. If they had been caught, they would have been taken away with all the other Jews. The Nazis gassed Jews. They didn't even do anything criminal; they were put in concentration camps. The Nazis locked a lot of Jews in a big room and turned on poison gas just because of their religion, because they were different. Doreen's aunt and uncle were really lucky to escape."

I asked Doreen's Mother, "Do you mean that right here in my own neighborhood there is someone who escaped the Nazis?"

"Yes," she said. "A lot of Jewish people can tell stories of experiences like this."

"What could I do if someone hated me so much that they wanted to kill me? With Nazis around, how can we be sure that we're safe just because we're not Jewish? People might think up other reasons just to kill anybody who isn't the same as them. Can that happen?"

She said nothing.

My thoughts return to the present. Two hospital attendants are telling me that I need to get up and walk around. No choice. I haven't been out of bed for two days. I stand. I walk—a little. That's enough! I sit. Thankfully, they go. Alone in this white-everything room may not be the best, but alone from those attendants is fine. My side where I was stabbed really hurt when I got up.

Back to Doreen and the Nazis. Why are people so mean? Why did the Nazis want to hurt Doreen's uncle? Why did this guy stab me? He wasn't a Nazi though. I don't think he cared if I was a Jew or not.

What's so different about Doreen anyway? All I knew that was different was that she didn't celebrate Christmas and Easter. Most everyone else I knew celebrated those holidays. It was too bad that she missed these fun holidays. Santa Claus, the Easter Bunny and all that. Once I told her that I was sorry she missed them. She said there were other Jewish holidays. She tried to explain why her holidays were different. It was something about what a person thinks about Jesus. This really didn't make sense. I don't know much about Jesus except that Christmas celebrates his birth. It's something about a baby having more power that kings with armies. And Easter, that has something to do with Jesus' living after he died. But I do remember hearing that Jesus *was* a Jew. And I knew that the first half of our *Bible* is the same as the Jewish religious writings. So, what was the problem about these holidays and who hates who? It just escaped me. Doreen's family went to church—temple they called it—on Saturday. Christians went to churches Sunday; Mother and I didn't. Doreen's father wore this little tiny hat when he went to temple. Why? Who knows?

Doreen and I spent hours every week doing railing somersaults. We were so lucky that the sidewalk on our street had a single bar iron railing all the way down the block. The railing was supposed to give old people something to hold on to. We kids used it to practice gymnastics. Fun made our friendship special. Nothing else mattered.

REAL PEOPLE AND BUREAUCRATS

I learned about real people when I was a "latch-key kid." I lived in three worlds. One was the university people at the top of the hill with Mother's professional friends—people like my family in Rochester. Another world was that of the Dick and Jane families whose kids went to the same school that I attended, and all the people we read about in books where they said that a family had to have both a mom and a dad. And I also lived in the world of the kids I played with at the bottom of the hill, kids whose families were more like mine—without two parents and a house, a lot of them were colored families, but most of them were poorer than we were. They didn't go to art classes at the Museum on Saturday like I did. I wondered why none of these people knew each other across their worlds. I thought that was too bad; I could have told them great stories about each other's worlds.

I really liked the kids at the bottom of the hill. I remember my last day as a latch-key kid in that neighborhood. "Mother, please—just one more stop as we leave this neighborhood. Can we go by Jimmy and Alice's house."

"Sure, let's do that," Mother said.

We started down the hill, past the garage and Madison School toward Jimmy and Alice's. I met them when we were out playing ball a year or so ago. Jimmy is a little younger than I am, so he didn't mind girls. Usually we went to Alice's apartment. She and her Mother and her baby brother lived on the third floor of a small building that's square and brick, and the halls weren't too well lit. They didn't have a yard so we played on the sidewalk. It was O.K. because we could roller skate and play hop scotch and play ball against the wall of her building. Alice's apartment was the same as everybody else's. We listened to music on the radio. We made peanut butter and jelly sandwiches while we sang-along with the radio.

"If I knew you were coming, I'd have baked a cake, baked a cake."

And "R-R-A-G-Ragmop." We sang and danced around Alice's tiny living room.

Jimmy and Alice went to Madison School. Madison was the place for kids who were poor, or colored or who had no fathers. I wished I could go to school with these kids, and also with my other friends—all together. My Mother arranged for me to go to Thornton School because it was supposed to be a 'better school.'

I was with Mother at the School Department when she arranged that. The people there were really rude to a colored

Mother in front of us in line. I heard what the school official said. I listened a lot—most grown-ups didn't know that. I wondered if they'd have said the same things if they knew that kids had ears.

"Mrs. Jackson," he said. "Don't waste my time. I'm very busy. Don't you worry yourself about things you can't understand. I'm in charge here and I know which school your daughter belongs in."

"She should go to Madison." He lectured. "It's near your house and we'll teach her how to behave."

"Now, Mrs. Jackson, set a good example for these other people in line. Go home."

Wow, I thought. No one ever talked like that to my Mother. If they tried, they wouldn't succeed.

We were next in line. The man did try to get my Mother to leave—but he was much more polite.

"Thank you, Mrs. Brooks, for coming to share your concern about Madison School. Just put your request in writing, and we'll be in touch in a few weeks when things settle down."

He took Mother's arm to escort her out of his office.

She did this quick, yet gentle, twirl and landed sitting on the sofa in his office. He was startled.

His only choice was either to walk away and leave her in his office, or to sit down at his desk and talk with her. To make it clear that we were staying, I climbed up on the sofa and settled in next to Mother. He sighed and sat down—still smiling. Well, his face smiled.

Mother started, "To begin again, Mr. Burling, my proper name is Professor Brooks." Without letting him get a word in, she continued. "I'm sure you realize that school starts in three days. What good would it do for me to write you and wait a few weeks? You won't be able to answer my letter before school starts, and I know you wouldn't want to be that disrespectful of a parent."

Hmmm, I thought to myself. My Mother can solve any problem—with words and wit. I wondered how she learned to do that? Should I learn this way to be heard?

She went on. "I'm well aware, Mr. Burling that the School Department spends $200 per pupil less at Madison than they do at Thornton. I researched that at the library. I'm also aware that 10% more pupils at Madison repeat grades than at any other school. It makes you wonder whether the school is finding materials that interest them, on the one hand, and helping the kids who need tutorials, on the other hand. I'm further aware that the building is in terrible repair. Frequently there is no toilet paper. Broken windows go months before they are repaired."

"Now, Mr. Burling, your choice is simple," Mother said. "Either my daughter can start school at Thornton on Monday, or I can ask a newspaper photographer to come with me and some other parents to document how the School Department is not doing its job. I'll get some university people together with some Madison parents and we'll have pictures all over the newspapers showing the poor condition of the Madison building. Maybe we should do that anyway."

Without leaving space for him to get a word in, Mother continued. "I guess that means we'll be at the School Committee meeting this coming week to ask why you are neglecting this school and its families. We taxpayers expect you to work for us, you know. Please sign this form for my daughter to attend Thornton."

He signed—hardly able to usher us out of his office fast enough.

Alice's Mother probably couldn't even get to the School Department. It was all the way across the city. She had no car. That was too bad, because while she, herself, may not have spent a lot of years in school, she was smart and she could out-talk anybody. I would have loved to see her with Mr. Burling. He wouldn't have pushed her away. She might have gotten him to fix up Madison.

He might have been rude to Jimmy's Mother, though. Jimmy's Mother was nice, but she was very timid. She never got to go to school much herself. She had to take care of her brothers and sisters when she was a kid. Now she took care of Jimmy and his three year old brother. She would have been too frightened to talk to the school officials—especially those white men in dark suits.

The day that happened, I asked Mother, "Why can't Jimmy and Alice go to a good school just like I can? Why wasn't the school department nice to everybody's Mother?"

She didn't answer.

Jimmy and Alice were great ball players. We invented all kinds of games.

Alice's mom had a new baby. Part of the reason we went to Alice's house to play was because that way we could see the new baby too. Babies were really cute. So tiny. Alice's dad left home a few months before the baby was born. He never came back.

Her Mother couldn't work at all now—not even at the house cleaning job she used to have. The baby couldn't be left alone and there's no grandma to take care of him like my grandma took care of me. Both Jimmy and Alice's Mothers were on 'welfare'—whatever that was. I never heard what happened to Jimmy's dad. They didn't talk about it. Somehow, I think he just disappeared.

We honked the horn when we got to Alice's building. Jimmy was there. He and Alice came down to the car.

"Gonna miss you," said Alice. "Wish you weren't moving."

"Me too," I replied. We hugged. I nestled my face into her black pigtails.

Jimmy just bounced the ball against the wall of his building. "See ya." He called.

My Mother didn't really know Alice's Mother. They'd met once when we passed them while walking to a store. But everybody was always busy. The only people Mother knew were the people she worked with. Alice's Mother was in the window upstairs with the baby when we stopped to say good-bye. She waved. Mother waved. We drove off.

LOTS OF SURPRISES

Maybe my latch key days had ended. I had a step-dad now. But I'd miss these adventures. I learned all sorts of useful things that we never learned on school or at home.

As I'd soon find out, all the latch-key adventures proved very useful.

"Come in now. There's a surprise for you," Mother called one evening about a year after she and Don had married.

"O.K. O.K. Just a minute." I slowly put the bike away and walked into the living room.

"Look at this," said Don. "We have a TV set."

"That's great. Now I don't have to go over to Fred Chesley's house to watch TV. His family already has a set, you know."

Don fiddled with the TV—trying to find something that wasn't either all snowy or just a test pattern with a single shrill high pitched tone "nnnnnnnnnnnnnnnnnnnnnnnnnn.' I watched and thought about going over the Fred Chesley's.

Fred and I were both in the sixth grade in 1951. Last year, we created a newspaper called the "Chesley Chat." I liked starting new things. I especially liked doing things that might actually matter to someone, somewhere—not just to me. That's what the paper did. Fred was Editor. I was the Assistant Editor. Fred and I gathered stories. We wrote about needing a new ball for the playground and what the teachers had say about that. We wrote about a place someone went for vacation and how you could go there. After we collected all the stories, we went to his house to type the stories onto stencils, lay out the newspaper, and run off the latest edition on his mimeograph machine with the purple ink. That ink was really messy. It was hard not to get it all over. When I went home my hands were always purple.

Maybe someday I'd start a real newspaper and tell people real news. That was a career I could have, if I decided not to be an art professor.

"I can't wait to tell Fred that I can watch TV at home all the time now."

Don said, "On Saturdays you can watch 'The Howdy Doody Show.' And, this year, 1950, there's a new program—'Superman.'"

"Don, the TV is great. I'm glad you brought it home."

"Maybe, someday, there will be more than three channels," my Mother noted. "And maybe they will have programs all day."

There's no TV in my hospital room now. But, the doctor said this morning that I'll go home in a couple days. That's good. There is a TV at Don's and my apartment. (By 1955 I was living with Don alone. Mother was gone.) But Don won't be home when I leave the hospital. He's in Florida with his girlfriend "getting some rest." I should be O.K. though because I have the apartment key in my wallet—still a sort of "latch-key kid." I can just take a bus from the hospital across the city to our apartment. I pile up the pillows on my hospital bed, stare at the very white walls and return to my past.

As it turned out, there was a motive in Don's bringing home the TV that day in 1951. It was intended to make me feel better about the announcement that followed.

"Just before Christmas," Mother said, "we're moving to another part of Syracuse. You'll be able to go to a new school."

"But I've only been at Bellevue for one and one-half years," I complained.

"Mother, do you know that if I have to finish sixth grade at Ed Smith, it will be my fourth school and I'm only in sixth grade. Don't you think four different schools in six years is too much change? Besides, it's the middle of the year."

"I know dear. We think you'll like the new apartment much better. It's bigger. And it's next to Drumlin's Country Club. In fact, it's on their property. Your new room looks out over the garden and the hills. You and I can go ice skating every day all winter! Don will do more tennis coaching."

"Ice skating—every day?" I asked.

"Yes, and we'll put up a huge Christmas tree. There's a wonderful big paneled living room, with a big fireplace, and place for a splendid big tree."

Mother, once again, tried to smooth over another change. She always tried to make the world O.K. for me. But no adult ever thought that kids had questions, or worries. Nobody wanted to hear kids. Adults say they really care about kids. How come they never care what they think?

To me, it seems like every time things started to get normal, everything was destroyed. I'd have to pick up the pieces and start over again. Family, friends, places to live—they all kept changing. Can a person just have things shaken up all the time? I'm not sure. Mother's right that each new adventure proves challenging and fascinating and somewhere within me I look forward to seeing how well I can master it, what the experience will teach me. But, that doesn't mean it's easy.

Once again I left my school. I said good-bye to Nancy, just like I'd said good-bye to Doreen, the garage kids and the kids at the bottom of the hill.

This time, however, the new apartment was truly wonderful.

It was a half a house. I'd never lived in such a big house—at least not since I left Grandma's big house in Rochester. Our new apartment was almost like the Dick and Jane houses—like the house my family had before my daddy died.

"Mother, I can see the skating rink! I see it from my bedroom window! That's heaven. I can watch the skaters at night when I'm in bed."

"I told you, you'd like it," she said. "Come help me decorate this Christmas tree."

"The balsam pine smelled wonderful," I exclaimed. Maybe, this time, life would be normal. I thought to myself.

"Here, let's put this angel up near the top. I've had this ornament for a very long time. Your grandma gave it to me. Your great-grandparents brought it from Germany. See the delicate wax body, and look, the angel has a painted face, and real hair. It's wonderful to have traditions—things that go on the tree every year."

Mother was chattering on about where each of the ornaments came from.

"Angels are a symbol of hope, hope for good times and good things," Mother said. "Isn't she beautiful?"

We really did have some nice ornaments. I especially liked the antique glass ones, the ones with stories. I liked the idea that there was one time every year when people made the effort to be with the people they cared most about. I liked the idea of sharing the stories of the history of these decorations—the stories of the people who put them up. All this is what makes Christmas a really special time.

"I'll put the tinsel on," I said.

"O.K. Do it carefully. One strand on a branch so it really looks like an ice cycle." Mother directed. "Don is over at the Country Club. He'll be back in a little while and then we'll turn on the lights."

"Why doesn't he want to help us decorate the tree?"

Mother didn't answer.

It's pretty clear to me that Don just didn't care. I know he tried to teach me to play tennis. But that's different. If he really cared, he'd have come to the hospital to visit me now, before he went to Florida.

A NEW SCHOOL AND SOME SNAKES

I'd been at the new school, Ed Smith, for several months. I still didn't know anybody. One day, the snow had melted and we went out for recess on the playground.

"Com'on come on with us, Carla Lee," Joan called. She sits near me in the sixth grade classroom. "It's time those boys paid for how they tease us. We're going up the hill behind the playground."

The boys were huddling on their side of the playground. They were digging up worms buried in the spring mud. In fact, they were choosing 'worm-throwers' to attack the girls.

The 'worm-thrower' raced toward the girls and selected someone to terrorize. He'd pitch his worm down her shirt. Another time, he threw a worm in a girl's hair. Everyone was screaming.

"That's gross!" One of the girls said. We need a way to get back at the boys."

"Let's go." Joan said.

A half dozen of us ran up the hill into a wooded area.

"What can we do?" Another asked.

"Let's think of something that will really make them run," said a third girl in the group.

"How about mud balls?" said the first girl. "We could take a supply down the hill and throw them at the boys."

"No, that won't work. Someone could get hurt, and the teachers will stop us anyway," Joan commented

"I've got it," I said. "Look what's over there by that rock."

Everyone stood dead still. We saw a garter snake.

"If the boys insist on chasing us with worms, why don't we chase them with snakes."

"What a great idea." Everyone agreed.

"Pick it up, Carla Lee." Joan said.

"You want me to pick up the snake?" I asked.

They all nodded. "It was your idea."

"Yuck." I puzzled. Maybe having an idea isn't such a good thing.

"Maybe I can hold him on this stick. Then I won't have to touch him." I tried to figure it out so the snake wouldn't fall off the stick. It took several sticks and several tries to get it right. The others watched and offered suggestions. Finally the snake stayed in place.

I gave Joan the stick to carry.

"Get 'em," someone yelled. We all raced down the hill in a pack with the desperate snake twisted around the stick.

"Com'on, get that boy over there. He tried to put a worm down my shirt," one of the girls shouted.

The boys screamed and ran as a pack to the corner of the playground to escape the snake.

In the chaos, the snake flew off the stick. It landed on the head of one of the boys.

"Heeeelllllppp." The boy screamed as he shook himself and wiggled away.

The girls cheered.

The boys redoubled their efforts to deliver multiple worms at one time.

We girls started back to the woods to find another snake.

"Dinggggg. Dinggggg." The school bell rang. Playtime was over.

We all, boys and girls, lined up. We transformed ourselves into a smiling set of polite young people ready to greet the teacher who opened the door so we could march back to our studies—two by two.

"Anything exciting happen on the playground today," the teacher asked Joan.

"No nothing. We just played." How did it come to be that kids didn't tell adults much, either?

And so it went for much of the spring. That's as far as friendships went at this school. Summer came. So did the now familiar family announcement.

"Let's have some dinner. There's news," Mother said one evening in early June.

She put the string beans and real mashed potatoes on the table. Then she brought the meatloaf and the gravy. We all sat down.

MOVING AGAIN

"In a few weeks school will be out." Mother said. "When that happens, we'll be moving away from Syracuse to a place called

Vails Gate. It's almost 200 miles from here—closer to New York City."

Don said nothing, as usual.

"I don't want to move. I like Syracuse. My friends are here. I've already been to four different schools and I'm just finishing 6th grade. It's hard enough now to keep in touch with kids from the old neighborhood on Comstock Avenue, or my friend Nancy at Bellevue. I'm just beginning to know Joan. Do I have to go to another new place, a fifth new school?" I asked.

Mother continued. "The country is at war again—with Korea. And Don is in the Air Force, as you know. The Air Force is sending Don to Stewart Air Force Base near Vails Gate."

"We'll go with Don because we're a family," I'm told. "We're no different from the tens of thousands of families across the U.S. who go where the military sends them."

Why doesn't it matter if I have an opinion? Life would be easier. It's confusing. Lot's of people never raise their opinions. They just obey. But, Mother had opinions when they wanted to put me in a school she didn't like. She made her opinions make a difference. When does an opinion matter? Hers? Mine?

On this matter of moving, I needed to learn how to make myself heard, I thought. I needed to get Mother's attention; she was always preoccupied with her plans.

I didn't really know what to do other than to be a pest, or maybe throw a tantrum. A tantrum usually worked. It got attention. That was the first step toward changing something. Were there other ways? I didn't know how Mother got people to *listen* – how to get them to change something. The problem with a tantrum was everybody ended up feeling bad. And I always ended up with a dreadful pounding headache.

Why do people ask me what I like if, when it comes to the big decisions, they really don't want to know?

"I'm sick of it." I said to Mother. "Why do we have to keep moving to where Don wants to go. First we went to his apartment where all I saw from my bedroom was garbage cans. Then I had to switch schools in the middle of the year. Now I just start meeting people and you say we're moving again—because of Don. Why don't we ever go where you want to go—or where I want to go? If this is what a real family is supposed to be like, I don't want one!" I stomped off to my bedroom.

"She's always been strong-willed," I heard Mother explain to Don.

Don was silent, as usual.

For a moment, I'm interrupted by the present. Someone just delivered a food tray to me in my hospital room. They called it lunch, but it really was a mix of sliced cardboard and glue. This will be easy to ignore; I can get back to what happened when we moved to Vails Gate.

I remember Mother's comment about me being strong-willed and I think to myself. Maybe, it's a good thing I am strong willed. If I weren't, I might never survive to grow up.

I pushed the sliced cardboard and glue lunch away.

The best way to pass the time until I can get out of this hospital is to slip back into 1951. At least my head can escape from this 1955 hospital room.

'Strong-willed' was hard to do. I was so upset about moving again that I burst into tears, ran to my bedroom, and sobbed myself to sleep. It didn't change anything; but at least people knew how I felt.

Again we packed. Again I said good-bye to friends. This time was different though. This time we moved so far away that we couldn't even go for a weekend to Rochester to visit grandma.

"Come Carla Lee, you might even like it at Stewart Air Force Base," Mother said as we finished packing.

"I'm almost ready." I had packed my 45 record player in a carton that was now in the truck. I took my Nancy Drew mystery stories with me in the car. We left.

I wondered then if having latch-key kid memories will make it any easier to start junior high and to become a teenager in new strange place?

As it turned out, what concerned me then would be the least of my worries.

Chapter Four

Military Brats and Playing Charades

"The doctor comes today," says the nurse on duty. "Perhaps he'll say when you can go home."

"Good." I reply.

"Stay out of trouble," says the nurse as she leaves the room.

"It's not my fault I'm here." I snap back. "I just didn't have a ride home from the church play rehearsal."

I don't think she heard. But, why do people say things like that? They don't care if they are right. They just assume.

They divide the world into good people and bad people, and if you don't have a dad, or don't live in a whole house, or are the victim of a crime, they want to put you with the bad people. The same thing happens if you live at the bottom of the hill, or are colored, or are poor. They want to make you believe that you are bad. I thought bad people were criminals, not just people who somehow were different or had different experiences.

Everybody thinks that a kid who didn't come from a 'Dick and Jane' family will turn out terrible. We're supposed to become delinquents.

I knew two kids at the school I just left who believed that their lives were horrible. Maybe it was true. Everybody said they were becoming delinquents.

I never talked with either of them. But other kids said that only delinquents would act that way. We were supposed to stay away from them. Is that because they were delinquents already? Or, by everybody staying away, did we help them to become delinquents?

One girl in sixth grade at Ed Smith just stared out the classroom window—all the time. She didn't care about school work, or about the other kids. She kept to herself on the playground. She tried to act older than the rest of us. She dressed sexy—a challenge for a sixth grader.

There was also a boy in that same class. He was just always angry—at everything. I heard that he'd been kept back in school and that he'd been arrested once. I'm not sure why. His buddies pick him up from school in a car.

Neither of them talked with the other kids. Maybe, like me, they think that the other kids wouldn't understand what has happened to them? Maybe they were "latch-key kids?" Maybe they had step-fathers who didn't care?

Kids aren't always friendly to new kids. For example, they sometimes don't let you sit at their table in the cafeteria at lunch time. They don't necessarily want to play at recess. Kids can be mean.

What will it be like in this new place called Vails Gate? Are there delinquents here?

LIVING IN THE COUNTRY

We moved into a large second floor apartment, the top half of a house. The house stood alone in a field. It had a long drive-way. The field had woods on three sides, and in the distance, I saw the mountains—the Catskills, they were called. I had never lived this far away from a city.

"You'll get the school bus at 7:00, and it stops right at the end of the driveway," Mother said.

"We're really out in the country. There are no school buses in the city." I am amazed by it all. "Look, there's a rabbit. In our yard!"

"I bet you'll even like it here," Mother said. She always tried to make change seem positive.

The air smelled very fresh. Riding a school bus was fun. I like being with other kids. Mostly I like waiting for the bus when it was just getting daylight. I could watch the fog lift off the distant hills. The sky turned from dark grey to purplish and then that amazing orange ball of sun came over the horizon. It looked like it was bouncing on the horizon. But only for a min-ute. Then it became today. The spectacle vanished. You can't see the transformation from night to day happen in the city.

For the next two summers, 1951 and 1952, I climbed rocks along the Hudson River. Don wasn't in Vails Gate very long be-fore he was sent by the Air Force to Korea.

Mother and I were alone again. Frequently we went to nearby West Point. The U.S. Military Academy had a wonderful location nestled in the rocky hillsides along the Hudson River. The cadet uniforms were so perfect, so sharp. And the grass was so perfect, so trimmed. It created an image that our military is friendly, a force in charge, and that they bring order to things. They looked stunning. Their parade marching was captivating to watch. Why do the soldiers at West Point look so different from the pictures of soldiers fighting in Korea that are in Mother's newspapers?

We did a lot of things that Mother liked to do. She liked to take pictures of me. I'm patient—or I try to be.

"Stand just in front of that mountain laurel." She smiled and snapped a picture. "In the next picture, can you sit on that rock?" The picture has to be in a setting that fits her artist's eye for perfection.

Then we'd get in the car and drive a bit.

"Here. I want to stop here. It's a nice field. I can paint that red barn in front of the mountains." Mother set up her easel. I find a spot nearby and read Nancy Drew, or pick wild flowers, or explore. I smelled the linseed oil and the turpentine in her artist's portfolio and dream about when I'd be grown up and able to do all the things Mother did. It was almost like being back on Comstock Avenue—except, all the kids are gone.

MILITARY BRATS

When we first moved to Vails Gate, I met some other Air Force kids on the base. I learned that we are 'military brats.' Therefore we decided we had to live up to our reputation. So, we'd run around the Stewart Air Force Base PX. We made lots of noise. We played Bingo at the Officers Club, and we'd throw popcorn at each other.

"You kids get out of this PX," some Sergeant yelled at us. "You're getting popcorn all over the place."

It was true. There are a half dozen of us. Our parents were at some reception at the Officer's Club and they sent us to a movie. The movie's over. But we had extra popcorn.

"We're just making a popcorn path," one of the kids yelled. Whoever had organized this adventure told us each to dribble popcorn along the path wherever he led us. So—we obliged. We created our path.

Out of the theater.

Across the street.

Into the PX.

Up one aisle.

Down the next aisle.

And now—quickly—out the door and behind the theater.

Brats have to act like brats, I rationalized. All the other kids were acting this way. What do I know? I'm the newest kid in the crowd. This was a different experience. Not only am I a 'military brat' now. I'm almost a teenager. I'm eleven. It's 1951.

A CAT AND TOMATOES

This year Mother let me get a cat, Cappy. Cappy was a beautiful little black and white kitten. She slept in my bed, and she purred all the time. She waits for me to get off the school bus in the afternoon. When she catches mice, she puts them on the front door step to show them to me. After I've seen them, she carries them off into the field.

Mother didn't like the mice very much.

Cappy had another unique habit.

"Get that cat off the dining room table," Mother screamed at me.

I ran to get the cat. The cat ran, too—but not before she'd taken a slice of tomato from the salad with her. Whenever we had tomatoes she figured out how to steal a slice or two. In its lifetime, the cat traveled with me across the United States—stealing tomatoes from peoples' salads.

This new 'normal' in Vails Gate wasn't to last, however. Mother's been so grumpy lately.

"Go and play, Carla Lee," Mother shooed me away. I went to my room to play the latest of my 45 records. What's happening? I wondered.

"Mother, it's OK." I tried to console her. I saw her tears.

"Never mind my tears, Carla Lee." She tried to reassure me. Then, she can't help letting a thought slip out. "It's just that there's no way for me to talk with Don because he's in Korea. It's so hard to get a message to him. And, we're too far away to make weekend trips to visit our family in Rochester. But it will be O.K. Let's have some dessert."

The conversation ended.

I had settled into my new school in Cornwall. I liked it. I especially liked that I was starting eighth grade—a second year in the same school. The kids here were mostly all from Dick and Jane families. Mostly, they all had white skin. A lot of them had dads who are in the Army or the Air Force. We played at school. Because we lived so far from each other, most of the kids couldn't play together after school.

THE ART COMPETITION

One day in early October 1952, I burst off the school bus and ran up the stairs into my apartment. "I can do it. I can do it. Mother, I can do it," I said jumping up and down. It is nearly Halloween and the kids with the best proposed picture for a store window in Cornwall would be able to paint their picture on the giant store windows on Main Street.

"Mother, they chose my picture. Only five of us can do this. I'm so excited."

"That's wonderful," she said.

"I'm thrilled—partly because it really will be fun to do, and partly because I am getting to be an artist, just like you."

Every day I'd leave early for school and stay late painting and painting. My store window was very big—about eight feet tall and eight feet wide. My Halloween painting had to be perfect! It would be embarrassing to do it if it were less than perfect. The proportions on the sketch needed to be accurate. The colors needed to blend and to be strong, and Halloween-like. And, they couldn't run. That was the biggest hazard of painting on a vertical surface. Then I had to watch the weather because everything I did had to dry before it rained. So many things to think about. Oh, and the brushes needed to be cleaned every day. And I had to make sure there are no drips on the concrete sidewalk.

"I have to finish it by the Tuesday before Halloween. That's tomorrow. Please can you drop me off at the store tomorrow morning before school—just one more time, Mother?"

That September, just as I started eighth grade as a twelve year old, there was a revolutionary change in school policy. The School Department said it was O.K. for girls to wear slacks, instead of skirts to school. The policy was set; but everyone still knew that 'good girls' don't wear slacks to school.

"Thanks for the ride, mom," I said as I jumped out of the car. "If I work quickly, maybe I can finish."

"Good luck," Mother said. "You know, you really are a good artist."

I beam at her as she drives away.

It is barely daylight at 6:30 AM. Hopefully I'd get a lot done in the nearly two hours before school began. I wouldn't have time to change clothes, and I couldn't stand on a ladder and paint in a skirt—certainly not a skirt complete with the required layers of ironed crinoline petticoats. So, I'd worn slacks today—for the first time.

At 8:25 I rushed to put my things away and run down the block to school before the 8:30 tardy bell. I barely got there on time. As I dumped my things in my locker, the kids were already filing into the all school assembly—several hundred kids.

"Whew, I made it," I whispered to the person sitting next to me as I slipped into my seat.

"Shhh, Mrs. Brown already took attendance. Tell her you didn't hear her call 'Brooks,' my seatmate advised.

Fortunately the eighth graders sat in the back of the auditorium, I thought to myself. I got Mrs. Brown's attention, confirmed that I was not absent, and settled into my seat with a sigh of relief.

Up on our feet. "I pledge allegiance to the flag of ...." Then "God Bless America, Land that I Love," the entire school in unison participated in the traditional ritual for beginning a new day.

We sat down. The assembly began.

HUMILIATION

"Will Carla Lee Brooks please come up onto the stage," Dr. Andrews, the principal, announced through the microphone.

I've never heard my name called through a microphone before. Whatever was happening? For a quick second I was excited to find out. But my excitement melted into panic.

"I'm wearing slacks!!!!" Maybe I even said that out loud.

I got up from my seat and started to the front of the room. Do you know how long a walk it was to go the full length of the auditorium—past several hundred pairs of eyes, past all those rows of kids and teachers, and then up the stairs onto—and across—the stage? It took forever.

I knew that every one of those eyes was fixed on my slacks. Why hadn't I left time to change into a skirt?

I tried not to look at anybody—just the path ahead. When I got up on stage I feared what the principal would say.

He's probably say, "You're wearing slacks! I know we said it was OK. But did you really think we meant what we said? Go sit down."

But he didn't say that.

"Congratulations, Carla Lee," Dr. Andrews said to me.

I'm not really hearing him. I'm worrying about how everyone in the whole school sees me wearing slacks. But Dr. Andrews never indicated that he noticed. He just went right on making his happy announcement.

"You have been selected by the teachers and by me to receive the Sands Medal."

What's that, I wondered to myself. I never heard of the Sands Medal. He handed me this silver medal—looks like a coin.

"We're really proud of you. The winner of this medal is chosen each year as the most outstanding student. To win this award, a student must have been outstanding in seventh grade academics as well as in participation in extra-curricular activity. That's hard for anyone to achieve—especially for someone brand new to the school as you were last year."

"Thank you," I said.

Hold that handshake, I was instructed. A photographer took a picture of me standing with the principal receiving my medal. Now everyone will remember, forever, that I wore slacks—on stage—for such an important event. I should be smiling. I don't think I am.

As I start to leave the stage, the principal said privately, "Congratulations, Carla Lee. We're always pleased to find a student whose work can be a model for the new seventh grade students."

"Thank you," I muttered.

I returned to my seat as quickly as possible. I wished someone across the room would just make a big noise, everyone would look that way instead of at me.

Conforming to the activities and attire of the rest of the kids really mattered, especially in junior high, especially when your family was a little weird and you were the new kid, and especially in the 1950s.

We all learned about the Cold War and how Americans needed to stand together and conform to expected behavior. This meant honoring standards for simple things—hair styles, clothing, house furnishings, foods bought, books read, etc. To challenge something might mean you'd be called a Communist—even if you weren't. The Nazis were gone. The Communists were bad now. On this day, I had not conformed; I wore slacks. Good girls don't do that, and I've always tried to be a good girl.

I took the medal home and told Mother about my day. She said she was proud of me; but she didn't act surprised. I don't think she'd ever heard of a Sands Medal either. She paid no attention to either the slacks or the name of the medal. That was the day that I understood that she just expected that I would do the best possible work that could be done. There was no alternative.

I had never realized her expectation before. Or maybe it wasn't an expectation as much as an affirmation. She never pressured me—except to play the violin. I got out of that only because we moved away from Syracuse and my violin teacher, who worked at Syracuse University.

She never told me that I had done poor work or that I could do better. It was just something that I knew—that criticism wasn't worth the time, but that doing one's best was all that mattered. I guess I just believed her.

I didn't think about it any more.

THE LANDLADY

I don't know why we stayed in Vails Gate with Don away. We might have gone to Rochester, or back to Syracuse. Probably Mother stayed so that I wouldn't have to change schools again.

Mother had lots of activities for us.

One of her projects this fall was to sculpt a head of me out of red clay. After school, I posed (not always willingly) while she sculpted day after day. She was also working on a nearly life-size oil painting of me and my cat, Cappy. (I had to sit still for that one too.) I guess it was how she managed to do what she loved—art.

"Let's take a break and go down to the garden," she said.

Because we stayed in Vails Gate, we were able to enjoying the end of the fall 1952 harvest of our very own garden. That was a first. We picked lettuce, beans, and tomatoes. We dug up potatoes. Over the summer, we had spread the tiny portulaca seeds. We'd enjoyed the flowers and now we collected the last of their seeds to plant next year. Before we went upstairs, Mother and

I picked a wonderful big bouquet of zinnias. These colors were spectacular! What a unique odor zinnias have. I like gardening. I think it amazing that a little tiny seed would turn into a vegetable or a flower. In a way, it was sad when it was time for frost. Everything would die and the ground would be bare in preparation for another cycle of life next year. I hoped that, in 1953, we could plant another garden. But she and I had little time left.

Mother and I had gotten acquainted with the big Italian family on the first floor—our landlords. There were so many people in that family. I never could keep them straight. They always had a lot happening. They laughed a lot. Laughing was wonderful. Like us, they weren't a Dick and Jane family either; they had too many people. But I liked their kind of family. I sometimes wished I could be around a lot of people who all cared about each other and who did a lot of laughing. Other times, it seemed overwhelming. Being alone gives a person time to think.

We were just going upstairs to our apartment carrying vegetables and zinnias.

"Come in and have dinner," said Mrs. Roselli, our jovial landlady. She and her husband were the parents and grandparents of everyone else.

Go ahead, Carla Lee," said my Mother. "I'll be down in a while."

I'd never been inside their apartment. But I liked watching this family. Maybe if I get to know them better, I could figure out if you really needed a lot of people in a family to be so happy. My Mother seemed confident, independent, and successful—but I didn't know if she was happy. It seemed like something sad was there behind her eyes.

"You go ahead and start dinner," Mother said.

"Ciao," said Joe, one of the Roselli sons. "I can't stay for dinner tonight, mom. I'll be over on Saturday. Dad and I are going to put a new muffler in my car."

Two old ladies chatter in Italian while they stood in a corner of the kitchen making pizza crust. I later learned that they are Mrs. Roselli's sisters. They come once a month. They live about an hour away. Mr. Roselli was having a rigorous argument in Italian with another man; one of his sons, I thought. They were arguing about a football game they had seen on TV. That's what I think is happening. But I'm not sure. Three little kids, grandchildren I think, were giggling and chasing each other in and out of the three bedrooms—sometimes tossing pillows. Their Mother was trying to keep them from getting too wild. I found a corner in the kitchen where I could stand and watch.

There were so many people, all in one family! And so many things were happening simultaneously. It was exciting. It was chaotic too. Sometimes people didn't finish what they were saying or where they were going. I guess it was just too busy. You know, I'm not used to so many people.

I was fascinated with the people talking Italian. Everybody understood Italian—except Mother and me. The old people preferred to speak Italian. They talked English too, when they needed too. The young people didn't have accents. They preferred English, but they knew enough Italian to keep track of the conversation. Why, I wonder, can some people speak two languages and I can only speak one? Maybe they are just smarter. I ought to be able to speak more than one language.

TWELVE AND LIVING ALONE

Dinner was on the table. We were all sitting down.

Mother stood near the door talking to Mrs. Roselli. She called to me, "Carla Lee, come here a minute, I need to tell you something."

I went over to the door.

"You have a good time tonight. I have to go to the hospital for a few days–well, really I'll be gone all week. You'll be O.K. When you are ready to leave the Roselli's, you go back upstairs to our apartment. This is a chance for you to be a really big girl and stay by yourself. In the morning, you know how to fix yourself a bowl of cereal. You know how to make a sandwich for your lunch. I've bought some special chocolate marshmallow cookies. And there are a lot of other things in the kitchen that you really like. You can fix the food yourself this week. That's really grown-up."

"Why?" I asked. "Why are you going to the hospital?"

"I have to have an operation," she replied. "I'll be home as soon as it's over."

"Wait, Mother, what if I need something? Can I talk to you on the phone? When are you coming home?" I was full of questions, and not really sure what was happening to me—another of those sudden life changes.

"You'll be fine. You're a really big girl now—twelve and one-half years old. Whenever you have a question, or need help with something, Mrs. Roselli is here. Just knock on her door, or call her on the phone. You know what time to meet the school bus. And when you get home, Cappy will be eager to play with you. I bought him some new catnip."

"What about this weekend? Will you be here then," I asked.

"Probably not this weekend, Carla Lee, but by next weekend I'll surely be home. I think the Rosellis are going to do some more Halloween decorations this weekend. I'm sure you can help them stuff big bags with leaves, maybe carve a pumpkin.

"Dinner's ready," Mrs. Roselli's sister announced.

Mother said good-bye. She had a taxi waiting for her. I waved good-bye. I'm fighting back tears.

What ever was happening? I wonder.

This caught me off guard. I had just gotten off home and we were gardening. Suddenly Mother has me in the Roselli apartment. After school, a group of us had walked among the shops admiring the finished Halloween windows. I was proud. Mine looked really good. And, it won a blue ribbon. Besides that, I'd worn my new jacket today, the one that Don sent from Asia. I wanted to tell Mother how much the kids liked it. It was really tacky—an orange silk jacket with a multi-colored fire-breathing dragon embroidered on the back. Don sent it from Japan—in the same package where he sent Mother an elegant silver cape, and the beautiful real pearl necklace and earrings. The kids liked the dragon and so did I. It was perfect for eighth grade. I had so much to tell Mother when I got home from school today. I hadn't had the chance to tell her.

All of a sudden, it isn't the really pleasant day I thought it was.

I'd only been in a hospital once before my current stay. That was to have my tonsils out. What a horrifying experience–even if I did get all the ice cream I wanted on the day that I went home. They put you to sleep. Then they cut you up. Uuuuggghhh. I shiver just thinking about it.

Thank goodness that isn't happening to me now in this hospital. I've been jolted back to reality just thinking of the day Mother left. I can't help but shudder again. Being in a hospital while thinking about Mother in the hospital is overload.

Why did Mother have to have an operation? Would she be O.K.? The Roselli's were really nice that night. But my mood shifted. I had to figure out about living alone. I never thought about that before. I can do this; I'm sure. But I need to think it through.

"Here, have some pizza," Mrs. Roselli said as she shoveled a piece from this big pie onto my plate.

"Thank you." I'd never in my life seen anything that looked like THAT!

And—I never had smelled anything quite like pizza. I had wondered what the smell was that filled the apartment! The unique mix of tomatoes and onions and oregano and sausage was new to me. Just now, it makes me a little sick. Years later, I came to love that smell, and that food.

I needed not to cry in front of all these strangers. I struggled to eat one piece of pizza. I wanted to vomit. I couldn't let them know. It had nothing to do with them. I just had to make it through dinner.

Everyone was chattering with everyone else. No one was paying much attention to me, thank goodness.

"Mrs. Roselli," I said. "Thank you for inviting me to dinner tonight. It was very good. I need to do my homework now."

"Are you sure you can't stay for dessert?"

"I'd love to, but I have a lot to do before I go to bed."

I went upstairs where I could cry.

Two days later, at recess, I tried to tell some of the other girls at school what was happening to me. "Did you ever stay at home, all by yourself, for a week?" I asked Sue and Betty.

They looked at me strangely. "Sure, but dad and mom were there at night," said Sue.

"My grandmother stayed with me once," said Betty. "That was fun. She took me to movies." (I wondered if my grandma wanted to come to Vails Gate.)

"I mean—all alone," I tried again. "Sometimes I don't know where things are—like the new tube of toothpaste. And I didn't get my dinner cooked so it tasted like it does when Mother cooks it. Some people like 'all alone; what do I need to know?"

They just look at me. Then Betty changed the topic. "I'm going to New York this weekend with my folks. We're going to Radio City Music Hall."

"That's fantastic," said Sue. I hope my folks will take me to Rockefeller Center before Christmas."

Once again, my experience made no sense to them. I bet that if I could talk with Jimmy and Alice, my friends from the bottom of the hill in Syracuse, they'd know what I meant. I'm sure they'd know how to solve the problems that arose when you were a kid alone. They'd know the best way to fix a meal. They'd know what to do if you ran out of toothpaste. They wouldn't be surprised that when there's only one parent, even if the parent is the most wonderful adult in the world, sometimes a kid had to stay alone.

Why would kids from regular families have any idea how to deal with the hard things in life? That stuff isn't taught in school. And it isn't discussed at home.

That week, while Mother was gone, I got up, caught the school bus, came home, fed the cat, and, once or twice, I ate more Italian food downstairs. I did my homework and went to bed. The days passed. School days were easier than the weekend. The nights were very long. How was Mother, I wondered? When would she come? Would she be O.K? No one called me. No one told me anything about her. You'd think someone would tell me how I could find out about her. Apparently she couldn't use a phone.

"Can you make it up the stairs?" Mrs. Roselli asked my Mother the day she came home. She had just come in from the taxi. There had been nobody to take her to the hospital, or to bring her home.

I'm certainly glad she didn't tell some government agency that she needed a place for me to go while she was sick. Staying alone is tough. Having to have a stranger live with me or to go away to someone else's house would have been worse. It would have made a challenging time into a terrifying time.

"Mother, wow, I'm happy to see you home. I love you soooooo much." I dance around in the vestibule. "Wait until you see the bouquet I picked for you."

"Coming, Carla Lee. I have to go slowly. It will take me a few minutes to get up these stairs."

I was so excited that Mother was home. I had tried to straighten up the apartment. I picked an end of the summer bouquet of colorful flowers for the table.

Things got a little unkempt this week—mostly me. I wasn't very good at ironing clothes, or at some of the details of grooming. It was hard to get the part in my hair straight. It was hard to get the braids to hold all the hair. I did leave some dirty laundry and dirty dishes. Did Mother think the apartment was a mess? She never said a word about it.

Mother still didn't explain much about her week in the hospital. Some months later I learned that she had kidney cancer. Why does cancer horrify everyone? I never learned why. Mother had one kidney removed. Is that O.K? She wanted me to think everything was normal. Or, maybe, she just wanted to make everything normal. How can I know what's true?

MORE GAMES?

Whatever is going on, Mother projects an unspoken sense that success is possible. She was getting better–more able to move around. That was good. And I really liked eighth grade at Cornwall. I started to pay attention to school activities again. Then one Saturday, another surprise came.

"Hey there! Good to see you," Don cried out.

"Welcome home," Mother said. They hugged.

It had been a month since Mother's operation. Don was back from Korea. I didn't know he was coming. I also didn't know that the Air Force had given him an emergency transfer back to the U.S. because his wife was dying from cancer.

"Look at all the things I've brought," Don said as he kept unwrapping items he'd brought from Korea and Japan.

"See, this picture is of the officers at a base near Seoul."

"Does everybody wear that kind of clothes," I asked, pointing to a picture of some Koreans walking down a street. "Koreans look different from people here. The houses look different too."

I'm beginning to understand that the rest of the world is, like my text books say, very different from America. Someday, I want to go to far away places. I just want to know what life there is really like.

"You're right, Carla Lee. Korea is different. So is Japan. Look at some more of these pictures. But, the guys on the military bases—we look the same everywhere in the world."

"Now, Helen, Carla Lee, I have more news. The Air Force is stationing us at the base in Lake Charles, Louisiana. We're moving right after Christmas."

"What? Louisiana! That's terrible," I said.

"It's not even the second semester, and I'll have to go to another school—again. Besides, people say that schools in the south are not any good. I don't remember who said this; but I must have heard it from several places. Otherwise, why would I remember it? Why don't I ever have a say in what happens? Why do I have to move *again*?"

I stomp off to my room. Adults are hopeless. I sob and sob. "You just keep repeating the same thing. Move here. Move there."

Mother came in. She tried to convince me that there would be an advantage of going to my sixth school for the second half of eighth grade.

"Have you thought," Mother pointed out, "the school in Louisiana finishes in May—whereas if you stayed at Cornwall Junior High you wouldn't finish the school year until late June?"

While this surely was veiled bribery, it worked. That was one reason to go! I could tell the kids, when I got to ninth grade, that I did eighth grade with a whole month less of school! I would have accomplished something in less time than was expected.

Once again, I said good-bye. I'd miss this school. I'd done well here. I won't miss the house. I liked seeing the sunrises and having a garden, but now it just reminded me of Mother's operation and living by myself.

"I think we're packed. Put the cat in the car, Carla Lee," Don said as he climbed in. Mother and I got in and a new chapter of growing up began. We started on our long drive to Lake Charles, Louisiana.

The landscape sped by. The cat and I had the back seat of the Nash to ourselves. There were hours, in fact days, to look out the window. We saw New York, New Jersey, Pennsylvania, West Virginia, Virginia, North Carolina, Georgia, Alabama, and Mississippi. Finally we got to Louisiana.

What will happen here? I wondered. I thought parents were supposed to help kids grow up. Mother tried. But her choices were always very hard ones. It seemed that I had to figure out all sorts of things by myself. How am I supposed to know how to do that?

Chapter Five

Louisiana: Eighth Grade and Cancer

The afternoon is slowly passing. It's another day in my Syracuse hospital room—maybe my last day. No visitors. Too bad kids can't visit. A hospital social worker did come.

"So, do you have a parent that you live with?" The social worker asked.

"Well, there's Don, my step-father" I say. "But he's in Florida vacationing."

"Vacationing?"

"I'm not surprised. All he told me was that he and his girl-friend needed to get away," I said. "But I can go home on the bus. I have a key to the apartment."

"Hmmmmmm." That was all she said. She left. I want back to thinking about when we arrived in Louisiana.

TRAVELING TO LAKE CHARLES

"By late morning we'll be in New Orleans." Don said. Three of us, Mother, Don and me are, it appeared, a 'family' again.

"We'll spend some time walking around the French Quarter," Mother added. "We'll have some beignets." She seemed to have recovered from her kidney surgery three months ago and she seemed genuinely happy to have Don back from Korea. The Air Force had transferred him from the base in Korea to one in Lake Charles, Louisiana because of Mother's cancer.

"What are beignets?" I asked.

"French donuts," Don replied. "They're deep fried, warm and covered with powdered sugar."

"They're delicious," said Mother. "The only problem is that we can't be gone from the car too long. The cat won't survive if it gets too hot in here."

"Hot! That seems so strange. It's January." I said. "There should be snow."

"We left winter behind when we left the north last week. By tonight we'll be at our new home in Lake Charles. We'll stop by the Air Force Base first. I need to report my arrival to the Base Commander. Then we'll go to our new house." Don said.

"You'll like this house." Mother added. "It's two apartments put together, and they are all on one level. For the first time since you were a baby, you'll—almost—be living in a real house again." For Mother this must seem like a step toward the life she had to abandon when Daddy died.

I was glad to stop in New Orleans. I felt like I had been in the back seat of the Nash forever. It had only been four days. But, that was enough.

On that last stretch from New Orleans to Lake Charles I wrote a letter to my Syracuse friend, Nancy.

"Nancy, you asked me to tell you what's different about the south. Well, it certainly isn't like New York. Spanish moss hangs on the trees, especially the live oak trees. It's very pretty. Somehow, it makes everything seem cozy. I can't explain why, but it does.

"And there's the smell. The rural south has a unique and wonderful smell. It's hard to describe. It's a mix of damp and rich soil and fresh plants. It reminds me of my Grandma Brooks' town, Raiford, in rural North Florida.

"Yesterday we bought boiled peanuts in Mississippi. I've seen them before when I visited my Grandma Brooks, but I never really tried them. They didn't look very appealing. How do I describe boiled peanuts? They are squishy and warm—just pulled out of a pot of boiling water. They taste bland, except that they are salty. I like them—a few—sometimes."

"Stopping in New Orleans was special. The old buildings made you feel like you'd traveled in time to another place. The buildings had intricate wrought iron railings forming balconies on the upstairs of houses. The balconies were full of plants. The streets were filled with all kinds of people as well as the sounds of jazz and the smells of Creole cooking."

"Nancy, you won't believe the cemeteries. They are above ground. New Orleans is below sea level and real graves would fill with salt water. We walked around in a cemetery. Four or five people are piled on top of each other in what looks like rows of walls. I guess that when one person has disintegrated, they put another person in the same cubicle. They just slide the coffin in the box, close the door, and lock it. In front of the dead person, there's a little shelf place where you can put some flowers. Some people put plastic flowers on the shelf. The faded ones really look crappy. The whole cemetery experience was very strange."

We crossed Louisiana heading along the coast toward Texas. We waited while Don went into a building on the Air Force Base for a few minutes. Then we drove to our new home.

"We're here," Don said as he pulled up in front of our duplex in the suburban Lake Charles neighborhood where officers from the Air Base lived.

I got out and looked around. "It really is on one floor," I said. "And look at the funny place to put a car. The garage has no walls, just a roof, and then there's a roof over the path from the garage to the house."

"That's a breezeway." Mother said. "It's how they do things here."

"Look at the flowers, Mother," I called. "They are just like the gardenias that a girl from Ed Smith School had for a corsage at a dance. The Monday after the dance, she brought the corsage to school to show us what it was like. Her flowers were wilted and a little brown by Monday. But you could still tell from the beautiful smell what it must have been like. I don't believe it—the same flowers are growing here in our front yard!"

"Yes, they are gardenias." Mother commented. "We can put some in a vase on the table after we get a table. And after we figure out which box has the vases."

In the Lake Charles house, I had my own room. It was big too. I immediately set up my record player and started playing "Mr. Sandman, Send Me a Dream." I liked that song. I also liked to play "Three Coins in the Fountain" too. The other half of the house was a studio for my Mother. She had her easels and paintings there.

"Carla Lee, please don't play in my studio unless I'm there."

I thought to myself. What a ridiculous rule; I am twelve now, nearly grown-up. Surely I'm old enough to decide where it's OK to go. And I wouldn't hurt any of Mother's art work.

MOTHER'S STUDIO

Playing in our new home was fun. Sometimes I just chased the cat around. A lot of the time I played ball–something I know I was only supposed to do outside. But it was very hot outside. I was very good at catching a ball, so surely I could do it inside without harm. I was really an expert at 'twirleys' (where you bounced the ball against the wall, turned around real fast so you could face the ball again in time to catch it when it bounced back). I was also very good at 'ball-under-leg throws', and 'bounce-off-wall while you clap throws.' The girls at school practiced and practiced during recess to see who could do these tricks the best. In that respect Louisiana and New York were the same—at least for the Air Force brats.

Don and Mother teased me.

Don said, "What good is it to know how to bounce a ball? When you grow up, it won't help you keep a job or get a husband?"

"I can see you when you're forty still doing 'ball-under-leg throws.'" Don teased.

I ignored him. Why would he think I just wanted a job or a husband? There's so much to explore. He doesn't understand that. Or, on the other hand, maybe he's teasing just to hurt my feelings, In that case, I really have to ignore him, or be hurt. There's no choice.

Mother said, "Carla Lee, won't you please spend some time doing something else. You have a new book to read. Maybe you could see how it ends? Or—why don't you draw some more pictures with your new set of pastel chalk?"

"Later, Mother," was my usual response. She didn't understand either.

One day I was playing ball in Mother's studio. I missed the ball and ran to catch it. My foot caught the leg of her easel. I knocked her oil portrait of a boy from India off of the easel. Worse yet, it hit something and the canvas tore—right on his face—right by one of his gorgeous big brown eyes–a big gash. I felt terrible. I loved that portrait. The dark skinned boy with huge eyes, so full of mystery and delight, was stunning. Of all Mother's paintings, it was one of my favorite pictures.

Mother heard the crash and came running. She had not known that I was in her studio.

"How can you do that?" Mother scolded. And she sobbed.

"I'm sorry. I'm sorry." I sobbed too.

"I didn't mean to knock it off the easel."

"No one ever *means* to have an accident. If people do what they *mean* to do, nothing bad would ever happen." Mother was very upset. "You were told not to be in my studio. And, I can't believe you would play ball in here. You go straight to your room," she ordered.

She sobbed more.

I went.

Mother was right this time. How could I be so stupid! I stared out the window. I didn't think I'd make a mistake. How could I fix things? I'm so so sorry. There's no way to fix it. Maybe I should have listened to her. How do you know when to listen and when listening just ties you down? How can you tell?

I seemed to be getting into trouble a lot these days. At least, it seems I got scolded a lot for making noise, and for running around in the house. Mother never used to yell at me like this.

Sometimes it wasn't my fault. She was just grumpy. Why?

But, this time, it really was my fault. I was sorry.

Other times, when she yelled, I yelled back—because I thought I was entitled to a point of view. I just don't understand why she's always so grumpy.

The only good thing that ever came out of these arguments was that we both say what's on our minds. And then, amazingly, we both seemed to get over it. Afterwards, everything is O.K.

And maybe it's better, because we each really heard what the other thought.

I hated it, though, when we fought. It felt so awful that people couldn't just talk normally.

Some people just keep silent and pretended that everything was O.K. when it isn't. Mother pretended whenever she had some adult decision that she had to make. I didn't like that.

But it's different when someone really does something bad. I was really at fault since I knocked down her painting. I can't fix it. All a person can do is move ahead and maybe learn something! That's really sad, especially for Mother. Moving ahead does nothing for the person hurt. I don't think this is about learning where to play, or about when to listen. I think it must be about learning to figure out why sometimes, when you think what you're doing is O.K. it's not O.K.? I don't know if it's possible to always figure that out. I wonder if Mother is just grumpy because of me?

SOUTHERNERS AND YANKEES

I'd made one friend—well an acquaintance. We weren't really alike, she was older than me—fourteen–but she lived nearby. Rosemary was also an Air Force brat. She came here from up north somewhere. She liked to act sophisticated and was really interested in boys. She spent all her babysitting money on clothes. She was always talking about different clothing styles, and hair styles.

I invited her to play in my room one day. We were listening to records and she was painting her finger nails with nail polish that she had brought with her.

"Come here, Carla Lee. Let me show you how to use the nail polish. You can use some of mine. It's cranberry red." Rosemary took my hand and started painting my nails cranberry red.

I thought to myself that this was really tacky. But I figured that soon I'd be thirteen and need to understand these grown-up things.

"Does it come off?" I asked hopefully.

"Yes, but you need to buy a bottle of this polish remover," she said. "You won't need to take it off until about two weeks from now when it starts to chip."

I didn't tell her that my intent was to buy a bottle of that stuff as soon as possible. Tonight I hoped. Nail polish looked O.K. on other people. On me it looked awful–fake.

"How come girls in Louisiana do things so different from girls in New York," I asked her.

"Girls in New York wear nail polish," Rosemary said.

"That's true. It just seems more popular here," I replied. I remembered that once I'd seen Mother with nail polish, but she never put it on my nails. Maybe she was just too busy, or maybe she had too much on her mind.

"Southerners are different in other ways too," I continued. "They talked really slowly, and it sounded so nice. They talked that way, even when they were angry."

"That's true," Rosemary added. "Thing is, sometimes you don't know they are angry because it all sounds so nice."

"A lot more girls here wear perfume." I said. "Some perfume gives you a headache." I tried to remember if Mother ever wore perfume. She wore a tiny bit—not too much, and only once-and-a-while.

Rosemary just listened. I don't think she understood my comment.

"Another thing," Rosemary added. "People here go fishing much more than they do in New York. And they ride motor-cycles more, too."

"Hmm, you're right. I wonder why?" I commented.

"I don't know why." She said. "Maybe it's because you can't take a bus or a subway to a fishing hole. Plus—in, New York, there aren't so many fishing places. And, it's cold up north."

"Guess so," I said. "We had catfish for dinner last night. Someone my step-father knows caught them."

We took a few minutes to finish with the nail polish, and to admire the results.

"You know what I don't think is right?" I said. "I don't think it's right that New Yorkers sometimes look down on Southerners. They say that Yankees are better. But—what does 'better' mean anyhow?"

Rosemary skipped the 'what's better' part and went on to make an observation, "I've seen Yankees look down on Southerners in movies, and sometimes I've read it in novels."

"Well I don't agree with that. It's silly. Everybody's the same. I ought to know. My daddy was a Southerner and my Mother is a Yankee—so I'm both. How can half of me be better than the other half? It's stupid," I exclaimed.

"I agree," said Rosemary. "Must be left over from watching Civil War movies."

I wondered to myself if ideas could last eighty-five years. The Civil War ended eighty-five years ago. I learned that in school not very long ago.

JUST MEAT ON A SLAB?

My reminiscing is interrupted again. This time a group of people in white coats stream into my hospital room. They gather around my bed. One man, a doctor, speaks. (Maybe they all are doctors.)

"This young girl came in by ambulance four days ago." He tells the group. He continues lecturing them about how they deal with this type of puncture wound. I finally figured out that they must be his students at the university medical school.

I want to interrupt and say "Hello, I'm not just meat on a slab. At least say hello." But I didn't dare. So I just stared at them, trying to catch their eyes, one by one. What's the point in trying to get them to be human, or to know that I am? I slipped back to Louisiana.

"Dinner time," Mother called.

"I'll see you tomorrow at school. You can tell me if your mom fixed Louisiana food for dinner. O.K.?" Rosemary said, joking. Louisiana food meant things like beef jerky, and Creole.

"Yes, ma'am," I replied in my best Southern accent. "Me an' my critter (I mean my cat) wouldn't wanna be impolite and just say a plain 'yes' the way those Yankees do."

She laughed.

"See ya' tomorrow." I waved.

Louisiana was fascinating. I loved meeting people who did things differently from my family. I loved learning about new cultures. I loved trying to understand why I expected things to happen one way and other people expected something else.

We sat down for dinner.

"Mother," I said, "my new school is so different from the schools in Syracuse. Eighth grade here is really easy. We studied all this stuff last fall in Syracuse. That's O.K. But Mother, is it O.K not to learn new things? Can I still be as smart as kids in New York?"

"You'll be all right wherever you are, Carla Lee. I'm sure of that. You are very inquisitive and you like to read and—equally important—you like to do things for yourself. You know how to be creative and how to start-up projects. You'll be O.K."

That was really nice of her to say. It made me feel good to have Mother say something specific, something that gave me real feedback. Maybe Mother will treat me like an adult now and not assume that I should be left out of discussions. I hoped so because, now that I'm spending time with teenagers, the world is becoming huge raising so many questions and so many possibilities. How can I figure out how to deal with all this?

Weeks passed. I began to feel at home at LaGrange Junior High School. What I did like about La Grange, aside from getting out a month sooner than did schools in New York, was the architecture. This was not like any school I've ever attended up north. You had to go outside under the breezeway to get from class to the cafeteria—even when it rained. That not only made a break in the routine, but it made me wonder about buildings. Two buildings were built to be schools. One was in New York State and one was in Louisiana. Both were full of kids and teachers. Did one place have a different feel just because of the imagination of the person who designed it? Maybe it was different because of where it was located. Anyway, it had a very different feel—a different impact on the people inside. Imagine that! Could it be that the kind of building you're in affects a person?

For example, this building where I am now—my Yankee hospital room has a cold, colorless, stainless, sterile, scary feel. Do all hospitals have to be that way?

A JOB

One day, I got off the school bus and another girl who also got off at my stop said, "Want a babysitting job? I can't do the job I took for Friday night. I have a date. Mrs. Larson will be a whole lot less angry about my 'finking' out if I tell her I've got somebody else to stay with her kids."

"Sure," I said. I was eager to build up my own babysitting business. I just needed some clients. So far all the people with kids had other teenagers as their regular sitters. Maybe I could start by being a substitute.

Sue, the girl who gave me her babysitting job, continued. "That's great. I'll tell Mrs. Larson and I'll give her your telephone number. What's your number? Oh—you charge $.50 an hour because it's a night job. When you sit during the day, you charge $.35 an hour. The rates are up this year. We all have to charge this same higher rate."

"GR9-4608," I replied. "Thanks. I'll charge $.50 an hour. I'll wait for Mrs. Larson's call." I ran off toward my house. Sue went the other way to her house.

Before long, I was busy with babysitting jobs. There were so many that I had to keep a calendar to schedule them. Sometimes the kids I sat for were really good; sometimes they were a real pain. They tried to get away with things when a sitter was there—things they'd never do if their parents were home.

Don't ask me how I learned to take care of kids. Truthfully, I don't have a clue how to take care of kids. I'd never been around little kids. I guess the people who hired me just thought that if you were born a girl and you were twelve years old, you'd know how to take care of kids. I hope they're right.

Soon I had my own cache of spending money. I used it for clothing and make-up. That's what the other girls did.

"Please Mother, can I wear lipstick? By next week I should be able to afford to buy some. The other girls wear lipstick when we go to the movies."

"No, Carla Lee. You need to wait until you're grown-up. I don't care what the other kids do. Lipstick doesn't look good on you yet." Mother was emphatic.

Weeks slipped by. The babysitting profits grew. And, sometimes, very rarely, it was O.K. to wear lipstick.

SKIPPING SCHOOL

"We're going to a rodeo tomorrow." Shirley, a girl in my class, mentioned when we were standing in the playground at school recess.

"Wanna cut school and come with us?"

I didn't know Shirley very well—well, I really didn't know her at all. But then I didn't know anybody very well.

"Sure, I'll come," I replied. I'd never cut school and I'd never been to a rodeo. Mother probably wouldn't approve. But the trip seemed harmless enough. Besides, school was so easy. I'd still get 'As'.

So I said yes.

We got a ride with someone. I don't know him. It took us almost a half hour to get there. Partly, that's because it took time to cram seven kids into this little car. The driver was fourteen. He had just gotten his license. Well, that's what he said. I hoped it was true.

He wore a cowboy hat, cowboy boots and a big plaid shirt with a hole in the shoulder. I guessed he was a friend of Shirley's. Maybe he was in ninth grade. He liked to strut around and act important. He only talked to the people he knew. So I got to watch. That was fine with me.

We parked a long walk away from the corral—at the closest parking place in the huge field where all the cars were. I was thinking to myself that this is the first time I'd ever ridden in a car driven by someone in my generation—not an adult. There were lots of 'firsts' today. Firsts are how you learn about being grown-up, I told myself.

The rodeo was in a big corral on a ranch. Just like in the movies, the crowd was enormous. The people who can't find a place by the corral to sit just crowded around hoping to see into the ring. That was us. I managed to get a view. It took a bit of maneuvering, but I could see perfectly between this big guy's arm and his chest—so long as he left his arm on the railing and didn't move it. He had no idea that this was my angle of view. He had no idea that anyone was standing behind him.

The rodeo was O.K.—not great. It was definitely different from anything I'd ever done or seen. A lot of people seem to be having a great time.

"Look at that!" Shirley exclaimed as she jumped up and down. A cowboy threw his lasso from one side of the ring to the other and caught a cow around the neck.

"Get 'em. Get 'em now," someone else yelled as another cowboy wrestled a steer to the ground with just the weight of his body. With some clever moves with his legs and arms, he suddenly had the steer pinned with his knee on the animal's throat. He had one hand on each horn trying to keep the animal still for the appointed time.

"Yuck," I muttered to myself. Why isn't this fun? It's supposed to be.

After a while, some other cowboys came out of stalls riding wild horses. "Stay on. Stay on. Stay on," chanted part of the crowd. These cowboys were trying not to be thrown off the bucking, running, jumping horses. The horses were trying to get these guys off their backs.

"It's really dusty," I said to Shirley.

"Yeah, exciting, huh," she replied. "Atta' boy! Stay on!" She returned to cheering.

I'm got tired of standing. I don't like the dust. Now I know what a rodeo's like. I don't need to do this again, I thought to myself. I wonder when we can go home.

"In about an hour, they'll have the blue ribbon cow boys," the guy who drove us said to Shirley.

"Great. This is really exciting. It's one of the best rodeos I've seen." Shirley replied. "I love how they do tricks with the lassoes."

I'm just listening and watching. I must be a real 'party-pooper' I thought to myself. I'm supposed to like all this sports stuff. I say nothing. I knew I needed to watch and to cheer for at least another hour.

That was the first—and last time that I skipped school.

CANCER

"Hi, I'm home!" I shouted in to Mother as I came in the house and tossed my books down.

It was the week after our rodeo escapade. I walked into the living room. I was ready to tell Mother what happened in school, to tell her about my next baby-sitting job and how I thought that I'd buy a new bathing suit when I had saved enough. But I had walked into a strange new world.

Mother was sitting at her desk crying.

"What's the matter?" I asked.

"I can't do it," she replied. "I'm trying to write grandma a letter. I know exactly what I want to say, but I can't make my pen put those words on the paper. I can't do it. I can't do it. I've been sitting here for hours. " She kept sobbing.

"My head won't work," she cried.

I'd never seen Mother like this before. And she's never talked with me like this. I didn't know what to do. I went and stood by her at the desk. I didn't know what to say.

"Can I do something?" I asked.

"No. No. I'll be O.K." She continued to sob.

There must be a way I could help her. There must be something adults know that I don't know about how to make people feel better.

Why don't I know what it is? I don't even have anyone to ask.

I hung around for a few minutes. I think maybe if I told her what happened at school today, it would change the subject so we could both think about something else. She was so upset; I soon realized that now was not the time to talk about other stuff. I stayed a bit longer. Then I went to my room.

It was dinner time and Don came home. He brought some food from a 'take-out' restaurant with him. We ate. We talked about other things. It was as if nothing had happened.

A couple weeks passed. To my eyes, it was as if life was normal again.

But that soon changed.

I came home from school and found Mother on the floor.

"I can't make this leg work. I know exactly where I want to put it, but it won't go. I can't get up," she explained.

This time she was scared—not crying.

I was really scared too. Whatever was happening?

"Here, give me your hand. I'll help you up," I said. "I've never tried to lift you before, but I bet, if I really pull, I can get you as far as this big chair."

I moved the chair toward her. Then I tried lifting. This wasn't easy. Part of her was almost dead weight. Mother was only five feet two inches tall, and she was pretty slim. But she was still bigger than I was.

"There, you did it Carla Lee," she said. "Thank you."

I'm relieved to see her sitting in the big upholstered chair. At least things looked normal.

"Are you O.K.?" I asked—still not certain of what was happening.

"I'm fine," she said. "Before you go, can you do one more favor for me? I think the telephone cord will reach as far as this chair. Can you put the phone next to me, please?"

"Sure," I replied. The cord was just long enough. I set the phone on a small table next to the chair and went off to my room. I knew something strange was happening; but I couldn't understand what it was. How do adults know what to do when something Happens that you never had dealt with before? There must be something that I don't know?

Don came home from the Air Base earlier than usual that day. He had news, too. Soon he'd be a Lt. Colonel. But we didn't talk much about his promotion that night.

"Run out to the garden and pick some lettuce," Mother directed me.

"Can you make us a salad?" Don asked. He opened a can of something.

"O.K.," I replied. I went into the yard to pick the makings for a salad. I liked our garden. We had, again, miraculously produced salad from seeds.

Soon dinner is served. We ate and talked about the cat and the garden. That's all. I thought about asking what was going on, but then it didn't seem to be my place to bring up the subject, and I didn't want to make things worse. I kept quiet and just watched and worried.

"Better finish dinner quickly, Carla Lee. You'll be late for your baby-sitting job," Mother commented while looking at the time.

I left. The babysitting business was booming! A couple more weeks passed. Things seemed pretty normal. No one offered any explanations for what had happened that day when Mother couldn't get off the floor. If something was wrong, no one let me know.

I wrote Nancy in Syracuse another letter. "Lake Charles isn't exactly the garden spot of the nation. We are very close to Texas where there are chemical plants that spew a rotten egg smell when the wind shifts toward Louisiana. It's disgusting. You'd never believe the smell." I told her other tidbits of news about my cat, the gardenias, and how easy school was. I didn't tell her about what was happening with Mother. Somehow it wasn't kid talk. And back when I had tried to ask her about Don's comments about girl's bodies and what a dad was like, she just wasn't comfortable with this kind of conversation.

I sealed the envelope, put on a stamp and walked the letter to the mail box.

I hurried back to the house because the wind had shifted. The smell was awful. I closed myself inside and wondered how the grown-ups could let the people at that factory take away our good air. Why didn't somebody make them stop? Didn't the people in the factory even care about their own families smelling that stuff?

Chapter Six

The Flood and A Telegram

MOLD

It was May 1953 now, and really hot. I had turned thirteen just a month before. We had two big ceiling fans in our Louisiana house. Each one was about three feet across. They made a loud whirring noise when they ran. We were lucky. Because the house was a duplex and the other half was Mother's studio, we could use both fans—not just one. But, I guess they didn't cool off my closet.

Everyday I learned something new about southern living. The tropics sure were different from New York State.

"Mother, look at this green stuff all over my shoes," I called. "Yuck, it's on all of them"

"That's mold, dear. It's just what happens when you live in the south. We have to keep the air circulating. Don't put damp things in the clothes closet. Leave your closet door open," said she. "Bring me your shoes. We'll clean off the mold." She showed me how.

"Here, Carla Lee. We'll wipe it off with this damp cloth. Wipe inside too. Be sure to get into all the corners."

I wiped. I'd rather have had her do the wiping. But, I wiped.

"Wash out the cloth, Carla Lee."

I worked until both shoes looked to be free from mold.

"Now, let's be sure they are as cleanly washed as possible, with soap. Then set them out in the sun to dry. It's about noon. By night time this hot Louisiana sun will destroy what's left of any mold."

That was one of the last pieces of parental guidance I ever received. Neither of us knew that would be the case at the time.

As far as I was concerned, the mold, the heat, and the big bugs that came in the house were quite enough. But, then there was more. We had a flood. New York State was never like this!

Lake Charles is very close to the Gulf of Mexico. All in all the bayous and swampland meant that, even in normal circumstances, there was a lot of water. In the past week it rained and rained. Lake Charles was largely under water.

People found themselves wading inside their houses. Some were in water four feet deep. And it was dangerous. We heard stories about places where the electric power was still on and people in the water could have been electrocuted. One story told about a house where the gas was on and was leaking. Then, everywhere, the dirty water had sewage and snakes in it. And it was really slippery to walk.

The Browns, where I baby sit, had to move out of their house.

"Mrs. Brown, can I help you carry things out," I asked. I had gone over to her house to try to help. I was wearing my tall rain boots, but they weren't quite tall enough. What a squishy feeling to walk with water inside your boots!

"Thanks, Carla Lee. There's not much else I can take. Can you just carry this one suitcase? Please be careful not to carry it by the handle because it will get in the water."

"O.K.," I replied. "Where shall I take it?" I started down the wet slippery street.

"Just put it on the Walker's front steps. Our family will camp on their living room floor until this is over."

"How much water is in your house?" I asked her.

"It's pretty bad and the water is still rising. It's up to my knees. For the one year old, it's nearly over her head. We're losing everything—rugs, electrical things, the beds, the sofa and chairs. They are all sitting in water—dirty water."

"That's terrible."

My house, less than a block away, had no water on the property. But something was happening that seemed even worse than the flood.

AN AMPHIBIOUS VEHICLE

Mother greeted me when I returned home from the Walkers.

"I'm going to the hospital tonight," she told me on May 23rd, 1953. "I need to have another operation—on my brain this time."

It's was not quite been two years from that day to this one, March 1955, when I'm in this hospital room—a stabbing victim. Do you think anyone would believe that my fifteen years have included all these weird events? It really doesn't seem like what happens to most kids. Does it?

"You can ride with us in the car," Mother said. "We'll drive to the edge of the flood waters. The Air Force has arranged to meet the car with an amphibious craft that will take us to a dry airplane runway," Don added.

"We'll go about 5 PM. I need you to be a really big girl, Carla Lee," Mother said.

She continued, "Don is coming with me on the airplane. We'll go to the Air Force hospital in San Antonio, Texas." She continued. "You'll stay here in the house. Because you've just turned thirteen, I know you'll be O.K by yourself. David's Mother is just a block down the street and she will be able to help with any problems you have."

David Alfred was my friend from school. We were in the same grade. His father was the Colonel who was the Commanding Officer for the Air Base.

It's happening again, I thought to myself. Once again no one told me what was wrong. They just sprang it on me at the last minute. I guess this is how grown-ups treat each other. But you'd think that if I'm supposed to act grown-up, I'd at least know what to do when the ground is pulled out from under me!

I squirm a bit in my own hospital bed. Maybe this reminiscing isn't a good idea. Too much hospital stuff! I'm in the hospital trying to forget my current dilemma by thinking about Mother's brain surgery! That really is pretty weird! There must be better things to think about. But, I decide that I have to finish this story. I have to get to the point that brought me to my current hospital room.

My memory returned to that day nearly two years ago.

We had an early supper. Don helped Mother into Colonel Alfred's car. I got in the back seat. We drove a few blocks—to the edge of the flood water. My block of officer's housing was one of the few parts of Lake Charles not under water. As we drove to the edge of the water, we passed the many houses with yards filled with refugees who were living in tents, camper vans and trailers. The yards were scattered with household belongings— furniture under tarps, all sorts of stuff. No one was sharing our house. We were an exception. I guess that was because Mother is sick and is going away. Other people seem to know that.

When we got to the edge of the flood water, a huge Air Force amphibious craft was waiting. It was painted military mud. In a minute, it would swallow my Mother.

I felt like Mother and Don were about to float off into some war zone—and all I could do was to watch. I wished I could go with them, or do something to help. I wished they'd tell me when they'd be back.

"I love you," Mother said. "You be really grown-up now, Carla Lee!"

"I love you too," I replied. I try not to cry. I don't want Mother to feel worse.

I hugged her good-bye. I hugged her again. I strained to watch her every move as she was helped into this vehicle. She disappeared.

It was the last time I ever saw my Mother, although, at the time, I didn't know that this would be the case. It was probably good that I didn't know.

I watched the vehicle roll into the water and then float away taking her and Don to an airplane. I watched the ripples from the vehicle spread out across the flood water and eventually disappear.

On the way home Mrs. Alfred told me that in San Antonio the operation on her brain would be to remove more cancer— another tumor.

What does it mean to have brain cancer? I thought to myself. At thirteen, I probably should know that.

"It's almost bed time, now," said Mrs. Alfred. She and the Colonel dropped me off at our house. "You'll be fine. Look, there's your cat. You can play some records. There's lots of food in the fridge. Don't forget, there's a new pitcher of cool-aid. If you need anything, call us on the phone. Remember, we're just a block away."

"Good night," I said.

She left.

I was alone. It was dark. Alone made the house seem so much bigger. I told myself that it would be O.K because, after all, I'd done this once before when I was twelve and Mother had her kidney removed. But then there was someone else in the same building at least. Now the closest person is a block away. Our neighborhood is full of refugees. There's flood water everywhere else. Things outside aren't even normal.

But surely I could manage. I had a flashlight! I could listen to music on my new red portable radio. I was scared; but that just meant that I needed to figure out how to move on. Be strong. Strong is amazing stuff—just inside a person.

"Gotta get over it!" I said to myself out loud.

"Here Cappy. Here kitty, kitty, kitty," I called. "Come sleep in my bed."

Days went by. The nights went by more slowly. Weeks went by. There were a lot of things happening. The flood meant that for several weeks every day was a novelty. David Alfred, the Base Commander's son and I hatched a plan one day.

BUILDING A BOAT

"I've got an idea," David said. "Let's make a boat and row over to our school."

"Do you think that's O.K.?" I asked. "They're giving everyone typhoid shots and telling people to stay away from the flood water."

"Sure, it's O.K.," David said. "We're not going to drink the water or eat anything."

I'm still uncomfortable, but David was convincing. Besides, we wouldn't hurt anyone but ourselves. I decided to go.

"I think I know where there's some wood," I said. "It's a big piece of plywood. There are some smaller boards too." This will be a real adventure I thought to myself. Risky, yes. But we'll be O.K.

We carefully nailed the wood together and we made ourselves a boat. There was a big piece of plywood for the floor. And the skinny pieces of plywood were the walls. The walls were about sixteen inches high. We didn't have any seats. And the bottom stuck out past the walls because we didn't have a saw to cut it into the right shape. Well—it might not look like a boat, but it floated. That was all that mattered. We got two more boards for paddles and a couple coffee cans for bailing.

"Over here, we can launch the boat behind that row of houses," David said.

Gingerly, we paddled away from the shore. I was still worried about the water—the pollution, the snakes, and bugs, and sewage.

"You know there are alligators in this water too, David."

"Someone needs to see what our school looks like under water," David said. "We'll be doing something useful. Someone has to report back to the kids in the neighborhood. It might be days before the adults tell us anything. The flood might mean that we'll get to miss the last couple weeks of school! School might have already ended for the year! This is important information. No one else seems to be gathering it. Why shouldn't we? We can be reporters. Reporters go to dangerous places." And they do useful things."

I wondered to myself where the line was between being a reporter and being foolish. Could it be that it just depends who you ask? Or is there a real difference?

"Hey, these boards make pretty good oars," David said.

"Oh, bail faster," he pleaded. "A lot of water is coming in."

"I am bailing. I only have one coffee can," I said. "We had left the other one on shore. The water is coming in faster than I thought it would."

"Yuck, do you see how dirty that water is David," I said. "Maybe those people at the Red Cross were right when they cautioned people about getting typhoid from the bad water. We'll be in that water if our boat sinks. I wondered if the boat sank whether it would really be true that we really could stand up and wade back? I'd hated to do that in sewage though. Ugghh."

"We'll be all right," he offered. "My daddy is a war hero and he lived through things much worse than this. Why can't we be brave?"

David paddled. I bailed—and bailed. Amazingly, we actually did make it the mile to our school.

"Carla Lee. Look," David said. "There's our classroom. Let me see if I can maneuver under the breezeway here."

He used one of the plank oars to help turn the corner. It worked. It would have worked better if the plank was long enough to touch the ground. But we made it.

"We're awfully close to the breezeway roof," I noted. "Watch out that your head doesn't bump into that sign. Duck!!!" I looked around—quickly–because I had to pay attention to the bailing.

"Here. I've got hold of the edge of this window," David said. We can stop and look in. See, Mrs. Boudreau's desk is half under water. The drawer where she keeps our grades is under water!"

"Maybe," I added, "maybe that means that our grades will all be a blur. The ink will wash away on all of them. She can give everybody an 'A'."

"Look," David interrupted. "The ball we use at recess is floating on the water."

"Let's see what the cafeteria looks like," I said.

He rowed over to the cafeteria. I bailed.

"I hope this boat doesn't sink before we get back," I said. "It's bad enough to have my feet soaked in this disgusting water. I'd hate to walk chest deep in it."

"Keep bailing."

"It's so yucky!"

"David, look. Through this window, I got a perfect view of the cafeteria. Some stuff is floating on the water here, too."

"What is it?"

"It's got to be plastic bags full of garbage. What else could it be?"

"They must have had the bags ready for the truck to pick up."

David stood up in the boat and cupped his hands around his eyes to get a better view.

"Careful," I said. "You're making us wabble. I don't think this boat can stand wabbling."

"It's O.K.," David said, not really paying attention to where he was standing. "Yup, the bags are garbage. See, the one stuck on the serving table. It came open. There's trash all over the serving table—some under water, some hanging on the edge of the counter near the water line."

"Thanks for the description," I said. "I'll remember it the next time someone scoops food on my plate from that table in the cafeteria line."

"What a gross thought," David said.

"I wonder who gets to clean this mess. What do you think it will be like with a few more days of hot sun and water? You couldn't pay me enough to clean that up. Imagine the smell! Imagine the mold!"

We made it back to our launch site. We waded the last few feet and pulled the boat up on the ground. We didn't sink. Gators didn't attack. No snakes right here. We weren't discovered and punished. We never really understood the risks we were taking.

The kids were thrilled to hear of our adventure.

And—as it turned out, school never did resume that year.

BIDING TIME

Eventually the flood waters receded. The refugees went home to clean up. I went with Mrs. Brown on her first trip back to her house. Her whole neighborhood looked so strange. The electricity had been turned off for days. Inside her house it was dark, steamy, and smelly. Lieutenant and Mrs. Brown scrubbed and mopped. So much was thrown out—furniture, towels, curtains. You should have seen the piles of trash. The trash from everyone's home just added to the debris from the flood—floating garbage that landed on a sofa. Things like that. Gardens and lawns were gone. Everything was just mud and grime. I felt so badly for the people whose houses were under water.

May 23rd, June 23rd, July 23rd. Time passed. Mother was still in the hospital in San Antonio. No one ever suggested that I visit her—or even that I talk to her on the telephone. I don't even know where to send a letter. I guess she couldn't write me. She didn't. I think she would have if she had been well enough. Kids can't go to hospitals; besides San Antonio is very far away. I don't know where Don is; but he isn't home with me. Some step-father. Every few weeks, he'd send a post card, but all he said was some comment like 'everything is O.K. and he hopes I'm fine.'

No one gave me any update on Mother's health; people just wanted to talk about how I was doing. They wanted to invite me to go shopping or somewhere with them. Mrs. Alfred probably knew something; but she never talked. The other people were just neighbors and they had no reason to have any information. Mother was the one who wrote Grandma, so I had no idea what the Rochester relatives knew. I didn't even know how to write Grandma.

There were parties for the teenagers from school, and the possibility of playing 'spin-the-bottle' with boys—and babysitting. I was earning money that could be spent on new clothes and make-up.

There was only one problem. I didn't have a clue what one did with all the drug store cosmetic products. There was a whole aisle of stuff to spray on, or rub on—stuff for my hair, stuff for my skin, stuff for under my arms. What are all these different products? How do you use them? How do I put lipstick on so it makes a nice shape, so it doesn't smear? What do I do with eye shadow? What's that stuff that covers up a shiny nose? Somebody I know bought cold cream. What's that for? And how would you ever know which product to choose?

Some of the girls at school had to buy pads because they started to bleed onto their underwear. It lasted four or five days every month. They said that that will happen to me too. I was glad it hadn't happened yet because I had no idea what that was all about. I hung around in the girls' bathroom sometimes to listen to the kids talk. I thought maybe I'd learn why this happened and how to keep from messing one's clothes with spots of blood.

I wasn't sure about what to wear to school parties. How do I fix clothes so they really Looked nice. What should I buy? Should I buy a bra with a metal under thing? I think I need a strapless one, but how do I pick that out? How much starch is enough for the crinoline petticoats? There were so many choices to sort out. How do you fix your hair in the latest style? If the dress needed to be taken in, or hemmed, how would I do that so it looked right?

I knew a bit about sewing. I had watched Mother make clothes and I'd even begun to sew some of my clothes. I used Vogue and Mc Calls patterns. And, this year, in eighth grade, all the girls had a sewing class. I made a yellow skirt and a matching bolero vest. Still, I can't remember everything I should do to get things right when I tried to sew. And I certainly had no idea about all the other things that I should know. Things like—what do you wear to this kind of event, or to that?

This was all stuff girls learned from their big sisters and their Mothers. One day I asked one of the kids at school about her lipstick. I was wearing lipstick sometimes now.

"When you put the lipstick on, how do you get the corners right so it tapers off?"

She didn't want to be bothered. "Ask your big sister," she said. "Or, ask your Mother."

I have no big sister. Mother is in Texas somewhere and I can't talk with her. It would be embarrassing to ask any one because this was all private—in the family—stuff. So I watched. I copied when I could figure out how to. I tried my best to figure out these woman things without any mentors.

"Come over to our house for dinner tonight," Mrs. Wilson said. "We'll feed you, Carla Lee, before you baby-sit for us."

"We're going to the movies Saturday afternoon," Mrs. Humbolt said. "There's a whole car full of us. Wanna come?"

This kind of exchange with neighbors was becoming routine. It did give me some place to eat other than my own non-cooking cooking at least once or twice a week. And I got to check out other families. My situation wasn't so bad, I decided.

"You're doing just fine, aren't you? What a big girl you are," Mrs. Alfred would tell me from time to time.

Why do adults like to keep things superficial? Why don't they tell me about Mother, or ask if I want to write to her, or ask what it's like to live alone?

SUMMER IN WACO, TEXAS

David's parents invited me to go with their family for two weeks to Waco Texas. All I knew about Texas is that I didn't like it. I had two good reasons. First, we got the smell from that factory just outside of Lake Charles. The factory was in Texas. Second the people who cut my Mother's brain open were in Texas. But I guessed there was really no choice other than to go to Texas. School was out. The Alfred's were my contact with adults who knew about Mother. So I said yes. Texas was almost like a desert. One good thing about the trip was that now I could add Texas to the list of states I had visited. The list was impressive. I wondered if someday I could visit all fifty states.

We drove for the better part of a day in Colonel and Mrs. Alfred's car and finally reached Waco.

"Texas is really spread out," I commented to Colonel Alfred from the back seat.

"It's a big state," he replied. "I grew up in Texas."

"It's mostly flat, and dry. And it's a long distance between towns," I observed.

I wondered to myself why Mother was in the hospital in a place like this. And I wonder how far Waco was from the Air

Force Base in San Antonio where this hospital was. I hoped there were more trees where she was. She liked trees.

Mrs. Alfred said, "Soon we'll be at David's grandmother's ranch. That's where we'll live while we are here."

"Guess what, Carla Lee," David added. "I didn't tell you, but I think we can go horse back riding every day."

"I love horses," I said. "I don't know how to ride. But I'd like to learn."

"We can arrange that," David said.

And, he did. Every day we rode horses. We rode western style. I liked that. I could hold on to the saddle horn. It was easier when I galloped. What more could a thirteen year old girl want than a chance to be with horses, and—after the horses—with boys.

The summer of 1953 was passing. I returned to our house in Lake Charles. Soon it would be August. I was really learning how to take care of the house in Lake Charles. I liked my small garden. Things grew. It reminded me of when Mother and I planted things so many months ago. There was always new lettuce to pick, new tomatoes. I had radishes. The gardenia bushes in front of the house were always so beautiful, so fragrant. Mother had planted some other flowers too. I picked flowers for the table in the kitchen. They were pretty. I had lots of daytime babysitting as well as night jobs. That was good. I kept busy, and I earned some money too. It was my money. Mrs. Alfred had the grocery money.

BY THE CLOTHES LINE

On August 3rd I was doing the laundry. It was a bright sunny day. The breeze was sufficient to dry things quickly. I was hanging wash on the clothesline. The wooden clothespins were still on the line where I left them after I took down the wash last week. Mother always took them inside. When I left them on the line, it was easier to hang things up. A car stopped in front of the house.

A Western Union man came up to me.

"Telegram for you. Sign here." He left.

I tore it open. I'd never gotten a telegram before. What could this be?

"Carla Lee. Stop. Your Mother died this morning. Stop. I'll be home in a few days. Stop. Hope everything is O.K. Stop. Love, Don. Stop."

I couldn't hang up any more wash. I went in the house. I wandered around for a bit. Mother died. My eyes welled with tears.

"What am I supposed to do now?" I wondered out loud.

There was no one to ask. Who would know? I wandered around the house a bit more. I cried. I tried to play one of my records. It didn't help.

I wondered what it was like in the hospital with Mother—at the end. Had she recovered from the brain surgery?

Could they keep her pain away?

Just now, they don't stop my pain in this Syracuse hospital! You'd think that would be the least they could do. I'm really ready to get out of this hospital.

I return to 1953 and thinking about Mother. Could Mother talk after they operated on her brain? I'm sure she talked with her eyes. She was always good at that. But did she have anyone to talk with?

There's not much of anybody to talk with here in my hospital. Talking is a good thing; helps you figure out what you think yourself, and maybe helps hear other people's ideas too. I don't mean talking with a counselor type; that type of person is usually useless, because they are so interested in 'helping' that they could sMother a person. Besides, why would one talk with a stranger? I mean talking with just a normal back-and-forth friend.

Everything was so final that day.

"She's gone. Gone." I needed to hear myself say it.

In an odd sort of way, for me she's been gone since she got in that military vehicle three months ago. But there was hope. Now, even hope is gone.

What's dead mean? I'm supposed to act grown-up. I've gone to school for all these years. Why don't we learn real life things? I don't know what cancer is. I don't know what happens to people—to Mother—when she died. I don't know about rodeos or lipstick or boys. Why not?

The longer I thought about Mother dying, the more big questions came to mind. Will I still live here for ninth grade? Where will Don go? Will I go with him? What will happen to all my things? What will happen to Mother's things? What about Cappy, my cat?

I went out to play. I saw some of my friends. Shirley and some of the other kids were sitting under a big tree at the corner. Shirley was telling them about her summer vacation trip to New Orleans.

"I just loved eating beignets," she said.

"Can we get them here in Lake Charles?" One of the other kids asked.

"I don't think so. This isn't a beignet kind of place. We've got cat fish instead."

"That's too bad."

"Hi, Carla Lee." Shirley said. "Come join us. You've been to New Orleans."

I stood there for a minute or two. Then I turned and ran away.

"Hey, where 'ya goin'?" Shirley called.

I kept running. I was crying. I couldn't just walk up to some kids and say—'hi—guess what—my Mother just died.

I can't say what I'm feeling in thirteen-year-old language. It doesn't work. None of the other kids would know what to say. They'd just be really uncomfortable and it would be my fault.

I went home.

On the way home, I stop at the Alfred's. David's family isn't home. Maybe that was O.K. What could Mrs. Alfred do anyway? And Colonel Alfred? He must have been at the Air Force Base. But he was all about business. He didn't deal with these things that happened to real people. He was perfectly nice, but how could I bother him. Even an Air Force brat knows when to stay out of the way.

Who else was there? I might have told some of the people for whom I baby sat. But, what good would that be? What do you say to grown-ups about people dying? Grown-ups don't like to talk about death as near as I can tell. They just would hug me and tell me some story about how she'd 'gone to heaven.' I didn't understand where a person went when life was no longer in their body; but it made me angry to have them tell me some story about 'heaven.' How could I know if that was real or if it was just some way to avoid talking about what happened? Maybe they just said that because they couldn't think of anything else to say.

I knew that Mother's life went away; but I didn't think anyone could prove where 'away' was or how that worked.

Why couldn't the adults just be honest?

It's not that someone who died was really all gone, I reasoned after one of these 'gone to heaven' encounters on the street.

For example, the flowers in my garden died in the fall; but their dead seeds start new flowers the next spring. Mother won't ever be here like she had been. I knew that; but she's still here in my memory. When I close my eyes I can see her sparkling eyes and her flashing smile. Lots of times I remember things she did or said. She's here in another way too; maybe part of her is part of me. Maybe what I will do and how I will think for the rest of my life will somehow be influenced by both what's happened to me during the years I lived with Mother and also by Mother being part of me.

Maybe this is what 'heaven' means—and it's not some made-up fantasy place. Nobody can know that, anyway. How would they know? How would I know?

Thinking back on that day, the odd thing was that, while I felt alone and confused, I didn't really worry about who was going to take care of me. I just wondered what was next. By now I'd learned that I am the only one who can take care of me—the one whose choices will decide how well I survive whatever happens next.

The next day Don came home.

Don? Well, Don was Don. He didn't communicate much. I don't think he'd ever had to talk with a kid since he was one; that was a long time ago. Mother's death must be hard for Don. His first wife died from cancer. Now he was going through it all again—only this time he's got his wife's kid—me. It's clear that I am an inconvenience for him. It's too bad he'd never talk about how he felt. Maybe I'd have cared more for him.

MY TRAIN RIDE

Things changed very quickly.

"We're going to Rochester," said Don. "We'll have a funeral where your grandmother and all your relatives can come." "You and your cat can go on the train. I'll pack up the house and follow next week. I'll drive the car up."

"When do we go," I asked.

"You'll leave tomorrow," Don said. "So, tonight, pack what you want in a suitcase that you can carry on the train. Remember, it's a long train ride. Three days. You'll change trains in Chicago. The conductor will show you where to go."

"Can my cat stay with me?" I asked.

"On the train, yes. She'll have to stay in the luggage car, but you can go there to visit her. When you get to Rochester, the cat will have a new home. She can't stay with you at your grandmother's apartment. Cappy can live with your Mother's cousins, the Hoffman's. They have a lovely home and a summer home too. And they have two boys about your age. So the cat will be well cared for. And you can go to visit her."

"Where do I sleep on the train? How do I get food?" I asked. My anger was welling up about the cat. How dare he take her away!

Don replied, "It's simple. I'll give you some money and you can go to the café car each day to buy whatever food you like.

Take a pillow and you'll be fine sleeping in your seat. The seats recline."

"Don't you care about anything, Don? How can you take away my cat too? Don't you know that all I have now is my cat? I can't take it any more!" I screamed at him, bursting into tears. I ran into my room and slammed the door.

Don said nothing, and he didn't do anything to minimize my hurt.

After a while I stopped sobbing realizing that I'd better pack or I wouldn't even get to take my things. I can't fall asleep until I pack.

Don put me on the train with a sheet of directions about changing trains, and some money for food.

It was a very long train ride.

It was a long walk to the baggage car to see Cappy. But I liked standing between the cars. Between the train cars is really outside. I enjoyed the wind rushing through my hair. I looked down and I could see the railroad ties as we rushed over them. I liked listening to the clickety clack, clickety clack, clickety clack. The train moved north. When I was at my seat I could be hypnotized looking out the window at the trees and the telephone poles whizzing by. I tried to count the poles, but it was impossible. They went by too fast. Or, maybe we went by too fast.

Visiting Cappy was tricky. All the passenger cars looked the same. I needed to remember the count of cars between my seat and the baggage car. Otherwise I had trouble finding my seat when I come back from visiting her.

Cappy was always happy to see me. I wished I could take her out of the cat container.

"Hi Cappy," I'd say. "Look I brought you some dry food." I'd fill her bowl with fresh water." I'd stay for a while and pet her. I'd clean the small litter container that she had. It was pretty cramped quarters for three days.

I remember nothing else about this trip. My body was just shipped from Louisiana to Rochester. The questions to be answered were so enormous. My situation was so uncertain. My grief for my Mother was so overwhelming.

I cried frequently, but quietly. I needed to be careful that none of the other passengers could see. How could I deal with their questions? Worse, I'd have to deal with their pity. A disgusting thought. I slept. I stared out the window at the blur speeding by. I had to get myself together to learn how to move on. I had left everything except some clothes in Louisiana—and two books, a few pictures, and some jewelry Mother gave me. Sorting through stuff didn't matter now.

I'd been in Louisiana for seven months. In that time, I'd gone from being a kid to being a grown-up. I was just supposed to go from being a twelve year old kid to being a teenager.

The Dick and Jane books were wrong. They said grown-ups were people over eighteen; I'm a long way from eighteen. But I really need to know grown-up things now.

"Soon we'll be in Rochester," said the nice elderly gentleman sitting next to me. "I'm going all the way to Albany. Where are you going?"

"Rochester," I answered—still looking out the window. He can't see how red my eyes are. "In three weeks I'll start ninth grade." I just didn't know where that would be.

Chapter Seven

The Kid, the Cat, and the Coffin

AND THE RELATIVES

"Whoooooooooooooo, Whoooooooooooooo." The train whistle signaled our arrival at the Rochester, N.Y, station.

I could tell that we were back in upstate New York State. We were passing small farms. I saw their red barns with the silos. I saw cows grazing. The rolling hill country made me smile. What a pleasant scene. It reminded me of when Mother and I would go out to paint. She'd paint and I would run through the fields laughing and giggling over bugs and butterflies and clouds that looked like puffy animals.

I looked forward to getting off the train.

What would happen then?

That led me to thinking about all the things I never talked with Mother about. Now I'd never get to talk with her. I never asked her for details about her year in Paris. How will I ever be able to travel to other continents when I don't know how she did it? I never asked her how she got to be a professor. How am I going to have a career as well as a family when I don't know how she managed that? I never asked how it was for her to be so independent—to live in New York City, and to start all over again after Daddy died. How can I learn how to manage difficult circumstances when I don't know what I need to know?

I really blew it! I could have asked Mother all these things. She never brought up these topics with me; I guess she thought I was too young. But I could have asked more questions. How could I have been so stupid? I just thought that tomorrow would always be.

"You're almost ready to go home." A nurse came into my hospital room. Her comment brought me back to the present. "You can walk around now, and use the bathroom by yourself. Everything seems to be working the way it should," the nurse commented. "Tomorrow's the day." She said as she walked out of my room.

It's quiet again.

My mind returned to the Rochester railroad station—not quite two years ago.

I'm back where Grandma is, even if Mother is dead now.

"Rochester. Rochester. Exit to your rear." The conductor jounced his way through the train cars making his announcement.

I gathered my things.

A football player type of guy sat on the other side of the aisle. When he saw that I was having trouble lifting my suitcase off the shelf, he jumped up and took it down for me.

"Thank you."

I stood by the stairs to the platform and watched us pull into the big old downtown railroad station. I liked big old train stations. I loved the train sounds. I loved the steam from the big locomotive, and watching how people just disappeared and reappeared when clouds of steam drift across the station platform. I liked watching the outside world slow down to a stop while the inside world on the train never did seem to be going fast.

I wondered to myself what it will be like to stay with Grandma this time. She's a lot older than when I last saw her. That was before we moved to Vails Gate and to Louisiana. That was three years ago. Since then, Grandma had sold her big house on St. Augustine Street. Now she lived in a small apartment.

I liked her big old house. It was where Mother grew up, where she and Daddy were married. It was where I lived between when Daddy died and when it was decided that I was old enough to be a latch-key kid and live with Mother in Syracuse.

When I stayed at the St. Augustine Street house, Grandma and I would walk over to the park by the Genesee River—nearly every day. We'd sit under the towering elm trees and watch the river. We'd watch boats, and people fishing from the shore. I'd have chalk and a ball for playing hopscotch on the wide sidewalk by the benches. Sometimes one or two other kids would stop by to play for a few minutes. We'd watch others walk by. I loved people watching. It was fun to guess what the people might be like. I watched who they were with, how they walk, the expressions on their faces, what they wear, and if they have a pet that looks like them. There are swings by the river too. I loved Grandma pushing me very high on the swings.

This time is very different.

First, I have to say good-bye to my cat. It's something else that is final. Cappy hasn't been with me as long as Mother has, but we've lived together through all of the times that Mother was in the hospital. Cappy is a very very special friend. Now she has to go off to a new home. Just like me. I really feel sad about that, and angry at Don for not working out how I could keep her.

While I'm at Grandma's apartment, I guess people will figure out what to do with me; placing me is harder than placing a cat I guess. At least—I know where the cat's going. Nobody says anything about where I'm going.

And this time Mother isn't here. Well—not really here. Actually, I learned as we got off the train, that Mother's body and mine both were transported on this same train together from Louisiana.

I rode in a passenger coach. Cappy rode in a case in a baggage car. Mother rode in a coffin somewhere in another baggage car. She wasn't in the same car as Cappy. I didn't see any coffins.

"Here, let me put your bag on the platform," said the conductor.

He deposited my bag at the base of the train stairs. I climbed down with my other things.

"Gee, it's good to stand on real ground." I said. "It doesn't sway back and forth." I'm pleased that the three day trip over.

"Hello. Hello. Carla Lee. Over here." Alton shouted and waved when he saw me getting off the train. "Here, this red cap will take all your things to my car."

"O.K. Please be careful of my bag. Some of the things break," I said as I handed him my belongings.

"It's the new gray Cadillac. Over there." Alton directed the red cap. Alton always had a new Cadillac.

Alton is Mother's first cousin. He's the family bachelor so everyone counts on him to do the errands. He really enjoys driving smart cars—big ones. This time big is important. He's toting me and all my belongings to Grandmas. Then, he's taking Cappy to her new home with the Hoffman's—other first cousins of Mothers.

"Let's find the cat, now," Alton said.

He and I walk to the baggage car. "Cappy, in her container, is already perched on top of a luggage cart surrounded by suit cases.

"Is that her?" Alton asks.

"Yes. Cappy—let me give you a rub. Alton, can you wait a minute while I reach in and pet her."

"O.K., but you can pet her in the car. The red cap is already at the car with the other luggage."

Alton directs me and the cat to a seat in his car.

"Now, can you wait here for just a minute?" He says. "I have to do something. I'll be right back."

"O.K." I say. I think to myself that this is fine because I'll get a few minutes with Cappy. Mother named her Cappy. It's short for capricious. The name fits—although I have to admit that it's a word I'd never heard until we named the cat. She's always so playful. We play ball together. She jumps when I dangle a string for her to grab. I wish I didn't have to give her away.

Alton disappeared. I guess he had to make sure Mother's body gets from the baggage car to the right funeral director. What a weird thought.

GRANDMA'S

Alton returns, gets in the car and starts the engine. "How was the trip? I'm so sorry about your Mother. Welcome back to Rochester. I have groceries to take with you to your grandma's apartment," Alton chatters on. "It's been a long time since you've been here."

We drive across the city.

He continues. "Your grandma's apartment is small. It's on the first floor so she doesn't have too many stairs to climb. My, you're such a big girl now. Here's the house."

He parks in front and starts to get things out of the Cadillac. I get out.

Grandma is watching from the front porch.

"Come in, Carla Lee. It's so good to see you. I've missed you so much." Grandma hugs me and we walk arm in arm to her apartment door. We'll put your things in here. I've made a little space for you in the closet. She looks smaller and more frail than I had remembered. Time has passed. Mother wrote letters to her. But I don't know what's happened this summer. Maybe there's been no communication during these months of Mother's time in the hospital.

"You've grown up," she says to me. "It's so so sad about your Mother." She wipes the tears from her eyes. I do too.

"Show me your apartment," I say. She walks with me from the living room to the tiny kitchen and to her bedroom.

"That's all there is," she says. "I'll sleep on the couch and you can sleep in my bed while you are here."

Grandma's apartment is small and it is packed full of a lifetime of her treasures brought from the St. Augustine Street house. Over the sofa in a heavy gold frame is a still life, an oil painting, done by my Mother before she married. Grandma has her lace doilies on every surface. She crochets them herself. The furniture is dark mahogany. The rugs are the big orientals with fringe. Her bed is the big four-poster one that I remember from her bedroom on St. Augustine Street. It was a very good substitute for a trampoline when I was little. The bed takes up almost the entire bedroom. There are the tiffany lampshades on the table and floor lamps in the living room. Those beautiful stained glass shades are truly lovely! I unpack my things, hang up some clothes and find a corner for my suitcase. I fill the drawer she has emptied for me in her dresser.

"Grandma," I say. "Remember the wonderful big front porch with the green rockers at your old house? The porch was a very special place to be. I liked looking out at people walking down the street."

"I know," she replies. "Remember, we'd sit out there and have lemonade in the summer?"

I chimed in. "I remember the day we were on the porch and a deer ran between your house and the one next door. That was so unusual that it made the newspaper." I continue. "You had the most wonderful back yard. I really liked playing in the garden."

"Yes," she said wistfully. "I enjoyed working in that garden. I remember when your Mother was little. She, too, played in that garden. And I remember when your parents were married. The wedding was in that garden." Grandma comments—half to herself. She pulls her cloth hanky out of her sleeve and wipes her eyes again.

"You had all kinds of flowers." I add. "I liked the snapdragons best because I could pinch them on the side and make their mouths open and close. It was fun when there was someone else in the yard. Two snapdragons can have a conversation, you know."

Grandma had gazed away. She recovered herself and added, "It was fun watching you. I remember when I was operating the jaw of a snapdragon in some of those conversations. And now— so much has happened, and you're such a big girl."

"Grandma, do you remember when Mother, you and I would sit in your yard on a sunny weekend morning. I'd play, and you and she would talk about things before she'd leave to drive back for her next week in Syracuse?" I asked.

"How could I forget?" She murmured. I think she can't say more for fear of crying.

"Grandma, let me tell you what I remember about your old kitchen." I say. "One of my favorite memories is the big iron cook stove. You made the most wonderful coffee cake and cookies in that stove."

"How about some cookies, Carla Lee? And some milk?"

"Of course, I'll have some. Don't put out too many though. I'd eat them *all*."

"I'm glad I'm here with you now." I add as I chew an oatmeal raisin cookie. "Thank you for the snack."

"What did you say?" grandma asked.

"A snack,"

"A pack of what? What would you like a pack of?" Grandma looks puzzled.

I quickly discover how much her hearing has deteriorated. Those first few minutes of conversation were the best because she heard most of it the first time. It's as if she really had to be able to hear for the first moments after my arrival. Then, it got harder for her.

The big bulky hearing aid she wore on a harness between her breasts didn't seem to make much difference. It is very frustrating to try to talk with her for more than a few minutes when we were face to face and less than two feet apart. I can tell from the expression on her face that it is frustrating for her not to hear me.

I try, again and again, to make conversation work. After a day or so passed, we both sort of gave up. Conversations became very short. We smiled a lot, and did each other little favors. It is really sad. I'm not sure, though, that even if she could hear, she'd talk with me about Mother. I think she's afraid that she'll cry. I think she thinks she shouldn't do that in front of me. This family doesn't share hard things with kids; and, in this case, what could anyone say anyway?

Grandma goes into parenting mode. She takes care of me—watching over things. I can tell she is uneasy with my being a teenager. A teenager is a child, but isn't a child. I want a little independence, a little privacy. I guess that scares adults. I can tell from her eyes and how she looks at me that her head is full of a thousand thoughts. Her eyes just seem to tell how deep the hurt of losing her only daughter is—and how desperately she hopes that she and I can be close. All we have now is each other.

Grandma had two children—my Mother and a son. The son is, I gather, very much the opposite of my Mother in every way. When he grew up, he left home and went to Pennsylvania. I recall once when I was small that he, his wife and her three kids from a previous marriage were visiting Rochester. We played in the attic of grandma's big house. I'll never forget the one time in the mid 1940s when the attic was full of us children—bouncing on the mattress, playing hide and seek, examining every corner to find costumes to wear for dress-up. I found a forest green velvet dress and a hat with a huge ostrich feather. Can't forget that. What fun we had. That house was meant to be full of people. We played for two days.

Then they left. I never saw my uncle again. As far as I know he and his family haven't been in touch with Grandma since then. I have no idea where he is. I don't think anyone else knows where he is either. Grandma never talks about it. I guess it would be rude to ask.

My grandfather died thirty-five years ago—before Mother was married to my daddy. He was the owner of a successful meat business on Front Street. I guess at one point he managed a plant for Swifts—somewhere in Pennsylvania.

At this point, however, Grandma has only her sisters to turn to. My grandmother's sisters and all their children still live nearby in Rochester. Grandma's family settled in Rochester when she was a child, and that's where she stayed. I think most people stay in one place—not like me.

"Grandma, why didn't you come see us in Vails Gate? It's been so long since I've seen you."

"Oh, Carla Lee. You don't know how much I wanted to come. But, I don't drive, and I've never traveled so far. It just didn't seem possible. I'm not young anymore."

"I'm so glad you write us letters," I said. "But I like it best when we are together."

"Remember, I did drive with Alton the one hundred miles to your Mother's wedding in 1949. That was a really big trip for me."

"Yes." I reply. "After the wedding I came back for a weekend with you on St. Augustine Street."

"That's right." She says.

Can I possibly understand what she's thinking? I don't think so. But I wish I could. Imagine the grief a parent has in losing a child? And here I am, her only grandchild moving in with her again, just as I had so many years ago when daddy died.

Grandma always tries to make things special for me. She and Mother worked together in that regard. For example, there was the Christmas when they gave me the beautiful china dolls from Germany. These dolls have striking blue eyes that look real. They have eyelids that open and close, eyelids with real hair eyelashes. They have joints in their shoulders, elbows, wrists, knees and ankles to make them almost real. One of them has strings that could be pulled to make it say 'ma' or 'pa'. Their porcelain faces and blonde hair wigs make them real treasures. Grandma worked for months before that Christmas to make a beautiful bridal gown for one and to have the wig fixed so the blonde hair would curl just right under the bridal veil. She made a full wardrobe for the other dolls too. One of the dolls was a human sized baby doll. Mother saved some of my baby clothes—a hand knit sweater, other outfits, a couple real diapers–to make a wardrobe for this one. When I opened the dolls that Christmas, I was so proud that they thought me responsible enough to take care of these wonderful antiques. The dolls are heirlooms that first belonged to my grandmother and then my Mother, now me. That's the special part. I like the history they carry with them, and the fact that Mother and Grandma worked so hard to make them nice for me—the invisible part of that gift.

Grandma does wonderful things—and best of all—it isn't about 'things.' It's about the 'experiences' we have together.

THE FOUR FAMILY MATRIARCHS

The Rochester relatives have already had a week to adjust to the fact that "Helen died." It took that long for us to arrive from Louisiana. I'm sure it was the four old ladies—Grandma and her three sisters–who decided how things should be handled. They then dispatched Alton to carry out the plan for the funeral home, the cat, the groceries, and me. My predicament was surely the topic of family discussion during that week. Most everything *is* a family affair in Rochester. There's a long tradition of the four families getting together Sunday evenings to sort out the latest events in various family member's lives. When I was a child, everyone came to Aunt Carrie's house (my grandma's younger sister and Alton's Mother)—the sisters, their children and grandchildren.

Over the years, numbers dwindled some. Grandchildren grew up and didn't come as regularly.

Grandma's oldest sister, Lena, was very frail and didn't come out very often. Her children were also older. Lena was short, not even five feet tall, with snow white hair. She always wore black. Her hearing was totally gone. You didn't really communicate with her; you had an audience with her. She was pleasant and gestured kindly. Her spinster daughter, Lillian, cared for her in a huge mansion with wonderful dark woodwork. I'll never forget the darkish living room with the gorgeous tiffany lamps, the fluffy upholstered furniture and the lingering aroma of powder that followed Lillian wherever she walked. I especially liked Aunt Lena's dumb-waiter in the wall of the large dining room. I always thought it would be fun to ride—but, of course, that opportunity never came.

Aunt Carrie's house remained the gathering place. My grandma's new apartment was chosen because, from Park Drive, it's only two blocks to Carrie on Barrington Street. She could walk over on Sunday evenings. The two younger sisters were especially close. Carrie was spry and the most outspoken. Her gray hair was tightly curled around the base of her head, just like Grandma's. Her house had a wonderful big porch with a large green striped awning. I think the reason Aunt Carrie liked hosting these Sunday evening events is because only one of her two children ever married and there never were any grandchildren.

I always enjoyed being together with people from this big family. Whatever happened, the four sisters looked out for each other. Mother and her first cousins were close because they had all grown up together. Many of my generation also stayed in Rochester; I'm the one who left town.

On a typical Sunday evening, the clan gathers at Aunt Carrie's for dinner. The elders discuss the state of the world, and the state of the family. The four old ladies break into German, their parents' native tongue. Their parents had brought them to America from Alsace-Lorraine when they were all children. They were sent to schools that would teach them to be bi-lingual. The sisters spoke German when they didn't want any of their children or grandchildren to understand what they were saying.

The four old women have all prospered—a state magnified by their own determination.

My family excels in determination. Some call it stubbornness.

Much of this family's prosperity is due to the enterprising ventures of their deceased husbands. Lena, the oldest, had married the man who ran a thriving liquor business. Apparently my great-grandfather had started this liquor business and later the oldest son-in-law, Lena's husband, joined him. My great-grandfather had been a clock maker when he left Alsace-Lorraine and came to America in the early 1800s, but he switched professions when he got here because owning a liquor business was more profitable. Aunty, the next sister, married a doctor. Carrie, the youngest, married a man with real estate holdings.

At these Sunday evenings, Alton, Aunt Carrie's son, sits in the big chair in the living room. He blows smoke rings. He entertains and supervises us kids. Alton likes kids. As the only bachelor, he just doesn't fit in with the rest of the adults at these gatherings. He is given the chauffeuring tasks. He does the shopping. He manages the real estate. And on Sunday evenings, he watches what the younger generation does. I suspect he is quite happy to have the babysitting assignment. We all like him.

The kids who come on Sunday evening sit on the floor by the big radio in Aunt Carrie's front hall. Our older second cousins rarely came as the years passed. They'd grown up. Sometimes there'd only be three of us listening—me and the Hoffman kids. We'd listen to "The Lone Ranger," "Charlie McCarthy," "The Shadow," and "Our Miss Brooks." Radio drama is wonderful. You can use your imagination to make whatever pictures you want. If Teddy and Greg, the cousins listening with me, wrestle and make too much noise, it's awful. We miss the story-line or miss the information about how to order a Dick Tracy Ring.

Alton has this gadget that makes three dimensional pictures. It is a stick about sixteen inches long. At one end is a frame that fits over one's eyes to focus on the other end. At the other end, one can insert one's choice of sepia photos mounted on cards about eight inches wide and four inches tall. There are two pictures per card. When you look at them, they appear as one three-dimensional picture. We sit with Alton looking at pictures for some time while the others chatter away in the dining room and kitchen.

Alton has a round smiling face, a round shiny bald head, and a round tummy. A big round tummy. He's fairly tall. He has an amazing skill for making smoke rings. His round smoke circles float up into the living room ceiling growing in size and, eventually, disappearing into nowhere. The smoke circles even have holes in the center.

"How do you do that?" I ask.

"Oh, it's easy," Alton always says. And he blows more smoke circles while I watch in amazement.

He's very clever, I think to myself.

DOING THINGS PROPERLY

At Aunt Carrie's Sunday evening suppers, a whole lot happens that you can't see. A firm standard exists against which to measure whether something is right or wrong. No one ever talks about it, but everyone knows what is proper and right.

It's understood that Dick and Jane families are right. That's basic. Deviations from that standard are–well—deviant and frowned upon.

I've never figured out how one can be 'deviant' if life just happens certain ways.

For example, how can it be wrong to not have a Dick and Jane family if that's just how life happens?

The only flexibility acceptable within this standard for family structure is that widows are allowed. Widows do weaken family structure a bit–but one does have to realize that these things happen. The four matriarchs are all widows. And two women in Mother's generations are widows. One of Mother's cousins lost her husband shortly before my daddy died. However, in keeping with their Germanic background, the widows are expected to stand tall and maintain the standard of living socially and economically even though they are without their 'bread winner.'

Boys are expected to be bright, athletic, not too rough; in time they should marry and either have professional careers or have some reputable means of making a lot of money.

Girls are to be well-groomed and polite. They should carry linen hankies. They should be pleasant to be around—not boisterous, opinionated, or too independent. They should get good grades in school, while remembering that their principal job will be to become good wives and Mothers, unless they are in the one branch of the family where it is O.K to become a nun.

We have one nun in the family, a lovely woman, who is the oldest of my generation. Her grandmother, Lena, is the one of my grandmother's sisters who is Catholic. The rest of the family is Protestant. This religious split dates back to some event when the four sisters were young girls.

Kay, my nun cousin, is really Sister Jane Frances. She's the oldest of my generation. I'm just thirteen now and whenever I see her, she always wears this long black habit. I can only see her face. The outfit somehow accentuates her warm and caring face. She looks like her Mother, and acts like her too. She's the only nun I've ever been around. She's a science teacher, and the only woman in the family, besides my Mother, to have a career. I like that. Kay's family is always especially nice to me—and I think to other people.

Orphans? Well, the Rochester family doesn't have any orphans. I'm the first. I don't think that orphans fit into the family framework very well—especially teenage orphans. Teenagers, just by their nature, are suspect. You never know what they will do.

I wonder how they dealt with my predicament at Aunt Carrie's Sunday evening gathering after Mother's death?

On Sunday evenings, when dinner is ready, adult conversation ends. Everyone comes together at the huge dining room table with the lace tablecloth. We each have a plate piled high with roast meat, homemade mashed potatoes, gravy, hearty vegetables, maybe a gelatin salad filled with fruits. For dessert there is always home made pie or cake, sometimes with ice cream.

After dinner, the sons and daughters of the four sisters continue their conversations. The women go into the kitchen to wash up the crystal and the silver and the good china—and to talk. The women talk about what is right to do. The men retire to the living room to smoke and to talk. Mother's cousins in the living room include a banker, a lawyer, a doctor, an architect, and a real estate entrepreneur. They talk about the stock market, cars, sports—that stuff. When the women solve the problems, the men provide whatever is needed to carry out the solutions found by the women for whatever the event of the week is. In the discussion about me, they had to plan without any information.

Since Mother and I were in Louisiana, the family wasn't regularly aware of our activity. Don never really was part of the Rochester family gathering. He was Mother's new husband and had been overseas with the military. In fact, the relatives probably hadn't seen him since Mother's wedding. The Rochester relatives didn't really know Don. It never occurred to anyone in Rochester to ask me about the current state of affairs.

Kids are ignored. This is adult talk.

DECIDING NOT TO DECIDE MY FATE

It's been a long time since my part of the family has been to one of these Sunday night events. That Sunday after Mother's death, I wish I could have been a fly on the wall. The gathering would have been small, but the conversation would have been interesting.

The only thing I've ever heard about whom I'd be living with if something happened to Mother is one comment Mother made after her kidney cancer operation. She and I were in the middle of some normal activity when she dropped a strange comment into the conversation.

"If anything ever happens to me, Carla Lee," she had said "I hope you'll be able to live with Ruth and Carl." Ruth is Aunt Carrie's daughter, Alton's brother and another of Mother's first cousins.

Mother's comment really sounded odd to me when she said it. What could possibly happen? Would I just go knock on Ruth and Carl's door and say "Here I am. Mother wants me to move in." I think Mother did talk with Ruth and Carl. She was always careful about details. But I'm not certain.

Carl, the very successful architect, designed one of early modern one story homes in Rochester on East Avenue. Ruth painted the house white on the outside—even the chimney. In addition, she painted everything inside white, and all her possessions were white—even the rugs and the furniture. Ruth and Mother were close friends as kids. Then Mother went to Syracuse University and off to Paris to start her career. Ruth went off to Wellesley College and used her education as a route to continuing her busy social life. Ruth's path was certainly the more traditional and more acceptable one for a young woman in those days. We always thought of Ruth as quite the socialite. She and Carl never had any children.

I'm sure the very thought of taking in a child—a teenager—as a permanent addition to their all white house and their all white life style must have been horrifying. I wonder how they handled the conversation at last Sunday's dinner? How did they 'save face'?

From my perspective, it's O.K. that they didn't want me. I could never live in an all white house. I'd leave too many things out of place. Besides, I'm not the socialite type. That's boring.

Socialite kids probably don't get to do somersaults on the railings, or play with black kids, or to build a boat to paddle through the dirty flood waters to see their school under water. They probably are never "latch-key kids."

I like Ruth and Carl very much. We keep in touch and enjoy talking together. Visiting Ruth and Carl for a few hours now and then is just right. Living together would never work. We all know that.

I bet the people gathered at Aunt Carrie's last Sunday really think that Don is "dad" since he's Mother's husband. In a Dick and Jane family, one would never question the premise that a kid belongs with her dad. What they don't know is that Don isn't really dad. At least, he's never acted like I think a dad might act. He doesn't know how.

I'm sure they probably discussed whether I could live with Grandma. Probably everyone decided that she was too old to parent a teen-ager. I love Grandma, but I think it might have been really hard for both of us to live together long term. She's in a different place. And she worries all the time—too much.

THE FUNERAL

The day of the funeral is here.

Don and Grandma and I had breakfast together. I don't think any of us ate much. "It's time to go to the funeral home now, Carla Lee," Don said. "We need to stand in line and shake hands with all your Mother's relatives and friends. Come. Your grandmother, you and I will all drive together."

Don had arrived by car from Louisiana on the previous day in Rochester. He had stayed in Louisiana until the movers took all our belongings and sent them to Syracuse.

"What happens after the funeral?" I ask Don.

"I'll drive to Syracuse. The Air Force has transferred me to the military base in Rome, New York. So I'll get an apartment in Syracuse.

This isn't very helpful in figuring out what happens to me, but I figure now is not the time to start a new conversation. I say nothing.

The three of us ride to the funeral home in silence. We go into one of those buildings made to look like a warm and welcoming house. I don't feel that way about it. I doubt if anyone ever can. Everything from the formal ceiling molding to the heavy drapes to the red plush rugs seem like death. Everything is too somber. The air is even heavy—whatever that means. You can tell. At the end of one big dark room is Mother's coffin. Someone decided to have an open casket. I think that's just how funerals are done in 1953. Nobody asked me if I wanted to see Mother dead.

The funeral people dressed Mother up in her good clothes. They had a wig on her that was supposed to look like her real hair. It didn't. They must think they dress people up for Halloween parties. It's the same kind of preparation. They put that pancake make-up on her. It's way too much make-up. Men are considered O.K without make-up. Why doesn't the same standard work for women? Mother really looks like a mask of herself—one done by a poor artist.

I think I'll forget looking at her. I want to remember how she looked when we ice-skated, and when we gardened, and when we went to a field to paint landscapes.

"Here, Grandma. You can sit here. It's away from the people like you wanted." Grandma sat and cried. And cried more.

I greeted people. There are only thirty or so people here—all relatives—but this wasn't a moment when time passed quickly. Talking with each person seemed like lifting a giant boulder. Again and again and again—thirty times.

"How do you do? Thank you for coming." I say.

"Helen was a wonderful person," someone says.

"Yes. Thank you for coming."

"Oh, Carla Lee, I'm so sorry," someone else shakes my hand.

"Yes. Thank you for coming."

"You had a wonderful Mother," says another.

"Yes. Thank you for coming," I reply again. Will this ever end? I wonder.

"I know you'll remember her." Someone says.

"Of course. Thank you for coming."

"What grade will you be in this fall?" Another person asks.

"Ninth grade. Thank you for coming." This is my mantra. I say it again and again. What else can I say? I'm numb. Thank heavens we don't know any more people in Rochester.

Finally, the last person has left. We have completed the procession to the cemetery and Mother is lowered into the ground next to Daddy. Thank heavens it's a nice day. I can try to distract myself by looking off into the distance at the trees. I hear birds. Maybe I can see them. What good is all this standing in the cemetery? Mother's gone. That's the only thing that matters. At last we get in Don's car and he drives to Grandma's apartment. When we arrive, he lets us out.

"No, no, I can't come in," he tells Grandma. "Gotta get back to Syracuse. It's a three hour drive, you know."

"Bye, Carla Lee," Don says.

We're hardly out of the car when he drives away.

Chapter Eight

Staying Ahead of Guidance Counselors and Guys

TREADING WATER AND KEEPING BUSY

I still don't know where I'll live or where I'll go to school.

I spend the rest of August and the first week of September walking the streets of this Rochester neighborhood. That's almost three weeks. Every day I came home to Grandma at her apartment. There are no kids to play with. That is O.K because I don't really live here, and I can't do kid talk very well right now. Grandma had a hard time going places and we have no car so we spend a lot of evenings at home listening to the radio.

"Where are you going?" Grandma asks when I leave after breakfast.

"Out," I reply. I'm working on the monosyllabic response teenagers are supposed to give when adults ask questions.

"How soon will you be back?" Grandma tries again.

"After a while," I respond.

Grandma remembers that food is a topic that sometimes brings a better response. "We're having roast chicken tonight— about 6 PM. Can you be back in time for that?"

"Sure!" I answer. "I like chicken. I really like your stuffing." I skip out the front door and call back, "Bye now."

I like the square city blocks near Grandma's apartment. Lovely old homes and big elm trees, and some oak trees line the sidewalks. It's so different from Vails Gate or Louisiana. It's so pretty. Sometimes I collect acorns. Today I find a chestnut tree and I collect horse chestnuts. They are so smooth and dark with wavy lines of varying shades of brown and black. As I walk the blocks today, I look at the porches on the front of each house. Who sat on those porches over the years I wonder? I'll bet there are a lot of interesting stories about the people who have lived in each of these houses. Two hours later I return to Grandma's thinking about the chicken we'll have later in the day.

Every day my routine is similar.

"Going for a walk now," I say after breakfast.

Sometimes Grandma replies, "Maybe later today, if I feel O.K., we can walk to the store. Will you come with me?"

"I'd love to," I always say. I do like it when we can do things together. I like to feel like I'm helping her, at least a little bit. She walks really slow, but it's O.K. for a short trip like to the store. And when we do something together and go somewhere, it doesn't matter so much if she hears what I say. We can just enjoy each other's presence. I like that.

I find myself a different entertainment every day. Sometimes I try to step on all the cracks in the sidewalk for a whole block. Sometimes I try not to step on any of them. I walk in different directions—onto different blocks. It's a challenge to find some variety here, or new places to go. One day I walk almost downtown. Another day I walk up East Avenue past all the big houses. It's a good thing I can create things to do. Otherwise a person could get really bored.

Days pass. One day, I walk to the Eastman House. George Eastman's home is now a museum. It is a wonderful place.

I buy a ticket. "One youth ticket, please."

"Are you alone?" The ticket taker says.

"Yes," I reply.

They give me a ticket. They look at me a little funny. Maybe I'm the first thirteen- year-old who is going to their museum without either an adult or a school group.

It seems to me I am watched a bit more closely than when I've been in museums before. Maybe it's my imagination, but the guard moves with me from room to room. What do they expect me to do? People never trust teenagers. It's not fair. Adults aren't sending us the right message. They should act as if they expect us to be trustworthy and independent—like Mother expected me to be, and like I try to be.

The Eastman House is fascinating. First I know that George Eastman did his early experiments in a building only a short distance from my great-grandfather's building on Front Street. Probably they knew each other. I like that idea. Eastman's camera exhibits are fascinating. My Mother had a few old cameras. She showed me how to use one. I like the old pictures too. I have a tintype of my great grandparents. I like thinking about how one person just starts up a career and does something really unique.

Imagine—just a normal person could get an idea in his or her head and make that idea become a reality. I wonder if I can ever get an idea in my head and make something real happen—something that really changes my corner of the world. I hope I can do things that make a difference when I grow up.

One Sunday I walk past the Presbyterian Church. Their door is open and I hear the singing and the organ. The music is beautiful. I like the words they sing too. I decide that the next Sunday I will go to the service to see what happens inside this building. Why do all those people go to a church service? Why does somebody keep this building as a church anyway? I make a mental note of the service time. I don't want Grandma to know I am going however. She'll either decide to come along, or ask me questions about it afterwards. I just want to see what it's all about. That's best done alone.

I've been in churches once or twice before, but I don't think for a Sunday service. For a few weeks when I first lived at Don's apartment with Mother I went to school-release religious classes on Tuesdays. That was because all the kids in my school class went to one class or another.

I remember that class.

"Ruthanne," I asked one day. "Don't you think all that stuff we read in the *Bible* in the school release class today was mostly a lot of complex, old fashioned words that nobody can understand? What's the point in taking turns reading stuff, most of which no one could understand?"

She replied, "I don't think about it much. I'm just supposed to go. My Mother thinks it's important."

"Well," said I, "mostly I think the class is a waste. I do like some of the people though. I like that stuff we read about people caring about people. I think they called it 'beatitudes'—a word I don't understand. That part was 'down-to-earth;' might even be nice if it mattered now and not just some place else two thousand years ago."

That was the end of my release class religious education. Either the classes ended, or I went to another school.

My family was always pulling up or putting down roots; things were complicated enough without trying to figure out how God fit into it all. Religion was a back-burner thing.

What would be gained by sticking God on, like a band-aid, to pretend something is better than it really is? Besides, how could I know if there really is a God? And how does Jesus fit into it all? Now, exploring the neighborhood near Grandma's apartment isn't the time to think this through. I need to get where I'm living settled and where I'm going to school settled. I'll just check out the music next week. That's enough.

The next Sunday, I go to the Presbyterian Church service. I slip into a back row at the very last moment before the service started. A few people stare at me. I guess they haven't seen a kid by herself in church before. I suppose you are supposed to sit with parents, or go to Sunday School. Maybe they stare because I didn't get all dressed up fancy. I wore slacks. Why would the clothes I wear make any difference?

The architecture of the huge sanctuary is impressive. It has massive marble-like columns and beautiful stained glass windows. I'm still amazed how a building—just brick and mortar—can affect a person's feelings. (It's like the school buildings in New York and in Louisiana. It's like the funeral home building.) I think people feel different things, maybe think different things, in different places. Now how would that work? I'm not really sure, but for an hour this morning I'll check it out.

I like to listen to the organ. It's not like my violin. Rather, it's certainly not like when I play the violin. So many different sounds come from an organ at one time. I really like to sing. Here people sing. There aren't many places a person can go to sing with a bunch of other people. Singing alone is no fun.

"Once to every man and nation, comes the moment to decide, in the love of truth or falsehood, for the good or evil side." Wow! Is that true? A hundred people are singing, together, and the organ is belting out the melody. This is fun. It's different.

I look around the congregation—all grown-ups. Why do they keep the kids in a Sunday School room? They don't get to be in this beautiful big room. They don't get to hear the organ and sing with so many people. The kids must be really bored.

This place seems so cheerful, so hopeful. Is it fake? Are these people's lives messed up too?

There's the last verse. "Though the cause of evil prosper, yet 'tis truth alone is strong." I like the words too—the part about people making their own choices, and the part about overcoming evil stuff. George Eastman decided what he'd do with his life. Mother did too. And lately, there's been a lot that I think is pretty evil. I think I'll start making some of my own decisions. Waiting for other people really isn't working very well.

When the service ends, I leave quickly. I don't want to talk with anybody—definitely not a stranger, not an adult.

"Good, you're back," Grandma said. "I have roast ham for dinner with pineapple. I also made the waldorf salad that you like."

"Thank you for making all this. It looks great." I reply.

Grandma and I enjoy dinner. Then we go in the living room where she crochets and I read. In the evening we go to Aunt Carrie's regular Sunday family gathering.

One cousin says, "Carla Lee, how proud we are of you."

"Thanks," I say while trying to get Alton to blow more smoke rings for me.

Another says, "Carla Lee, we know you'll do well in high school next year."

I'm thinking to myself. This is stupid. I know these people really care about me, but can't anybody talk about real things. All these *words* go no where, accomplish nothing.

If somebody tells me where I will live or what school I'll go to, that would mean something. If they even say that I can go visit my cat Cappy on a given day that would be something. If they give me some pointers about how to get along with people who don't like to talk about death, or orphans, or step-fathers, that would be something. I don't see any point in telling them that. It would just be awkward. So, I smile.

PACK FOR SYRACUSE

The days pass. Fall is in the air. The leaves begin to change. Labor Day weekend is here. It's Saturday.

Grandma makes an announcement. "Don is driving over from Syracuse today. He'll take you with him to live in his new apartment in Syracuse."

"Oh," I reply. I knew someone had to say something soon because school starts next week. I don't know what I expected. Frankly I hadn't thought of a good solution to my predicament. Going to Syracuse with Don came as a surprise. Living with Don? I'm not sure I want to do that.

"Yes, he says he has a really nice place. It's on the eighth floor of a high rise building. He says school starts early next week," Grandma continues.

"What school will I go to? Is the apartment near school?"

"I don't know," grandma replies. I'm sure Don can tell you all of that.

This school, wherever it is, will my seventh school and my ninth year of education. At least I'm back in New York State.

I've learned far more in the month of August 1953 than I would ever learn in a classroom. I wonder what high school will be like. I'm leaving what little remnant of family I really have to live with this man, this "dad" who I hardly know. Why don't people in Rochester understand this? Don can't be happy about my moving in with him. I'll cramp his style. Or maybe I'll just be invisible and he'll be out and about like he always has been.

"Hi, Carla Lee, are you ready?"

"When are we leaving," I ask.

"We'll go back right after lunch. There's no point in my staying over night."

Grandma had expected him to stay for the weekend.

"Can't you stay through Labor Day?" She says. "Aunt Carrie is all set to have you stay in her spare room."

"That's all right. I have to get back. I'll just take Carla Lee off your hands this afternoon." Don says to me, "This way, by tonight, you'll be in your new room, Carla Lee. You'll have some time before school starts to fix it up."

After lunch, I pile my stuff into Don's Buick. Grandma and I hug long and hard. I climb into the car and we make the drive to Syracuse.

"Is the apartment near my old friends on Comstock Ave.? Or, is it near Nancy's house on Bellevue Avenue?" I quiz Don.

Don replies, "No, it's on the other side of the city. It's a brand new high rise."

Mother and I had taken this drive often when I was a little girl. When she and I drove between Rochester and Syracuse, we stopped at a farmhouse in Auburn to buy fresh eggs. We stopped at another farm where we bought fresh fruit pies. I spotted both the farm houses. Mother and I used to sing in the car and listen to the radio then. We had a rollicking time! The old two lane roads past farms and through fields brought back wonderful memories.

This time is very different.

HIGH RISE LIVING

Living in a filing cabinet for people is a different experience. I've lived in lots of apartments. But this is the first time I'm living on the eight floor of a high rise building able to look out only on one side of the building. It is very modern. That's supposed to be good.

"Excuse me," I say to the lady with the fox fur draped around her neck.

"Sorry," I say to her husband, the tall man in the pin-striped suit. I just bumped the wheel of my bicycle into him. Ohhh, it did leave a little dirt on the side of his trouser. But, I think, it will just brush off. I hope so. Maybe he didn't see it.

It's hard to fit my bike into the elevator under any circumstance. When other people want to ride up too, it's nearly impossible. I was here first. But I guess that doesn't matter. The fact is that I'm one of very very few kids in the building.

"Do you have to bring your bike on the elevator?" The lady questions me.

"Well, I need to take it to the eighth floor," I respond. "I don't know how else to do that."

Fortunately, the doors open to the eighth floor. I get off. Continuing that conversation could only bring disaster, I think to myself.

On the other hand, taking my bike on the elevator isn't half as bad as when I wear my roller skates. (I do wear them sometimes.) I think about this as I wheel the bike down the hall to our apartment. Hope I never am in the elevator with those people when I go roller skating. It's very hard to stand still when the elevator moves. It is a challenge to see if I can stand still though—out of the way of all these stuffy people. There's no place else to put the skates on. The doorman won't let me sit on the steps of the building to do it.

This is where Don brought me to live in Syracuse the day he picked me up at my grandma's. I've lived here for three days now. (I'm almost up to 'now'—my time in this hospital bed. That's a good thing because I really want to finish this reminiscing before I leave the hospital. Before I leave the hospital I need to figure out how I got into this dilemma and what I want to have happen next.) I still don't know why it wasn't obvious to my Rochester family. Anyway—where was I? Oh, starting ninth grade.

Today school starts. I'm going to Central High School, the main downtown high school for kids from all over Syracuse. There are four grades here and I am a freshman. Central used to be the only high school in the city, except for the Trade High School. But a few years ago people started to move to the suburbs. Now, the schools in the little towns around are being rebuilt as big modern schools. My school is very old. It's a brick building and it takes up most of a city block. We will have classes on all three floors, and our lockers are in the basement. Twelve hundred kids attend Central High. I walk one and one-half miles each way from our high rise apartment to get to school. Today, it took me about forty minutes. Most kids walk. There are no school busses. But, if the weather is really bad, Don says I can take the city bus part way.

This is really exciting. It's also a little scary to be brand new. But, almost every year, I'm brand new somewhere. This time, it's high school! This time it's just me. I guess I'll be O.K. because the whole freshman class is new. Here goes.

SETTING THE GUIDANCE COUNSELOR STRAIGHT

I approach the huge building uncertain of where to go. I suppose that I should go in the front door. Where else?

The doors are massive. Very few other people seem to be using this entrance, but it must be the door for new people. When Mother took me to new schools before, we always went in the front door.

I find myself inside the official entry. Beyond the massive front doors is a broad vestibule with a half dozen worn marble steps leading to the first floor offices. And there—in the middle—is the large imposing marble statue of 'Minerva'. That's who it says she is.

I don't know why 'Minerva' has caught my eye. Maybe it's because it's the first time I've started a new school that had a big Roman statue in the entryway. Maybe it's because I've lived my life with an artist Mother who always looked at sculpture. It says at the bottom of the statue that 'Minerva' is the goddess of wisdom. I like that!

I walk toward the sign that says office.

"Hi," I say to the person behind the desk. "I'm new, and I'm in ninth grade."

"Come in. Welcome to Central High School." The lady behind the desk greets me. "I'll call Mrs. Wilson, the guidance counselor. She'll tell you where to go."

In a minute I am in Mrs. Wilson's office and I show her my report card from LaGrange Junior High School in Lake Charles, Louisiana, and I give her my current address.

"Tell me your Mother and father's names, please?" She requests.

I pause. Then I say, with a tear that I can't control in my eye. "My Mother isn't here any more."

She looks puzzled. "Where is she?" And she says, "Tell me your father's name?"

"They're both dead." I blurt out.

Mrs. Wilson is not quite sure how to handle this. She tries again. "Tell me the name of the adult you live with, and how that person is related to you."

"Don. Don Casety. He's my step-father."

Mrs. Wilson is a thin carefully buttoned person in her early sixties. Her blouse collar buttons up under her chin. It's white. She wears a dark blue flower print skirt and jacket. Her curly hair is carefully pinned in place. Her desk has everything in neat piles. Her office is plain. This is one no-nonsense woman who knows her job.

I don't think people give her answers that she isn't expecting very often. And I am absolutely certain that I gave her answers that she wasn't expecting. But it got worse.

"O.K.," Mrs. Wilson says slowly.

"Now let's see what classes to put you in." She proceeds to show me the course schedule and explain what I must take with all the ninth graders and what the electives are.

"I'll put you in the typing class that meets second period. Then, in the afternoon, after English, you can take shorthand." Mrs. Wilson is busy filling in her papers.

I just have to interrupt her. I can't let this happen to me.

I muster up my courage and in a shaky voice I say "I don't want to take typing. Shorthand is stupid!" I vaguely remembered someone telling me that you can't go on to college if you take typing and shorthand. Mother went to college. So I guessed that I should plan to go to college.

Mrs. Wilson stopped writing and looked up.

This is good, I thought. So far, so good. I might as well continue to speak up. I've got a lot to lose if I keep my mouth shut. And, she did stop writing whatever she was writing.

"I want to take Latin." I say. "And I want to take German, too."

Mrs. Wilson's expression hardens. It's clear this will be a challenge. "I'm sure you'll like the kids in the typing course, Carla Lee." She says. "It's just the right thing for you."

"How do you know that?" I ask her.

I had no idea what was happening to me. Some time later, someone told me that they call it 'tracking.' Some kids are put—their first day–on the track where you take typing (if you are a girl), shop (if you are a boy). Other kids are put—on their first day–on the academic track where you take languages and algebra and sciences. Somehow the guidance counselor decides what's 'right.'

I guess they just look at you and guess who to put where—or look at what school you attended last year. Or maybe they place a kid based on whether or not they think the kid's family has money to send them to college. I don't have a family, So I guess that's an easy call. Plus, everyone in New York State knows that a Louisiana report card must mean that the person holding it must be sort of dumb. Wrong!

Mrs. Wilson thinks deciding my 'track' is an easy call. She figures I'm not going to have a career. She doesn't even care what I want, or that I've won awards in school—in New York schools.

These thoughts race through my head. I hate having to muster the courage to fight an adult. And, if I'm going to fight, I have to win. Otherwise, what's the point?

Mrs. Wilson knows that Mrs. Wilson knows best. As a last attempt to settle this issue, Mrs. Wilson tries another approach. "Carla, typing is very important to earning a living. You'll want to get a good secretarial job when you finish high school—so you can support yourself." I can tell she's hoping this approach will work. The first morning of the year is busy and she can't spend all day with this stubborn newcomer.

"Mrs. Wilson," I say. I'm trying very hard not to sound too obnoxious and mindful that I don't want to mess up my future in high school before I've even started. "You don't know me, or anything about me. I'm going to have a career." I have the floor now. I might as well blurt out what I'm thinking. I can't do more damage than I've already done.

"Why do you want to pigeon-hole me? You said that high school is a place where a kid can learn all kinds of new things. You said there are 'electives.' Why are you forcing me to fit your mold?"

Mrs. Wilson pauses. She decides that if she can't track me peacefully, she'll let me do what I want for a few weeks. She must assume that soon I'll be back her office asking for the other courses and she can say she told me so.

"O.K. Let's try this your way," she says. "Just this semester."

"You say you want Latin and German. You know I will need to also put you in an algebra class, an English class, and an American history class." She fills out the papers.

"Yes. That's what I want. Thank you."

The paper work is finished and she walks me down the hall to my 'home room.'

Phew. I won—taking on an adult who I don't know in a place I've never been before. How hard can anything be after this?

As we walk to the home room, I think to myself. Why did I say I wanted to study Latin? I just pulled it out of the sky. Maybe it's because the statue of Minerva by the front door had some connection to Latin. Maybe Mrs. Wilson just made me angry trying to tell me what to take, so I picked the most impossible course on her list to make my point. I'll show them that I can do the very thing that nobody thinks I can do. I bet I'll get A's too!

It doesn't take long for me to learn that the regimen is precise in my homeroom. Stand up. Pledge allegiance to the flag. Part way through the semester they added 'under God' to the Pledge. (I didn't know you changed things like pledges.) Keep quiet for a moment of silence. Sing "God Bless America." Then sing "Sixteen Tons". Do it in that order. Every day. Every week. Every month. That's how the day begins. The teacher has the same command of us troops that a Sergeant in the movies has of his platoon.

I haven't figured out why our teacher wants us to sing "Sixteen Ton" or why she has us do it just one deep breath away from "God Bless America."

"God bless America, land that I love. Stand beside her. And guide her, with the light that shines from above. From the mountains to the valleys to the oceans white with foam, God bless America, my home sweet home." Pause. "I'll load sixteen tons of number nine coal. Another day older and deeper in debt, I owe my soul to the company store."

We belt it out, again and again. Is the teacher trying to tell us something, or does she just think that this is the way to be 'hip' with teenagers?

This surrealistic introduction to high school is following right on the heels of my last school experience where eighth grade ended earlier even than usual because my Louisiana school was four feet under water. I sure hope no one ever asks me what I learned in school in eighth and ninth grades.

LATIN

I really like Latin. I like the rhyme of all those conjugations—"amo, amas, amat, amamus, amatis, amant." And I like the logic of putting all those 'a,' 'ae,' and 'nt' letters together into a whole new language. It's fun to find words in English that are like ones in Latin. It's really incredible when the class can put a sentence together that means something. Too bad, nobody talks Latin these days. My cousin Kay, the nun, uses Latin. I'm glad that at least the Catholic Church keeps the language alive. It's a fantastic language.

And I like what we were learning about the Romans–the adventure, the politics, the history of the escapades of all those

Roman guys. "Omnes Gaulia divisa en tres partes est"—etc., etc. Learning this is a discipline, but—for some very strange reason—it's fun. I'm doing more than learning a language. I'm learning about a way a civilization is put together. Do you think things today are put together the same way they were in the Roman Empire?

"I like our Latin teacher, Miss Whipple," I tell Diane, my friend from another class. "She's a tall old lady with lots of all white curls. She looks exactly like all those statues in my text book."

"Really?" Diane asks. "I never thought about a teacher looking like what she teaches. It's sort of like people looking like their dogs."

"We kids tease her," I tell Diane. "Someone writes on the blackboard before she comes to class. Latin is a dead language, dead as it can be. First it killed the Romans and now it's killing me."

Miss Whipple just smiles and erases it.

I have a free period today, after Latin class. I think I'll look in the library to find out about 'Minerva'. I've only seen her a couple times since that first day. Kids aren't allowed to use the big front door. I just can't get this giant marble statue who greeted me my first day at Central out of my mind.

'Minerva', I learn, is the Roman name for the Greek goddess Athena. She is the goddess of wisdom, war, arts, industry, justice and skill. She was the favored child of the chief Olympian god, Zeus. In fact, Athena, it is said, sprang full grown and armed from her father's head. Wow! Somebody decided to put this statue at the front door of the high school. Are we noisy, sometimes unruly, kids expected to live up to this standard? How do we do that?

SOCIAL STRATA

The academic part of school is going well for me at Central High. And it certainly is much more interesting than eighth grade—in New York State as well as in Louisiana. I like all these new courses—except Algebra. That's a drag, but I'll get by.

The social part of school is another matter. The twelve hundred kids are divided into groups. Nobody talks about it. It's just the way things are. I wonder who decided it has to be like this.

The Negro kids (we didn't call them 'colored' any more) hang together. They know each other, I guess mostly because they live in the neighborhoods below the university. A lot of them went to Madison, the school near where Mother and I lived when she was teaching at the university. I found somebody who knew Jimmy and Alice, the kids from my old neighborhood. But I never did find out where they are now. I haven't seen them at Central. Maybe next year. I hope they come here and that we can be friends again.

The white kids from families who aren't affluent live mostly on the northern side of Syracuse. I've driven through some of their neighborhoods, but I've never lived there. Most of them are studying for secretarial jobs. They think I'm a little strange with my interest in Latin, and Minerva, and all that. I try to tell them that they shouldn't let adults tell them what they will or won't be able to do with their futures; if they really want something, surely they can figure out how to make it happen. These kids let me sit at their tables at lunch. I like them because they do a better job caring about real life than do the more affluent white kids. This must be because many of them have complicated lives—just like I've had. They aren't as consumed with image as are the third group of kids.

The more affluent white kids, the third group of kids, live mostly in the western side of town. These kids have parents who went to a university, parents who have careers. The whole world is open to these kids, if they can build on the privilege given them. They care a lot about brands of clothing and make-up and who goes where with whom. Dick and Jane families really matter to these kids. Most of them don't know how to react when I tell them about my folks dying—so I just don't say anything.

Somehow, I know that if I really don't want to be 'dead-ended,' if I want a career and a chance to choose my future path, I've got to be accepted by the kids who plan to go to college and have careers. Besides, I like their academic interests It's from these circles that kids either do or don't get chances to do things that lead to careers and to making the world a better place.

It's so wrong that this class segregation forces fourteen year olds to get pigeon-holed. I like my friends in all three social groups. It's so unfair to the kids who can't bridge these social gaps. I'm so incredibly fortunate that I've been able to know what life is like in all three groups and that I have friends in all three groups. I don't think there's any way that anyone could have arranged this; it just happened.

Probably it's good that I don't live now in any of the three group's neighborhoods. The best thing about Don's high rise apartment building is that it is on a main street surrounded by office buildings and businesses. It isn't in anybody's neighborhood. There are no kids to play with. That's too bad, but it wouldn't be an easy time to make friends anyway. Leave it to Don. But—actually that works if I'm going to be friends with kids in all three of these social circles.

Trying to make friends in high school is complicated. This social strata stuff gets in the way. This three-class dividing up of people is just the tip of an even more stratified social situation at school. Within the affluent white kid social group, kids hang with kids they knew in eighth grade, or kids who live near them. These divisions all get formalized in the school's sorority and fraternity system.

PLEDGING A SORORITY

Fall of freshman year is the time for pledging a sorority. All you have to do is look around, in the cafeteria or at a football game, to tell that if you aren't asked to join a sorority, life is over. You get labeled as 'a lesser human.'

I have to pledge a sorority. If I don't, I lose all opportunity for leadership in school clubs and in school social events.

I've been eating lunch mostly with the white kids who aren't in sororities for the first few weeks of school. Occasionally I'll sit with the Negro kids. These are the only places where, when I sit down, people will talk with me. The first week or so, after I started at Central, I tried sitting at different tables on different days. It was a horrible experience. How can kids ostracize some-one just because they've never even met before?

I have one week to make these sorority contacts–the last week before the pledge decisions are made.

What will happen if I'm blackballed?

"Don," I say one night at home. "Tell me about sororities and fraternities and how to get into one."

"Oh, don't worry about that stuff." Don replies. "You'll just work it out." He goes off into another room.

That isn't helpful. All I've learned from the gossip in the halls outside our lockers is that I'm supposed to meet people and have them like me. Then I get invited to pledge. If you didn't go to eighth grade where they did, and you don't live in their neigh-borhood, lunch time is the only way to get acquainted.

I resolve to meet the necessary people and to get conversa-tions started. Because I am strong-willed and can speak up, you'd never guess that I'm really shy. Usually I can cover up how shy I am, but it is very hard to get up whatever it takes to put myself in new situations. I'd rather fall in a hole than go up to a group of strangers and jump into their lives and their conversation. But, I have to do it.

It's Monday. I have my tray from the food line. I am resolved to make this work. I go up to a table of girls from one of the sororities. There is one empty seat. I put the tray down and sit in the chair.

"Hi," I say.

The conversation stops. They look at each other, bury their heads in their lunches, and keep to themselves. No one even glances over.

Silence. I wait. I eat.

Silence, still!

I have two choices. I can sit there and finish my lunch, or I can get up and leave. I decide to stay. Why should they spoil my lunch? And, if I leave, they win. The silence could be sliced with a knife. I eat as fast as I can and I leave.

Fortunately classes resume and I don't have to think about this sorority thing until tomorrow.

It's Tuesday now. The week for meeting would be sorority sisters is slipping by. I'll try another table today.

"Hi," I say as I put my tray on a table with a couple extra seats.

"Hi," one girl says. "My name is Cynthia. I went to school with all the kids at this table before I came to Central. I'm a sophomore now. Central is a great place. Everyone's so friendly. Which kids did you go to school with last year?"

I'm thinking to myself that friendly is not what I'd call Central—at least not yet. "I went to school in Louisiana last year," I say. "I used to live in Syracuse a long time ago." I add, so I don't sound too strange.

That brings a weird look. No further comment on that topic from Cynthia. Maybe I'm the first person she's ever met who keeps changing schools. I am pleased that she did continue the conversation.

"I have to fix my bike after school today. I have a flat tire," she says. "I usually put it on its side in my yard and try to make the pump fill it full of air. It usually works, but it takes a long time because I can't both hold the pump over the valve and pump at the same time. Maybe I can come to your yard. You could help me fix the tire and then we could both go for a ride together. You do have a bike don't you?"

I reply. "I have a bike. I'd love to go for a ride. And, sure, I'll help you fix the flat. But I don't have a yard. I live in a high rise building."

"Where?"

"On the eighth floor of the Skyline Apartments. Over on James Street near all those insurance offices." I reply.

"Oh." Cynthia answers. "I guess this won't work. I'm on the other side of town near Onondaga Park." She starts eating the rest of her lunch.

By now, another girl, Pam, is interested in the conversation. She says, "Julie and I are planning what we'll bring to sell at the sorority bake sale next weekend. We have a table at the school fair. The fair is for both parents and kids. That always makes it more successful. Parents can afford to buy the baked goods." Pam continues. "Carla, can you and your Mother come to the fair?"

"Ummm," I reply. "I'll come. Maybe I can bring some brownies. My Mother can't come, though. She died last month."

Now there's a conversation stopper for thirteen-and fourteen-year olds. Nobody said anything else. To be fair to them, I guess it is hard to know what to say. I don't know what to say either in these situations. I had to answer her question.

So much for that table. I take my tray to the return place and leave the cafeteria.

It's Wednesday. I try one more table. A group of girls are discussing cosmetics. They are from a third sorority. "My sister loaned me her make-up. Can you get some of that new lipstick?" a sophomore asks me as I am sitting down. That is good. At least I don't have to start the conversation.

"Where do you get it?" I ask.

Wrong question. Obviously everyone else knows. I didn't tell them that I have no idea what new lipstick they mean. It seems best to keep quiet. There's some more chit-chat among the girls. It's about lipstick colors. I finish eating and I leave.

This sorority stuff is frustrating. I either can't answer their questions, or my answers make no sense to the other girls. They can't deal with what I say.

Then there's the problem of getting myself to school looking acceptable to the sorority girls. When it comes to picking out the right clothes, or fixing my hair style, or the very private matter of how to take gym class and not leak when you have your period. I never seem to get everything right at the same time. Only once, do I ever get any assistance.

A girl in the bathroom is standing next to me while I am trying to make my page boy hair cut behave. I really like my long hair, and page boy hair cuts are very popular. The hair should just turn under all the way around. Only sometimes mine turns up, or is straight. Then it looks horrible. Straggly is the word.

"Carla, why don't you buy some of those new big round pink curlers? They will make your page boy stay curled under. They are much better than the old curlers."

"Thanks. I'll get some," I say. "I've been thinking of getting them." I added that so she'd know that I wasn't totally stupid about the new pink curlers. Actually, I've never heard of them. I decide right then that I will stop at the drug store on the way home to get some. But I still think this kind of stuff shouldn't be so important. So many other things in real life matter much more.

Now, if I could figure out how to make my clothes look as tailored as some of the girls, then looking like I fit-in would be a non-issue. I'm doing something wrong with the starch and the ironing; but I don't know what. It's hard to get things wrinkle free. I think it has to do with how damp the clothes are and how hot the iron is. There's nobody to ask how to get it right.

Fall of freshman year is really tough. I'm getting mostly A's in my courses, but I just can't manage the social part. I've always made friends before, even though I've always been the new kid. It must be that this time it's high school and things are so stratified. I wish Mother were here; she'd know how to make things work. I begin to be very nervous. I feel like I don't handle anything right. I get so anxious and worry so much about the things that I have to figure out without a parent. For a period of a month or so, it's so bad that, at the least opportune moments, I can't control my bladder. This makes life even more embarrassing. It's hard to keep it a secret. What's happening to me? I wonder to myself.

I was black-balled. No sorority chose me as a pledge.

I'm not really surprised. Most of these kids seem to think I come from another planet. I'm not 'Dick and Jane' enough for them. It's not my fault that I've ended up an orphan! Why do they have to be so mean?

A week passes, and I try to keep it a secret that I was black-balled. It won't be a secret for long, because hell week is coming when all the pledges dress up and do stupid things. Just now I need to figure out how I can ever pick up the pieces of my high school social life.

Some watchful teacher—I guess—intervened. Who else could it be? Somehow that person worked it out. I got my invitation to pledge a sorority in the mail today! It tells me when and where the new pledges meet for the first time. My invitation was mailed a week after everyone else got their letters; but at least I got it.

Hell week is absurd. The upper classmen guarantee that the whole week really is hell. "Tighten that blindfold. She's not supposed to see anything," an upper classman yells to the person leading me around.

"O.K.," I hear an upper classman say to her sorority sister. "I've got them all locked in the cellar."

"Good," someone else says. "Now girls, here are some witches' eye-balls for you to eat. You won't mind if we stuff them in your mouth." Music from horror movies is playing in the background. Occasionally someone shrieks. They lead us through dangly wet things hanging from the ceiling. How stupid, I think to myself.

At last that part is over. But 'Hell Week' isn't over.

"Now, scrub that sidewalk," I'm told. "An upperclassman will need to walk on it soon."

The sidewalk isn't very kind to my knees, I think to myself.. There are three of us, each scrubbing a section of city sidewalk.

They work us to exhaustion doing errands for the older kids. A highlight for them is a party where they cover us pledges in mud, eggs, and some paint. Even in our hair. What a disgusting mess. I don't think it is funny; but I can't let anyone know that.

They think it's hilarious. At the end of hell week, we all get our sorority pins—the badge of membership. Now we're part of the self-proclaimed top layer of social stratification for the next three and one half years. How silly to have to be among this elite in order to be among those considered when opportunities come for high school kids.

I think to myself that it must be very hard on the kids who aren't invited to pledge.

And, I've noticed that sorority and fraternity membership seems to be only for affluent white kids. The kids from Madison, near where I used to live, aren't invited to pledge. No one intervenes for them. Neither are the kids who sit with my foster-sister, Ellie. School should let everyone try whatever they want to.

I still like to eat lunch with some of my friends at the non-sorority tables sometimes. The other kids think this is strange. I just try to keep things normal plus I do enjoy my friends in the other groups of kids.

The dust settles. Time passes. We kids begin to work on projects together, to get acquainted. People start to care about each other. Everything is O.K. They still think I'm different, but we do things together. I'm beginning to think that being different is fun; I can talk about all the places I've lived, and all these schools I've attended.

TWO BACHELORS AND A TEENAGE GIRL

Life at home isn't a bowl of cherries either. Don mostly leads his own life. He has no idea about parenting. He has a friend—another bachelor down the hall. His friend joins us sometimes in the evening to watch TV. Sometimes we make popcorn. It's almost spring now. Soon I'll finish my freshman year.

"Come over here, Carla," says Don. He's sitting in the big upholstered chair. He's put a pillow on the floor in front of the chair. His friend is sitting on the sofa across the room. "Carla, you can sit on the floor in front of me so you have a good view of the TV."

I go over and sit down. I'm interested in two things—popcorn and TV.

"If you sit closer to me and lean back I think it will be easier for you to reach the popcorn bowl I'm holding," Don said, opening his crotch, so I can reach back for the popcorn bowl that he keeps positioned where he wants it in his lap.

I sit. Leaning back gives me a back rest on the base of his chair. When I want more popcorn, if I reach back, I can reach it. I watch "I Love Lucy," and "Dragnet." After a while, Don's hands are on my shoulders. Just a friendly resting place. Then, before long, Don has his hands down my shirt fondling my newly growing breasts. I guess he gets some charge out of it when I lean back. I did notice that he had shifted around so that my head was leaning against something soft that wasn't the chair. My head must lean against his penis. This is really weird, I think to myself. I've never had this happen before. I just want to lean back. I never thought about penises.

I have no idea what's going on. Is this what people are supposed to do when they are teenage and becoming adults? Who can I ask? I think it's a bit strange that he puts his hands down my shirt. But, what do I know? I'm not quite fourteen. I decide it's not really harming anything, so I keep eating popcorn and watching the movie until I can move away without making an issue. Besides, what would happen if I say something? Instinctively I just know that I don't like what's happening!

Evening after evening, these two men would take turns watching TV with me. I'll be asked to sit on the floor in front of whoever is settled into the big upholstered chair. I lean my head back to look up toward the TV. I eat popcorn. From my position on the floor, what's happening isn't evident. Still, I don't really like spending evenings at home now. Whenever I can, I stay late at school for some club, or another. But I live here. I have to come home somewhere before it gets really late.

After the 11 PM news, Don's friend goes home. Then I go to bed.

"Carla, let me come and say good-night." Don says as he comes into my room.

He likes to lie beside me in bed. He keeps his clothes on, just likes to cuddle. Sometimes he likes to put my hand on his penis. I move it away—inconspicuously. It's creepy. I don't understand why he's doing this. He's just really strange!

"Isn't it good to just relax at the end of the day," he says.

"I'm really tired," I say. "I've got school tomorrow, and I have to leave early. Can you go get in your bed now so I have some more room. You take up most of the bed, you know." I just want the space to myself. I don't know enough about sex to really know what's happening. I find it all creepy.

Don leaves. "Good-night."

Fortunately, Don soon has a girlfriend. This means that I am alone in the apartment a lot more.

SPRING BREAK IN FT. LAUDERDALE

Don and his girlfriend, Mel, decide to go to Ft. Lauderdale for spring vacation week. Mel has a daughter named Jan. Don has me. They take us with them. That way there'll be no need to get babysitters. We can share one room at the motel. They'll be next door. It's a very convenient plan.

"Look, we're right on the beach," I say to Jan after we arrive and unpack. She's in ninth grade too—but not at Central High.

"Let's take our stuff over to the beach, and stake our claim," she says.

The two of us spread our blankets on the beach jammed with boisterous college kids. Don and Mel are off somewhere. Mel's an alcoholic and starts every morning with two or three screwdrivers. For her, it goes down hill from there. We kids are on our own. So we just hang out on the beach. We make friends with those who pass by—especially the boys. That's what the other girls seem to do on the beach.

We really hit it off with a couple of the guys. We hang out on the beach with them for most of the afternoon. Then we go to a nearby food stand to have some food and some beer. I really don't like beer, but I know I'm supposed to. So I pretend.

"Good burgers, huh," says one of the guys. "You girls like ice cream?"

"I like butter-pecan ice cream best," I say.

"There's an ice cream place down the street a bit. Let's go get some," says the other guy. We don't know their names. They don't know our names either.

"O.K.," says Jan.

We leave the burger place and the four of us head down the street. By now, we've divided into couples. Each couple is walking arm in arm. We get our ice cream and head back across to the beach. It's dark now. The beach is deserted. The stars are bright and the moon is nearly full.

"So where did you say you are from?" One of the guys asked.

"Syracuse," says Jan.

"We go to Penn State. We're both sophomores," the other guy says.

"We're freshmen," I say.

We continue the walk down the beach. Jan and I are talking and the two guys are talking to each other. Suddenly one turned to us and says—"freshmen at what college?"

"No, high school," Jan replies.

They must have thought we looked really young. That must be why they asked. The boys bolted.

"Gotta go now. See ya." They took off running down the beach.

We go back to our room. I don't know why they ran off. I don't know if Jan knows or not. We never discuss it with Don and Mel. They are very busy with each other. Later I remembered that I heard a kid at school once say that when a guy, who is technically an adult, is with a girl who is not technically an adult, they call it statutory rape. She says that's a crime. I don't know anything about statutory rape, but maybe that's what worried those guys. Maybe I should know a whole lot more than we do about this sex stuff. What's rape?

LUCKY ME

Don's girlfriend changes the course of events for evenings at home. Don doesn't put his hands on my breasts anymore. And he stops crawling in my bed to say goodnight. That's fine with me. Really fine! Thankfully, he got a girlfriend just in time.

I'm really caught up in all the after school activities, and the year end parties. At night I have more and more homework to do. I'm just as happy to have Don out at Mel's. No parent is sure better than a crappy one.

Some months later I make sense of all this strange behavior. I went to a movie with some kids. In the movie, the police arrested a man who raped his girlfriend's daughter. Listening to kids talking, I learn what rape is. Around the same time, the kids were talking in the locker room about a girl who had to leave school because she's pregnant. I put all these bits and the pieces about sex together and finally get the picture of what Don was doing. He could have raped me! So could have that guy on the beach in Ft. Lauderdale! Wow. That would be an awful thing to have some man force himself on you. And then, to get pregnant—not now! I guess I'm really lucky. I should have known about rape and sex before all this started happening. I could have asked, I guess. But I don't know what to ask, and I certainly don't know who to ask. We don't have sex education in our school. I guess I'm supposed to learn this stuff from the other kids or maybe from the movies. So, that's how I learn.

Chapter Nine

All Kinds of Victims

GARDEN APARTMENTS AND THE HURRICANE

Before my sophomore year started, Don and I moved from the high-rise into a garden apartment complex. Maybe the management at the high rise complained to him about a kid in the elevator. I don't know. This is the eleventh place I've lived in my fourteen years; but this time I don't have to change schools.

I like the new apartment. We're on the second floor. I can look out and see grass and trees and kids playing. It's better than living in a filing cabinet in the sky in a non-neighborhood. My room is small, but I have my radio and my record player. I have a collection of stuffed animals that live on my bed. I have a couple plants, too. It's cozy, and it's mine.

The new apartment is a neighborhood of garden apartments, and a good place for me to baby sit. Earning babysitting money plus taking part in after-school activities keeps me very busy. For a few months it almost seems like I can settle in to being a normal teenager. Life is generally routine—except of course for the night of the hurricane in September 1954.

"Take care," says the bus driver as I got off the city bus tonight. I had stayed after school for a meeting of the Dramatic Club, and I hadn't paid attention to the weather. It's 6 PM. It's dark out—darker than usual because there was no electricity in the entire neighborhood. Street lights are out. Houses are all dark.

"This is a really bad rain storm," I reply to the driver.

"No, it's a hurricane. It came earlier than the weather people predicted.," he says. "It's been a long time since we've had one this ferocious." The driver is trying to be helpful, but he really is scaring me. "Watch out for falling branches, and for downed electric wires. Be careful now." He drives off. The bus is empty.

I start the six block walk from the bus stop to my apartment. The wind is howling. No point using my umbrella. The wind turns it inside out. I run as fast as I can toward our apartment. Then I stop. I'm tired. I'm out of breath. I'm soaked. I'll have to walk the rest of the way. Trash cans are rolling in the street. The rain is coming down in sheets.

Walking in my shoes is like having my feet inside water balloons. Yuck. It's cold and squishy. And it squeaks every time I take a step. And every so often, I step into a deep puddle. Oooh—wonder what's in this dirty water? At least it can't be as bad as the water in Louisiana when David and I rowed over to our school in the flood.

No people are in sight. I guess everyone is smart enough to be inside. Gotta get home. Four more blocks to go.

Wow! Look at that big old tree. It just tipped over. The roots are out of the ground and the tree is totally across the road. I can walk around it, if I climb over this big root. That way, I should be still on the sidewalk. I can't really see in the dark. I remember that in a movie I saw, there were live electric wires on the ground when trees were knocked over. Do you think there are any live wires near here?

I try to remember exactly where things are. I've walked this route every day for nearly two months now—but I never had to do it without seeing. All I can see is the light from a candle flicker in the occasional house window. But that's no help on the street.

Wait a minute, I think to myself. If I turn here, I can find the entrance to the underground parking garage at this end of our apartment complex. If I can find it in the dark, I can walk the last three blocks underground—where there is no wind and it is dry. I've only been in this end of the parking garage once. One of the kids in the complex showed me how to cut through the blocks of garages shortly after we moved in. It was fun to explore because the whole series of garages and passages that connect under a dozen buildings spread over a three block area. I hope I can remember the way.

I find a door that seems not to go into anyone's apartment. This should lead to the stairway down to the garage. I feel my way along the wall hoping to find a railing. I don't want to fall down a flight of stairs. Things are bad enough. Testing what's in front of me by gingerly putting my squishy foot down, I find the stairs. Great, I think. It's wonderful to be away from that wind and rain. Now—I have to get downstairs and navigate three blocks in the right direction to our unit.

At the base of the stairs, the door knob I find opens up into something. I hope it's the main garage. And I hope it doesn't lock behind me when I walk through. Now I see nothing. Not even candles. It's pitch black. But, it smells like cars, so I must be in the first garage. Which way do I go?

I can't see a thing—not even my hand in front of me. This could be scary! What if I never get out?

Let's see. The stairs turned once half way down, and the door from outside was on the wall parallel to the street. So, if I turn left I think that should take me the length of this garage to the end of this building toward my building. I walk with my hand touching the wall.

"Ouch," I said out loud at one point.

I must have bumped something someone was storing in front of their car. I'm beginning to scare myself. I climb over what-ever-it-is and keep hugging the wall to the end. Now to find another door. I hope I didn't miss it.

I feel for door knobs. The first one is locked. I think to myself that maybe the locked door goes in to a boiler room. I'd be just as happy if I don't find myself in the dark in a boiler room full of hot pipes, or behind a locked door that I can't get open to let myself out.

I keep feeling the wall until I come to another door knob. It opens. I walk through.

Now, let me see. This should be the building straight down the main street. Where do I have to turn left to get to our garage which is two buildings in from the street? I stand still while I try to remember and visualize the configuration of the upstairs buildings. They all look alike when you can see, and when you're upstairs. So doing this in the basement and with no lights—not even lighted exit signs—is really tricky. Do you think architects who design buildings think about this part of how their building affects people who are inside? I doubt it.

There's no place to go but forward. If I find a stairway up and go outside now I'll have no idea where I am and I'll have to walk all through these garden apartments until I somehow see a landmark that tells me where my building is. They all look alike—unless someone's curtains or outside chair gives a clue otherwise. I might not find my way home from outside either. I'd rather be here in the pitch black than back out in that storm.

There was a live electric wire by the big tree that was knocked down. I was lucky that it was across the street from me. I just saw it spark when the wind moved it. What if I run into another one? I'm right to stay in the garage and not go back outside.

My mind starts re-running all the horror movies I've ever seen, all the terrible things that happen in dark garages. Somebody can sneak up on a person and strangle them. People get raped. In the movies, they have shoot-outs in parking garages. It's too dark for a shoot-out. I think you have to see at least a little bit if you want to have a shoot-out. Hope so. A person can get mugged. If that happens, I can scream. But, no one will hear me if I scream. I'll just lie here in a lump on the floor. I shudder.

Trying to pull myself together, I try to convince myself that it's silly to think that kind of stuff. No criminal in their right mind is in this garage tonight. You can't see anything. You can't take a get away car out in the storm. Fallen trees and wires block the street. So, see how silly it is to think these things? I feel really cold. I'm not sure if it's fear or if it's the fact that I'm soaked.

I keep going forward. Eventually I decide it's time to find a door on a left wall. My mental compass guesses that it's time to turn rather than going straight. I find a knob. I go through that door. I keep hugging the wall and try to count the buildings. After I turn, it's not just a matter of walking through the garages. I have to walk through the passages between buildings. I have to feel the wall on the other side to know it's a passageway and not another room. These passages lead to rooms for the boilers, rooms for the trash cans and the incinerator, and rooms for the laundry. I don't know which is worse—walking between the silent totally dark cars in the cavernous garages, or down the narrow totally black passageways between garages. Why don't I carry a flashlight, or even a match? I'll have to remember to do that in the future, I think to myself.

Let me try this door. I think it's a stairway. And, if I've calculated all this right, it should go to the entrance to my building.

Amazingly, I'm right! I emerge into the lobby that I think is mine soaking wet, and dirty from hugging the garage walls. I decide it's my building because a lady with a first floor apartment in our building has a wreath on her front door. I feel a wreath. There can't be two first floor tenants with a prickly wreath on their door. I must be the right building.

I go upstairs to our apartment on the second floor. I let myself into the apartment.

Don is asleep. He doesn't even know I've gotten stuck in the storm. He doesn't know I'm not home.

I like being a sophomore at Central High. I know my way around now. I have some friends. The guidance counselor doesn't hassle me when I decide to take college entrance courses. I guess my grades are good enough and she realizes that she made a snap judgment that was wrong. Adults don't like to be wrong. That's silly because everybody is wrong some of the time. Me too.

AN ESSAY CONTEST

The school just announced a contest. The winner has to write a paper and present it out loud before some judges. It's the American Legion sponsored "Voice of Democracy" contest. Contests are fun.

"What do you think about that contest?" Bill, who sat next to me in home room, asks as we head out the door for first period.

Bill's a nice guy. He's in some of my classes, and occasionally he goes with a group of kids to the movies on Saturday afternoons.

I reply. "I think I'll enter it. When I went to Bellevue, some friends and I started a newspaper called "Chesley Chat." We tried to get people at school to speak up and be heard about things that needed fixing at school. This is the same sort of thing— speaking up. Speaking up is how you get things to change for the better."

"Yeah, but this contest is all about government," Bill adds.

"That's O.K.," I reply. "Government can be fascinating. We read about all this stuff in Latin. What the Romans did was government. Besides, I just finished the American history course, so that should help. All those revolutionary heroes we read about started democracy just by speaking up."

"What about having to stand up in front of people and present your paper? That takes guts." Bill talks himself out of entering the contest as we walk down the hall to our next class.

"I had to give a presentation in class last month. I think it went pretty well. I like to stand up in front of a group and answer their questions. I like to prove that I can succeed when they are sure that I can't. Definitely, I'll enter the contest," I say.

"Can you give me a ride to Marjorie's house for the sorority party tomorrow night?" I ask Catherine who is going down the hall in the other direction.

"Sure," Catherine says.

"Thanks." I tell Margorie. "I'm bringing some cookies too. I guess Marjorie invited some boys?"

"Yup! It will be a fun party. I'm taking some records." Marjorie adds. "Gotta go. We'll be late for class."

She and I both run off.

The party is typical of events that happen every several weeks. Usually they are at someone's house from the sorority. At the parties, the boys stand on one side of the room, near the food. The girls stand on the other side of the room. Periodically couples move onto the living room floor and dance. Dancing is hugging and swaying slowly. Mostly I watch this. The lights are very dim. If you're not careful, you can trip on the rolled up carpet. A couple times a year, dances are held in the school gym.

I often help make the decorations for these dances because I like the artistic part. Sometimes I make favors for the parties at a person's house.

I wouldn't say that my social life is extra lively. It's O.K. I like dates—mostly with a group of kids. I don't have any particular friends, just a lot of acquaintances.

These autumn weekends are busy. I need time to finish my speech for the "Voice of Democracy" contest.

To me, the refreshing thing about the contest assignment is that it is freewheeling—there are no prescribed books to read, or questions to answer. It is the first time I've been given an assignment where I just have the freedom to think. I like to figure things out. I always have. Maybe it's because I have more time alone than with other kids or adults. Since the day I got the telegram in Louisiana, I've had a lot to think about—and a lot of time to think. I've never thought about government before. Maybe I can figure if there's a connection between how well people get to live and government?

Ever since we kids climbed all over the Syracuse University snow sculpture, I've liked the idea that 'all the world's a stage.' I remember talking about sending my uneaten vegetables to China that day; maybe government could give people in China the vegetables kids don't want. But then the government in America would have to figure out how all the American kids could actually mail their vegetables so that they got to China before they got moldy. I guess a voice of democracy deals with deciding things that affect everybody—not just a few people. I wish people would always speak up, and make things better— like get rid of that awful chemical smell in Louisiana. I wonder if government could get hospitals to make it possible for kids to stay in touch with their sick Mothers? But I wouldn't want government to not let me be independent!

My thinking is helped along by the fact that I recently had to memorize Lincoln's *Gettysburg Address*. In less than 200 words, Abraham Lincoln said a lot. I think to myself, it's a good thing my paper can be longer than that. Longer is easier. Wonder if I can fit any of Lincoln's ideas into my speech? Lincoln said this is "a new nation, conceived in liberty, and dedicated to the proposition that all men (maybe that meant women too) are created equal." He said that we must resolve that "government of the people, by the people, and for the people, shall not perish from the earth."

That sounds nice. Wonder if we can make it true? So far I haven't seen a lot of equality for all people here at my high school. This sorority pledging thing certainly illustrated that some people are clearly more equal than others. White people are more equal. And so are wealthier people. I like the idea of equality for everybody. It's only fair. How do we get enough equality to not 'perish from the earth'? That's sort of what Lincoln said we need to do—have everybody listen to everybody else. I think I can turn all this into an essay.

The appointed time came. All the contestants, the judges and various other adults gather in one classroom after school.

I practiced my speech at home last night. Today I am wearing my nicest skirt and blouse. I'm nervous about it—even though I think I'm ready. I think what I plan to say makes sense; it connects all those famous people with what goes on in every day life today. It calls on normal people to speak out. I just hope I present it all right.

It's hard to get any sense of whether my presentation will be any good or not. My head is racing. I'm trying to remember what parts I want to emphasize, where I want to gesture. I'm so busy worrying about how I'll do that I don't really hear the speakers before me. I should have listened. Well, maybe if I had heard them, I'd only be more scared.

"Carla Lee Brooks. You're next." The moderator says.

I stand up and go to the podium. "Ladies and gentlemen," I say. "Democracy can't just be in our history books." I go on identifying what people claim democracy is about. Then I note that these claims don't work for everybody. (I think, really, that I'm describing how Dick and Jane kids get a fair break, and others often don't.) I conclude by calling every person to speak out now, today, like our heroes did in the past, so that democracy can be real for everybody."

I sit down—relieved that it is over. I think it went O.K. But then, maybe that's just what I want to think.

I wait. The judges are deciding. All the contestants are standing in the hall. There was a panel of judges, some teachers and I think the others were from the Veteran's Post. Eventually one of them came out into the hall.

"We want now to announce the winners," one of the judges says.

Third prize, second prize….. They introduce each winner and comment on their essay. I was convinced that I hadn't even placed. It was probably pretty presumptuous of me to think that I could compete in this. And, I think what I said may have been too lofty, too much a hope, and (on the other side of that coin) too critical of things the way they are today. I won't place.

"First prize goes to Carla Lee Brooks."

I am astonished. I won the contest.

Good heavens! I won the contest!

It's the first time I've won anything like this. The Sands Medal that I won in seventh grade when I lived in Vails Gate doesn't count. I didn't do anything to win that—I don't think I did. Here I made a speech about something important, and it came out OK! I guess.

STUDENT COUNCIL AND THE CHURCH PLAY

I am feeling good about things. In January I decided to run for a vacant spot on the Student Council. I'd represent the sophomore class. The campaign is short. Three other people are running. We stand up in class one day and tell what we'll do to represent the class' interest in getting more school dances and in improving the year book. This would be easy after the contest speech.

I did get really nervous the night before we had to get up and speak. What if I get too serious and all the kids just want to think about fun? What if I haven't gotten my hair style and make-up and petticoats just right? The girls won't stand for that. I know that they think appearance matters more than what I say. What if… What if…

I worried my way to school the next morning.

The teacher had the class fill out paper ballots and she collected them. We all sat at our homeroom desks doing our work while she counted them.

I got elected. What's going on? Again, no one was more surprised than me. What a difference this sophomore year is from freshman year when the kids wouldn't talk to me in the cafeteria. What happened?

One day before a Student Council meeting started, Diane, my friend from the Dramatic Club and I start talking. She's a senior and also an officer in the Student Council.

"At my church, we're putting on a spring play." Diane says. "We need more people in the cast. Why don't you come to the youth group and join the cast."

"What's a youth group?" I ask.

"This is at the First Presbyterian Church, on West Genesee Street. My dad's the minister there. The youth group is a kind of club for teen-agers. We meet every Sunday evening, and have fun and go places together, and try to do things to help people—for example we sing Christmas Carols at nursing homes," Diane explained. "Come this Sunday. We meet at 5:30. We're done by 8:00."

I liked the idea of being in a play—where you could create a fantasy world. It sounds like what we did when we played on the snow sculpture at Syracuse University. I'm not sure I am good at acting; but it sounds like fun. Besides, it would be fun to do something with kids on a weekend. And I've been a bit curious about churches since I went to that one in Rochester when I stayed with my grandmother. "O.K.," I reply to Diane. "I'll come this Sunday."

"I'll meet you at the drug store near the church," Diane says. Then you don't have to find your way to the room where we are."

"See you then," I said.

The church is downtown—past the turn-off for school It's about a two mile walk from Don's and my new apartment. The buses don't run very often on Sunday night. Don certainly isn't willing to give me a ride to and from rehearsal as do most of the other kids parents. He says he's too busy. So, I walk.

For several weeks I go to the Youth Group. I have a part in the Spring play. It's not a big part. Frankly, I think I'm not good at acting. But it's fun. I enjoy the kids. Every week, when it's over, I'm the first to leave, so I can get a good start on my two mile walk. The other kids parents come. Some of them carpool. Most of them live on the west side—where people like Presbyterians live.

It is a spring-like Sunday night in late March. I am wearing my new navy blue blazer. Rehearsal just ended.

"You all are really doing fine," the play director told us. "Remember in two weeks, we have dress rehearsal, and the performance. Between now and next Sunday, work on the rough spots, and start thinking about your costumes. See you next week."

"Bye, Diane. Bye Phil." I get my jacket. Kids are standing around the refreshment table.

"Here, have the last cookie," Diane says to Phil. "I can bring in a large black hat for you to wear in the final scene."

"That sounds perfect," Phil replied. "Will it fit?"

Bye, Carla Lee. Diane calls to me. She continues talking with Phil. "I think the hat will fit."

"Phil, your mom's out front," Jim calls across the room.

"Bye, Carla Lee." Phil says. "Tell her I'll be there in a minute. Diane, can I come by your house after school one day and check the hat?"

WALKING HOME THAT NIGHT

A thousand things are happening at once. My mission is to leave quickly and unnoticed. I started walking briskly toward home. After about fifteen minutes I've walked past the old factory building and the used car lots near the church, past the railroad track crossing, past the downtown streets, and past the office buildings. I enter a stretch where the big trees block the street lights. It is darker on the sidewalks. It's very near the high rise apartment where Don and I used to live—and still over a mile from my new apartment. It's quiet now—on a Sunday evening. The businesses are all closed. The four lane street, however, is a main one—James Street. Traffic is steady and traffic lights cause the cars to stop and start at frequent intervals. Seems like a perfectly safe place. Surely, it's safer than where the industry and the railroad tracks are.

Suddenly, I listen more sharply. Is there someone walking behind me? I walk a little faster. The footsteps behind me come a little faster.

This was just a minute ago. It was just before I ended up in this hospital room. My reminiscing while lying in my hospital room has now caught up with the present. I re-live last week just one more time—just to finish my attempt to understand how I got here.

I was walking up James Street from the church play rehearsal—lots of lights and four lanes of busy traffic.

"Keep your mouth shut!" I am given this order as an arm reaches around my neck in a stranglehold.

"Heeeeeeeeeeeeellllllllllllllllllppppppppppppp!!!!!!!!!!!!!" I scream at the top of my lungs. Yes, I'm learning to stand up for myself, to speak out. Screaming seems the best thing to do. It's all I can do just now.

I feel a dull hard thrust into my right side. I see the face of my assailant. I see his large hunting knife. Then, nothing. He runs up the street and into the dark. He disappears.

(I try to shift my body in the hospital bed; it's not possible to be comfortable even though they say that I'm ready to go home later today. I have to finish my train of thought. What did I do after he stabbed me?)

I stand there. Alone. It's got to be only a split second. It seems like an eternity. My right side is getting warm, and it hurts—not much—a little. I put my hand on my side. It's covered with blood. My clothes are covered with blood. I'm making a big puddle of blood on the sidewalk. That's scary to look at!

I've been stabbed!

"Heeeeeeeeeeeeeelllllllllllllllllllllllpppppppppppppp!!!!!!!!!!!" I scream again. My assailant is gone. But I really don't know what to do about all this blood. What if I pass out or something? It's really dark out here. Then, I'd really be unable to take care of myself. I've got to get someone's attention while I can.

A huge door opens on the closest big old house. The house looks like it's straight out of the stage set for "The Addam's Family" TV show. A couple men appear in the door. "Hello? Hello?" They see me on their front sidewalk. They walk a little closer. "Are you alright?"

"Help! Please help!" That's all I can say.

They see the blood gushing from my side. "Here, take an arm," one man says to the other. "Let's take her to the back room."

I think to myself that these aren't people whose arm I'd ordinarily take. Each of these middle aged men is wearing a tuxedo. They both are big men, and the tuxedo trousers are a little too short. One man has squinty eyes. The other is bald. Both have round red noses—like they might drink too much.

Basically, aside from all the things that have been happening to me, I'm still a shy kid who, if anything, works extra hard to be good and to stay away from people who I think might be bad people. The grown-up world is still a mystery to me. But I'm learning fast.

I have no choice. I really do need help. No one else is anywhere around on this dark street of office buildings. I take their arms.

With one on each side of me, they half carry me into the building that they came from. I'm leaving a healthy trail of blood the whole way.

I'm totally terrified. Which is worse—gushing blood onto the sidewalk, or being hauled off by a couple of strange men?

RUINING SOMEONE'S FUNERAL

Inside the house, there are two parlors, one on either side of the entry hall. Both rooms are full of people, dressed in black, all gaping at me. There's a lady all in black. Her mouth is wide open. She's holding the wall near the doorway and fanning herself. She looks a little pale. I hope she doesn't faint. An older man in a brown suit is wiping his brow with a handkerchief. It's as if he doesn't know how to react. A collective "oooooohhhhhhhh" comes from these spectators as they watch me dripping blood.

"Look at the blood," a tall woman with spectacles on her nose snaps. "It's damaging the rug."

"Good Lord," I half whisper out loud. "I'm in a funeral home!"

I realize what's happening. The two guys helping me are undertakers. I don't think I'm dead. Am I?

All the people in black are attending a wake! I wish I could make a photograph of the expressions on the faces of these mourners. I have this overwhelming desire to laugh as I realize what's happening. It's hilarious.

"Did you see her?" One distraught woman says to another.

"It's bad enough. It's Grandpa's funeral. I'll remember it all my life. But—but—now I'll never forget the image of a bleeding teenager being half carried through our wake." This woman throws herself, crying, into a man's arms.

It's a long corridor. I think to myself. I'm heavy for the undertakers to haul to the back room. I don't think I'm pulling my own weight very much.

I think to myself that they could have deposited me on the sofa just near the front door. I probably would have ruined the cover on the sofa. And, besides, had they done that, I would have been in the same room with the mourners at the wake. That might not have been good for business. After all, the wake is traumatic enough in itself. Having a real live horror show run at the same time could have really sent the public away.

This is one of those times when a minute is a month. Surely we're almost to 'the back room'—wherever that is. We emerge from the dimly lit hallway into a florescent bright room. They lay me on this stainless steel table in the middle of the room.

One of the men heaves a sigh of relief from depositing his heavy load. "Just lie there—so you don't lose any more blood." He takes a wad of paper towels and presses it up against my right side.

"We've called an ambulance," the other undertaker says.

"You just lie quietly." The first one repeats. I think he's worried about what will happen next.

The two men in their proper mourning clothes look a bit flustered. I don't think they've ever had anyone alive on this table before.

I'm lying on the table where they embalm bodies! Oh, my God, I really am! What else would they use this table for?

Look at all those bottles on the shelves. Must be the cosmetics and stuff they use to make a body look like a some-body. There's the back door. One of the men just went out. I think he's directing the ambulance back here and not to the funeral in the front. The folks at the wake don't need guys bursting through the door with a stretcher—not after what they've just seen.

I think the ambulances usually drop the dead people off here—on this table; they don't pick up breathing bodies. That door is really wide. It's wide, I think, so that, after the funerals, the caskets can be carried through the entry and into the hearse for the ride to the cemetery.

This is really weird! Maybe I am just at home watching "The Addam's Family?"

Ohhh..., I can't move. My side hurts now. The undertakers find some cloths to replace the paper towels against my right side. I'm still bleeding.

"One, two, three, lift." One EMT says to the others. I am lifted off the stainless steel embalming table and onto a gurney.

"Get the door. We're off." The driver calls to the others.

GETTING THE AMBULANCE DRIVER TO LISTEN

I'm lying now in the ambulance, strapped down. One EMT is sitting next to me. I see the roof of the ambulance and the lights of traffic outside—as much as you can see when you're in this position. I hear our siren. The red lights are flashing. I'm wondering what's going to happen next. I've never been in an ambulance before.

I hate having to always deal with these big issues when it's a crisis.

"St. Josephs, right." It's kind of muffled, but I think I hear the driver on his radio talking with someone. I'm feeling a little light headed now. But I better pay attention to this.

"Where are we going?" I ask the EMT next to me.

"To the hospital," he says.

That's dumb, I think to myself. "I know that!"

"Which hospital?" I ask.

"Whatever's closest," he says. "You'll be all right."

"No. No. Are we going to St. Joseph's?" I ask.

"Maybe."

"Well I won't go to St. Joseph's. It's a lousy hospital. It's the worst hospital in the city." I tell him. "Tell the driver to take me to University Hospital."

"Don't you worry about it. You'll be fine. Take it easy now. You don't want to lose more blood," the EMT tells me.

They are just conning me, I think. They aren't listening to me. If ever there was a time when I have to get people to listen to me, it's now! It's important that I get these adults to listen to me; I can do that.

"Listen, I say. Listen to me! It's my body. Take me where I want to go." I feel faint. I'm thinking that I have to pace myself so I don't black out. I'll lose my argument if I faint. That light headed feeling is getting worse. I've got to win this battle.

"Turn this ambulance around! Take me to University Hospital. You know St. Joseph's is lousy! Now do what I say!

Please!! If you take me to St. Joseph's it won't matter if I lose more blood, anyway."

The EMT decides I'm too agitated. He's talking to the driver up in front. "Hey Joe, better head to University Hospital. This'll never work," says the attendant with me. They whisper some more.

"It's O.K.," my attendant says. "The driver is turning around. We'll take you to University Hospital. Now calm down, or you really will lose more blood."

I calm down. Why can't anything ever be normal? I think to myself.

When I arrive there are x-rays and more x-rays. I hurt. I really hurt. My new blue blazer is ruined. It's soaked in blood, and they cut it off of me. My black slacks are splattered with blood too. The hospital attendants exchange my street clothes for a hospital gown. Finally I get to lie in a regular hospital bed. I am exhausted. They give me a blood transfusion. A doctor comes in.

"You're a lucky girl," he says. "That hunting knife came in a fraction of an inch below your lung, and stopped just before your heart. Do you know what would have happened to you if your lung had been punctured, or your heart had been stabbed? You're lucky to be alive."

"Really? Wow. Thank you. Can I sleep now?" I reply. I guess I really did almost die. I'm too young. I'm only fifteen. I think to myself—and soon doze off. I'm in and out of sleep for a long and painful night. My side hurts, and I can't turn over.

The next morning the police come.

The officers have lots of questions. "How tall is the person who attacked you?" "Does he have dark hair or light hair?" "How old is he?" "Which of these pictures does he look like?"

I tell them as much as I can. This is someone I only saw for a few seconds—and in the dark. But, it was one of those moments you don't forget.

I guess it was two days ago when I heard what the police were doing.

"They caught the guy who stabbed you." A nurse popped her head in the door. "I just heard it on the radio. He is a young man from the nearby Indian Reservation."

It's not clear what he wanted; but it's not hard to guess. The news is all over the Syracuse newspapers. The incident makes headlines—"girl returning home from church youth group is stabbed on busy street at 8:00 PM". The papers say that I have helped the police identify the assailant, and they give my name.

Hospital attendants bring me a tray with a bowl of boiled cardboard. I'm starving, but I can't eat this. I hope this is my last hospital meal. I fall asleep—finally.

THE VILLAIN AND MY NEXT HOME

"You have visitors," a nurse says. It's morning and I'm supposed to go home from the hospital today. I think I have the strength to take the bus to Don's and my apartment. I hope. I'm getting ready to find some outdoors clothes. The clothes I wore the day I came to the hospital are ruined.

The minister of the First Presbyterian Church and his wife are my visitors. My friend, Diane, is their daughter.

Yesterday, the newspapers carried a follow-up story on my stabbing. Apparently the assailant that I identified and that the police had caught and put in jail had escaped. They say that the police can't find him. My name and address has been in the newspaper, and the paper already stated that I can recognize him. Someone at the hospital figured out that I'll be going home alone. The assailant will know where to find me. And I'd be home alone.

Don is on a beach in Florida.

The Harris's apparently decided that being home alone wasn't a good idea. Maybe the hospital social worker decided to call them.

"Would you like to come to our house for the weekend," Mrs. Harris asks? "We'll be happy to have you come. In a few days Don will be back and you can go home."

"That would be wonderful," I say. I like Diane and this would be like an extended slumber party—even if I am all bandaged up and taking lots of medication. Besides, it will be nice not to be in our apartment alone.

"We'll pick you up in a couple hours. We can drive by your apartment so you can get some clothes and anything you'll need for the weekend."

"That's nice. Thank you. See you then" I say, really relieved.

I have to write Grandma and tell her about all this. It's hard to keep in touch with my family in Rochester. They think everything here is fine because Don is my 'dad'. I wish I could visit Grandma in Rochester, but I don't know how to make that happen. I bet Grandma would want to come see me if she could. Then again, probably most of the people in Rochester will think it's my fault that I can't get a ride home from the church youth group and that I got stabbed while walking home at 8:00 at night on a busy street. That's what Dick and Jane people think when people have misfortunes. For them, the world is always perfect. What's not perfect is hidden, because bad things don't happen to good people.

Except, they do.

"We're here," Jim Harris announces. "Are you ready to leave the hospital? You need to ride in this wheel chair as far as the front door. Hospital policy." He and Mrs. Harris pick up my belongings and wheel me to the elevator.

I leave the hospital.

Chapter Ten

Raiford, Florida and "Old Sparky"

A WEEKEND GUEST

"Welcome!" Caroline Harris opened the door to their home. Rev. Harris carried my things inside the big house. This house, very near Onondaga Park where I had lived so many years ago, is the manse for the Presbyterian Church. It's big. It has a huge front porch. It's a house for just one family. This will be a treat—a whole house.

"Hi, I'm Jimmy," said the smallest of the kids in the Harris family. He's a blonde skinny kid with twinkling eyes—about seven years old.

"I'm Suzie," said his sister who would be quite an attractive girl had she not been recently encumbered with heavy rimmed eyeglasses and braces on her teeth. Suzie's maybe ten years old.

Diane, my friend from student council and from the church play greeted me. "Glad you'll be here for the weekend. I can tell you all about what's happened in school this past week."

"Come and meet Ellie." Diane said. On the way upstairs, Diane told me that Ellie had been living for some years in a local orphanage and that the Harris's had just arranged for her to finish her last two years of high school living in their home as their foster child. She had moved in only a couple weeks ago. Ellie is also in high school with Diane and me. I hadn't met her before.

Mrs. Harris comes upstairs with us.

"It's just for the weekend, kids," Mrs. Harris explains. "Carla is Diane's friend from school, and she's in the church play."

"Here's our room," Suzie says. "Diane and I sleep here. This is the first bedroom at the top of the stairs. It's a big front room with ample space, big double hung windows and hundreds of stuffed animals.

"This room is mine." Jimmy shouts out from around the corner where he's jumping up and down on the mattress. "Your room is down the hall."

"Carla, you and Ellie can share the double bed in the back bedroom." Mrs. Harris and Rev. Harris direct me down a hall toward the back of the house and the back stairway.

Ellie is already in the room. She isn't pleased about getting a roommate. It's obvious in the expression on her face. But she dutifully moves her belongings to make room for mine.

Diane and Ellie show me where things are and where I can put my suitcase. Ellie says, "This sun porch is ours too. It's a nice place—unless the weather gets cold. If you run out of space, we can put things out here. But it shouldn't be a problem since you'll only be here a few days."

I'm tired. The trip here from the hospital is the most I've moved around in a week. We had to stop at Don's apartment to pick up things on the way. I had to climb stairs there, and now again here. I spend a lot of the weekend in bed. My side still hurts.

Sunday night comes and it's time for me to leave. But Don never calls. We think he's still out of town.

"I don't think she should go home by herself," Caroline Harris says to her husband.

"You're right. We need to confirm that her step-father is at the apartment," Jim Harris adds. They call repeatedly. No one answers the phone. We five kids are sitting on the comfy old sofa in the TV room watching "The Ed Sullivan Show."

"Kids." Caroline Harris announces to the five of us who are sitting in the TV room. "We're going to ask Carla to stay until her step-father calls. Carla, it's late now. I think there's no point in your leaving tonight."

I stay Monday and Tuesday. The other kids go to school. I'm still too sick so I spend the day alternating between the bed and the TV couch. This is a nice place. Mrs. Harris is a jovial woman in her late forties. She bustles about making the house perfect, fixing meals, talking with church people on the phone. She fits the women's magazine image of Mother, wife and social secretary. She's always doing things for other people, and taking great pleasure in those acts. Rev. Harris is out a lot. He's the minister of music. When he's home he enjoys doing music related things with the family. Sometimes he plays the grand piano in the living room and everybody sings. That's fun. He's always bringing people in and out. This is a happy place. Each of the four kids has friends who visit. The three girls get lots of phone calls. Jimmy plays ball with the neighborhood boys. It's a real Dick and Jane family.

TELLING DON WHAT I THINK

Finally on Wednesday, Don calls. "Mrs. Harris, my circumstances have changed here in Florida. It will be a few more days until I return to Syracuse," he says.

"When will you come?" She asks. She doesn't sound anxious—just ready to have her life return to the normal routine of parents with four children—not five.

"Maybe at the end of the week," he tells her.

She's very polite and doesn't seem to know what to say.

"May I speak with Carla Lee now?" Don asks.

"Hi Don," I say. He tells me how nice Florida is and how he decided to stay a little longer. He never even asks how I am feeling. I'm getting angrier and angrier as I listen to him. I made a spur of the moment decision.

"Don."

"Yes?"

"I don't want to live with you any more. I'm not coming home when you return to Syracuse." I hear myself say, "I'm staying here. I'm moving in with the Harris's."

I can't believe what I just said. It just blurted out. Pretty rude!

I'm sure Mrs. Harris couldn't believe it either.

Fortunately she is standing right next to me so I don't have to explain what I'd said. Now, she really doesn't know what to do next. She's a very polite person. She'll have to explain this to her husband and to the kids—most especially to Ellie who, no doubt, is eager to have her new bedroom back—especially her bed.

Don, on the other hand, is probably enormously relieved.

"Whatever you want," Don says "See you soon." He hung up as quickly as possible, just in case Mrs. Harris might get back on the phone and tell him that I am mistaken.

The adults are in a huddle again, trying to figure out what to do with me. The Harris's move an extra dresser into the back room, move some things onto the porch and try to provide sufficient storage area for both Ellie and me.

In a couple months, school will be out. Come summer, the Harris's will go to New Hampshire where he is the minister of a tiny Congregational Church in North Barnstead.

"Maybe we can make it work until summer. I'll see if she has any relatives she can visit this summer," Mrs. Harris tells her husband.

"The house in New Hampshire is too small for so many people. We're already going to be cramped to make room for Ellie. If we can make it until then it will give us time to talk with someone at Family Services, a child placement agency, and work out a long term solution."

"I'll talk with her step-father," Rev. Harris says. "There must be some legal structure for her guardianship."

MOTHER'S PLANNING SAVED THE DAY

Don never paid too much attention to structure, and it's not clear to me that anyone else did either. But Mother apparently had put things in place before she died. She will never know how important it was for her to have done that.

Charlie Close, Mother's college friend and the Judge who married Mother and Don, played a role I'd never known about. I haven't seen Charlie since the day of the wedding in his yard. So much has happened since. I guess Don put the Harris's in touch with Charlie. One day, Charlie called me at the Harris's and announced that we should meet after school at a soda fountain near my school. I'm there at the appointed time.

"Hello, Carla Lee. It's been a long time since I've seen you. I'm so sorry about your Mother." Charlie greets me with a hearty handshake. He's dressed in his pin stripe suit and black shoes. He looks a little out of place in a soda fountain. He's apparently just left his courtroom.

"Hi." I respond. "It's nice to see you." I'm wondering what this is all about. Although, I think to myself, it is very nice that someone wants to talk with me about what's happening.

"Carla Lee, you may not know that your Mother left some money for your education. She left me in charge of handling it. Her idea was that when you turn eighteen, you'll have it to use for college and to get established." Charlie explains.

"Really? I had no idea." I replied, somewhat uncertain of what is happening this time. But, I'm used to that feeling.

I never had really thought about money. Mother always gave me what I needed and Don continued that practice. I never needed much—just for school lunches and clothes. My other money was what I earned babysitting.

Charlie continues, "you are very fortunate that your Mother was able to do this for you, and that she had the foresight to plan for unexpected circumstances. I know she thought that you'd grow up living with her or Don or with other family members, but circumstances have changed."

"I don't want to live with Don," I say.

"I know," says Charlie. "Rev. and Mrs. Harris have been very kind to take you in."

I have this great desire to blurt out the obvious; Mother knew from the beginning not to trust Don. It was clear now. Somehow, even as a nine year old, I knew that. Otherwise, why would Charlie have been in charge of the money? But, I keep my mouth shut. So my gut reaction about Don was right!

"I think, given the circumstances, that we need to use some of this money now." Charlie continues.

"The Harrises can't be expected to pay for your upkeep if you stay there. They will need money for food and other expenses. You'll need money for clothes and other school items. I'm arranging to pay them something every month for your expenses and I will arrange for you to have a $50 check every month. You'll need to open a savings account and not spend all your money at once. When you need something expensive like a winter coat, you'll need to have the money in that account to use." Charlie spells out all the details of my finances.

"O.K.," I say. "I've never thought about money before. What happens if something doesn't work right, or if there's some big expense?"

"Here's my card so you will know how to reach me." He says. "You're big enough now to make calls like this yourself.

"My office isn't far from here. From time to time, I think it would be a good idea if you come by to let me know how things are."

I sip my strawberry ice cream soda and try to think if I've forgotten to ask him anything. I don't really know what questions to ask about money.

"Oh, I almost forgot," Charlie adds. "Your Grandma Brooks is in Florida. You haven't seen her for a long time. I think your Mother told me that she and you drove down there a few years ago."

"Yes," I reply. "I remember that trip. Another time Mother and I went to Jacksonville by train and I slept in the top bunk. I send Grandma Brooks a letter from time to time."

"How would you like to go to Florida for this summer's vacation?" Charlie asks. "I think you're old enough to make that trip on a Greyhound bus by yourself. Your uncle will meet you at the bus stop in Jacksonville when the bus arrives. The Harris's will take you to the bus stop here. It's a long trip—three days."

"Wow. I'd like that. Florida is so far away—farther even than Rochester. I never even see the people in Rochester anymore." I answer.

"Well then, we'll arrange for your summer trip to Florida," says Charlie having completed his business obligation.

"It's good to see you again, Carla Lee. I'm sorry that you have had all these problems. You be a good girl and do well in school." Charlie waves and walks back toward the Court House.

As I leave the soda fountain and head back to the Harris's house, I'm realizing that the whole incident of my being stabbed and saying I was moving in with the Harris's apparently got the adults talking. I wonder if Charlie Close knew all that had happened to me? I don't think so. He would have come to the hospital. And he never mentioned it. Don certainly wouldn't have told him. And the Harris's only know about the last few weeks. The Harris's don't even know about my real family or what has happened.

I wonder what would have happened if Mother hadn't left money to pay the Harris's for my bills? What happens to kids without money? Ellie, the foster child at the Harris's, ended up in an orphanage. I guess the government takes care of you then— if anybody. That's scary. The government is so big it's so many somebodies that it's nobody; a person certainly wouldn't have much say in his or her own future. It would be like being put in a prison. Why does nobody ever care what kids think?

Given all the things that could have happened, I'd say that I have been remarkably fortunate. I wonder if I can help other people who are in a tough spot?

Soon school ended. I packed for Florida. I'm excited about taking this long bus trip—all by myself. I'm also excited about seeing my Grandma Brooks. I haven't seen her since way before Mother died.

"Bye. You have a good summer." Mrs. Harris handed me my bag as I boarded the Greyhound.

It's all arranged that my uncle, S.B., will pick me up in Jacksonville. People in the south just go by the initials of their first name and middle name, not by their real names. He's always been just S.B.. He's kind of like Alton in Rochester, the family bachelor.

"Good-bye," Diane Harris's father said. "Have a good trip. Write us and we'll see you at the end of August. Don't forget, we'd like you to come to New Hampshire for the last weekend of the summer."

"Good-bye," I shouted and waved through the open window as the bus pulled out of the station.

What relief the Harris family must have felt. This problem of what to do with an extra teenager isn't resolved, but at least summer gives them time.

THE GEORGIA TOILET

I sit on the bus for three days and three nights. It's pretty boring and very uncomfortable. I talk with different people now and then, read a lot, and only get in trouble once. That was when we pulled into a station somewhere in rural Georgia at about 2 AM.

I had to pee—really badly. I was disgruntled and barely awake. I stumbled off the bus and followed a bunch of women through a door. What a relief! A toilet! I emerged from the stall and got very strange looks from everyone in there.

"Go on. You better leave, right now." An older, well dressed Negro woman said to me.

I look puzzled and start to go toward the sink to wash my hands.

"You shouldn't be in here," another woman says to me.

I can't figure it out what's happening. I'm too sleepy to ask. The best course of actions seems to be to leave—now. So I do.

Back on the platform, I stand for a minute stretching my legs before I fold myself up and into my seat again. At that point I turned around toward the room I just exited. The sign over the door said—"Ladies Room—Colored Only"

"Woops," I said out loud. I hadn't done that intentionally. It just never occurred to me that I need to be alert to such customs when traveling in the rural south. I'm too accustomed to Yankee ways.

Now I understand why the women in the rest room looked so distraught, why they were so anxious for me to leave immediately. They knew that had anyone decided to make trouble by raising the racial issue, one of them might be beaten up, or thrown in jail, or both. I am white and a kid and had there been trouble in that situation it wouldn't likely have been considered my fault. White adults might have even thrown the Negro women in jail for that. It's 1955 and here-and-there some white folks as well as some Negroes are starting to question segregation. So people are very careful. They didn't know if I was stupid or if I was trying to stir up trouble. Turns out, I was just a sleepy kid. How do I end up in these situations? What's to do with what I learn?

I get back on the bus. It's not much farther to Jacksonville.

GRANDMA BROOKS' HOUSE

Finally I can get off the bus. S.B., my uncle, is there to pick me up in his fin-backed Buick.

S.B. is Daddy's younger brother. He never married and has always lived with my grandmother. S.B. was elected County Judge for Union County in 1951. He dresses the role—southern style. S.B. is a large round man who has trouble slipping into his car because the steering wheel is in the way. He wears a straw broad-brimmed hat, white trousers and a light shirt. His necktie and suit jacket are on the back seat of the car. I do like his large gold watch that he wears on a chain that dangles across his vest to a pocket.

"Grandma Brooks is anxious to see you. It's been so long. You're so grown up," he tells me as we drive toward Raiford.

"I'm glad I could come," I say. "It will be fun to be here for the whole summer."

Nothing has changed in Raiford. Things change very very slowly here. An hour west of the bustling city of Jacksonville is like traveling several decades back into the real old south. I think it is both charming, and exciting.

It's charming because the rural countryside had tall splendid pines—acre after acre. You can look down the rows of the forest as if you were looking down rows of marching soldiers. You can look up to see the tops of them swaying gently in the breeze against the very blue sky full of puffy clouds. I liked the rows of pines and their smell. They get turpentine from these pines and that's a big business here. Everywhere else there are live oak trees spreading their very wide branches draped with Spanish moss—providing welcome shade from the scorching hot sun. I love to watch the moss wave gently in the breeze.

It's exciting because visiting my Grandma Brooks and S.B. is like taking a trip into a novel. It's so very different from New York State! The places to go are different; the things people talk about are different. It's never boring.

Grandma Brooks' house is an imposing large white house with a broad porch marked by tall columns that rise past the second floor porch to the roof. Large pecan trees are in the back yard. A small grove of banana trees is in the side yard. I'm told that at one time there were several lovely old Victorian style homes with the big pillars and the large porches in the Raiford area. But, in 1955, only Grandma's house was left except for a few tucked way back on country roads. Her house in just large, not a mansion, but it looks a bit out of place without any other houses like it nearby. It's quite near the general store and gas station. Dusty one lane roads cut in both directions from their home.

"Oh, Carla Lee, It's so good to see you," Grandma greeted me. "My, how you have grown since I last saw you. You're nearly grown-up."

"I'm happy to be here," I said. "We have a whole summer together."

"Isn't that wonderful," says S.B. "Come I'll show you around the yard before we go inside."

Elsewhere in Grandma's yard is the elevated pen where a dozen rabbits live. "Can I hold one," I ask.

"Sure," S.B. says. "Later, you can take one on the front porch and sit with your grandma."

"Look here." S.B. points to another structure in the back yard. "One end of this building is where we take showers." He shows me.

"But the other end is where I keep my parakeets." We enter a screened-in shed about half the size of a small room. It contains at least fifty parakeets.

"This is amazing," I say. One lands on my shoulder.

"Hold still," S.B. says. "They scare easily. Look at this one sitting on my finger."

"Pretty bird. Pretty bird."

Much to my amazement the bird replies, "Pretty bird. Pretty bird."

I've never seen this before. When S.B. is not in his judge's office at the Court House, one of the things he enjoys is to train the birds to talk.

"Back here," S.B. continues his tour, "this is the chicken yard." He shows me a penned in area where about a dozen chickens and a couple roosters live.

"Tomorrow morning you can come to find the eggs that they have laid. You can have some for breakfast."

This is unbelievably exciting, I think to myself. How lucky can a kid from New York State be! It sure is different from the city.

"Let's go inside. I'll put your things in the upstairs bedroom. Come up and see."

They give me one of two very big square second floor bedrooms. The walls and ceiling are all narrow wainscot boards—a dark wood. The floors are wide wooden planks. The big double bed has an imposing decorative iron head and foot board. The bed is covered with a hand crocheted lace bedspread. The ceiling is very very high. There are two huge windows. Through one, it's possible to look out into a huge pecan tree. Through the other, one can look down into the top of a banana tree. The glass in the windows has the ripples you find in really old glass. What an adventure I think to myself. And it's *my* history. Without history, now wouldn't be the same, I think.

Everything has that southern smell—the smell of tropical plants decaying. It's a smell I like. I like finding familiar smells. Grandma's windows have lace curtains that blow in the breeze from the fan on the floor. (This is all long before air conditioning.) Opposite the top of the stairway, just across from my bedroom, is the door to the huge second floor porch. It runs the length of the house. S.B. tells me that we don't use this porch as much as the first floor porch one. To me that doesn't matter. I'm going to like sleeping with the door open. I can look through and see the trees covered in Spanish moss.

"How about a nice cold glass of iced tea?" S.B's offers.

"Good idea."

We go to the front porch. Grandma is already sitting there with a rabbit in her lap. "Want to hold him?" She says.

"You bet," I reply. I never held a rabbit before. He is very soft. He has a pretty face. I like him—until he poops in my lap. I put him back in the cage, change my clothes and return for more iced tea. This summer I'll spent a lot of time playing with the rabbits.

"How did our family get here?" I ask.

Grandma and S.B. take turns telling me the story.

LOTS OF FLORIDA HISTORY

The Florida roots are deep for my family. I'm a sixth generation Floridian, I learn.

My great-great-great grandparents came to Florida from Georgia when the United Stated purchased the Florida Territory from the Spanish and settlers came in the mid-1820s—twenty years before Florida would become a state. The family already had lived for some years in Georgia. Settlers struggled across the Okefenokee Swamp bringing wagons filled with family, horses, farm animals, and belongings in promise of the newly opened territory of Florida. The Brooks' established their homestead in Providence, Florida. They, and the hand full of other settlers, built log cabins, cleared land and settled in. Life was rough. The Indians, chased from one location to another, were fighting to keep their land and they were not friendly to these Europeans.

The early Brooks settlers joined others in Providence at the place they built called Fort Call during the Seminole Indian Wars. In fact, my great-grandparents are buried at Fort Call. It's still there! The men signed up at muster calls to fight in the Seminole Wars. In peace time, families raised cotton, set up turpentine stills and made a life for themselves in the land of tall pines, cypress bogs, live oaks and Spanish moss. Their peace was interrupted again by the Civil War. Again, the men went off to fight. The cotton business became more difficult after the Civil War. In the early 1900s, my grandfather, moved his family from the family homestead in Providence Florida to Raiford.

At the time, Raiford was a promising new community, a railroad stop. The railroad was new. Flagler's Atlantic Coast Line brought the promise of a new era and a better economy. Raiford was important because it was where you'd change trains. One line went to Lake City Florida and then up into Georgia. The other went between Tallahassee and to Jacksonville. There was a substantial depot. A large hotel was near the depot. My grandfather had built the original big framed general store. And not too far away, he built this sizeable home with its pillars and porches.

Here's somebody else who just decided to do something— build a store. A lot of people just go day to day, it seems. But life is interesting when people have a purpose, I think. Like my grandfather, or my Mother, or me when I get the guidance counselor to not put me in a shorthand class.

It's beginning to get dark. It's time to go inside. I've learned a lot on my first day in rural north Florida. People may be the same; but who they "are" and what they care about drives what they "do,"

GEORGIANNE

"You haven't met Georgianne," says Grandma Brooks.
"Georgianne. Can you come in here please?"
This hugely round jolly woman appears from the kitchen. Georgianne takes care of the house and cooks the meals. She

lives in a small house behind this one—just past the chicken yard.

"This is Carla Lee," Grandma proudly announces.

"Yes, m'am."

"She's looking forward to some of your famous fried chicken. Those Yankees don't know how cook," Grandma says.

"Yes, m'am."

Gerogianne always wears a scarf around her hair. She wears a big printed apron that covers her large belly. The apron often has traces of the latest of her many delicious menus. She has dark brown twinkling eyes with wrinkles that smile. I'm going to like Georgianne.

I learn later from Grandma that Georgianne has been living here for three or four years. Because S.B. is the judge, he had learned about her predicament. She had been sentenced to life in prison for killing her husband and was an inmate at the nearby Raiford State Prison Farm. Apparently a number of people either thought she either hadn't killed him, or that she was simply defending herself from his wrath. People liked Georgianne. They trusted her and she had a good reputation.

S.B. arranged her parole. He arranged for her to come to his house. Georgianne has a heart of gold, and is more important than she ever knew to holding that household together. Grandma is getting too old and too arthritic to manage rural living, and S.B.'s schedule at the Court House keeps him away a lot.

By now S.B. has taken a seat at the piano and started playing familiar popular songs. We join in and sing-a-long. After a while, he leaves the piano and picks up his banjo and keeps playing. A couple neighbors hear the music and drop in. Someone makes a request and if S.B. isn't sure about the melody, he'll ask someone to sing a line or two. "Somewhere over the rainbow"— Once he hears it, he plays it perfectly. He's never taken music lesson and he can't read music.

For hours and hours the county judge sits in his old worn upholstered chair—the one he has trouble getting in and out of because he weighs so much. The fan is whirring. The curtains blow with the evening breeze. He's singing away "Oh I come from Alabama with my banjo on my knee." People take turns bringing him iced tea. He doesn't drink or smoke because he's a Morman. Other than that, my uncle, the judge, is surely the stereotypical 'good ole boy.'

Grandma is a jovial, but quiet woman. She likes to sit on the porch and rock—and spends most of her time doing just that. Her health isn't very good. She has heart trouble. People stop by for a visit. We chat. Some evenings we sit and watch what was happening at the evangelical church across the street where the Pentecostal spirit apparently brings people to never ending church services. We listen to the rhythm of their singing. Nice music. It's a white church. The Negro churches are across the state highway—really across the railroad tracks Churches, and everything else is separated here. They call it segregated. Except, Gerogianne has a little house for her and the many children she cares for; it's just behind S.B. and Grandma's house. S.B. arranged to have it built there.

RAIFORD

"Come let's go over to the highway and watch 'ole man Jones' hang the mail pouch by the train," one of the neighborhood kids says.

I go—just up past the general store. The railroad depot is across the street, but we can see it fine from here. Some kids tell me 'ole man Jones' has been doing this for years. When the train comes through, the conductor just picks it off the hook and keeps on moving.

The fellow at the general store comes out.

"You must be Missus Brooks' granddaughter," he says.

"Yes, we came to see the train pick up the mail pouch." I reply.

"Here comes!" He hears the train whistle. "The depot has always been a goin' thing around here. I guess business used ta be good 'cause of the mill and the folks who make the ties for the railroad tracks."

He stands in the doorway to the store and talks, half to himself. "Things are changin' though. More cars, less trains. Fewer turpentine stills. The big ol' two story hotel is still there—but it's empty a lot now. Most folks from around here work at the State Prison Farm now. " He takes a puff on his cigarette.

"T'aint like it was when your daddy grew up. The big old two story school house is gone now. He was in my class at school—a real serious student."

I think to myself, it's hard to imagine Daddy being here. It's hard to imagine much about Daddy, since I never knew him. I do know that he apparently had a sense of adventure too—just like me. He was another person who decided to do something with his life. As soon as he was grown, he moved away from Raiford—first to Miami and then to New York after the devastating Miami hurricane of 1926.

The summer days passed quickly.

I spent a couple hours every day with Grandma on her front porch. We sit together and chat about little things. She's sweet and quiet. I can tell from her eyes and her smile how happy she is to have me, her only grand-child, there for the summer. When Mother died, she sent a letter to somebody saying I could come and live in Raiford if I needed a place to live. Now that I'm here, I can just feel how much she would have liked that. To me, at the time, Raiford seemed so far and so foreign. I don't think the idea of my going to live in Raiford was ever considered a serious option. But then, I don't know who made that decision; probably the four old ladies in Rochester. It's hard to imagine living here. It's so different from my schools in New York State, even more different than was the school in Louisiana. Or have I just become what they call a Yankee snob?

Sometimes I play with the kids who live nearby. Most of them are boys. One thing we all do is eat watermelon. They grow everywhere so we don't just slice one melon in pieces the way it's done up north.

"Here, you take this quarter." One of the kids hands me a huge piece of melon.

"Fantastic!" I say. I love watermelon and can hardly believe my eyes. I sit down and start eating. This is, for me, a time consuming job. Bite by bite, I eat every bit of red melon flesh. When I'm down to the white rind, I stop and look up.

All the kids are watching me.

"What on earth are you doing?" One says.

"Nothing. I just finished my piece. It was a big piece."

"But most of what you ate ain't any good."

I learn that people only eat the very sweetest center section. They throw out two-thirds of the melon. I got teased. But I also got the best of the melon!

The only problem playing with the local kids comes when someone suggests going swimming.

"You have to stay here." One kid says to me and the other girl in the group.

"Why? I like to swim." I say.

"Because we're girls," the other girl tells me. "Girls don't go to the swimming hole."

"Why?" I ask.

"I don't know. It's just how it is," she replies.

KNOW YOUR PLACE

I'm wiping the sleep from my eyes and stumbling into the kitchen. No one else seems to be around. I guess I did sleep late.

"Morning, Georgianne," I say.

"Lord knows, Miss Carla Lee, everybody else is already had breakfast," says Georgianne. "You come sit down here and I'll fix you some toast."

"That's wonderful," I say. Georgianne's toast was the best thing in the whole world. She melts a big gob of butter in the iron frying pan and then puts the bread in. When one side of the bread is golden brown, she puts another glob of butter in, turns the bread over, and toasts the other side. What could be more wonderful than a whole summer of Georgianne's toast! Every morning!

"Please come sit down with me," I'd say to her.

"Can't do that."

I keep pleading. She just nods and smiles—and stands talking with me from across the kitchen.

I spend the entire summer begging Georgianne to join me and not just to wait on me. She spends the entire summer resisting that invitation. What invisible rule makes her so afraid? Can this change? We have great conversations. She tells me about the little children she takes care of. She says she's 'adopted' them. There always are a bunch of kids by her house. They never come over here. It's never suggested that I go over there. We talk about my school, and what it's like up north. She never sits down with me. I feel bad about that. She just patiently waits for me to finish so she can do my dishes and move on to the next chore. She won't let me wash my own dishes.

"O.K., Carla Lee. You want to see what I'm doing next. Follow me," Georgianne announces when breakfast is over.

We walked out to the chicken coop. First, we gather eggs.

"There's a couple over there. Can you get them?" She asks me.

I run to the place on the straw where the eggs are. Wow! I've never collected fresh eggs before! I've only gone shopping to get them in the grocery store. "The eggs need to be washed off," I observe.

"They're OK for us," Georgianne says. "One or two spots on the shell won't damage anything. You've probably just seen eggs the way they come in the store." She notes.

We put the basket of eggs on the back steps and return to the chicken yard.

Georgianne's next chore is to start planning for dinner. "Tonight we'll have fried chicken," she says.

FRIED CHICKEN

Without any warning, Georgianne grabs two chickens by the neck. She twirls them around really fast—one in each hand.

"Uugghhh! What are you doing?" I ask, shocked at the realization of what it takes to get from here to fried chicken.

"It's the easiest way," she says. "They don't feel a thing."

How does she know? I watch the headless chickens run all around the yard.

Later I told Carole, one of the local girls, about this and she says that her Mother does the same thing. Only, her Mother calls her from her play after fifteen or twenty minutes and says "Carole, go look and see if the chickens are dead yet."

Once the chickens are dead, Georgianne picks them up, take them inside to pluck, disembowel, wash and cook. She spends most of the morning doing this. She picks some beans and some tomatoes from the garden, gets okra from a local farmer and spends more time preparing dinner. Things need to cleaned, peeled, sliced and cooked. Then she makes gravy and biscuits 'from scratch'. No instant packages or boxes of frozen food. I never knew it took so long to fix a fresh meal.

Georgianne fries her chicken in deep boiling lard. She has a big can of lard near the stove. The lard comes straight from a neighbor's hog.

Carole tells me what it's like the day they shoot a hog. "The farmers get the lard by cutting the hog's skin and the fat under it into little squares. When it's heated, it's pretty and real clear. Then it gets poured into these big five gallon aluminum cans. It looks like oil. But, of course, it hardens—not real hard."

Those cans are just like Georgianne's big lard can.

Carole continues, "when Momma is making biscuits she just opens the lard lid and reaches down in and gets a hand full."

I remember watching Georgianne do the same.

Carole says she'll tell me later how they cut up the bacon and the pieces of ham and the pigs knuckles. "They usually take the rest of the pig to the house of someone who can smoke it."

Georgianne fixes a delicious dinner. Her fried chicken batter is thick, just the right amount of pepper. Unforgettable. Real southern fried chicken. I'm eating this delicious meal.

With each tasty bite, it's easier and easier to forget what happened in the chicken yard after breakfast.

A DRIVER'S LICENSE

"S.B., S.B., guess what I just discovered." I run out to great him as he returns from a day's work. "I can get a driver's license in Florida. This is exciting. I'd have to wait another whole year in New York State."

"So?" S.B. says.

"Can you teach me to drive?" I ask my uncle.

He thinks for a minute and scratches his head. "O.K., I'll teach you. We'll go out this Saturday."

"Thank you. Thank you so much. Not only do I have to wait until I'm sixteen in New York, but there's nobody to teach me in New York State." I think one of the best discoveries of the summer is Florida's law allowing kids to get licenses when they turn fourteen.

S.B. taught me to drive in his enormous Buick. He seemed a little nervous, as he got in on the passenger side and I got in behind the wheel.

"Now, remember what I told you about staying in your lane on the highway," S.B. cautions. I'm headed off down a county road outside of Raiford. "There aren't a lot of cars here, but if one comes around a curve, it will expect you to be on your side of the road."

At first I go very slowly and am very cautious. Then, since things are going alright, I speed up a bit more—just enough to go the standard 35mph.

"Watch out!" S.B. says sensing that I'm a bit too far toward the right side of the road.

"Oooh. Oh. What's happening?" I hear a sssscccchhhrrreeechhh!!!!

"Carla Lee, turn the wheel." S.B. shouts.

I do. We get back on the proper lane. Soon I find a place where I can pull over. I stop.

We both get out and look at the damage. Fortunately it's not too bad; but I did side-swipe the bridge we just crossed. Put a dandy scrape the full length of S.B.'s well polished car.

S.B. is not looking happy. He drives home. I sit in the passenger seat.

"Just think," I say. "It could have been worse. I could have gone off the side of the bridge." "But seriously, I'm really sorry, S.B." I felt bad.

S.B. didn't seem to be amused.

By several days later, he had had the side of the car repainted and he was ready to take me out driving again.

This time S.B. took me to Daytona Beach. It was an hour or so from Raiford, but I guess he thought it would be safer. Here I learned that it's good to drive near the water, not away from the water where it's drier. I thought I should stay out of the way of the people who wanted to swim. I get the car stuck in the sand. It took us about two hours to dig the car out of the sand.

All S.B. ever said was, "it's best to drive on the hard sand, next to the water." I wonder if S.B. will be happy when I go back up north? I don't think I appreciated his kindness.

I took my test and got my license! Good thing there weren't other cars to park between when I had to parallel park.

SUMMER ENTERTAINMENT

Sometimes I'd go with S.B. to the Union County Court House in Lake Butler.

The old Court House building is truly the loveliest architecture in Lake Butler. It's an attractive stately stone building sitting back in the center of a large lawn framed with giant live oak trees draped with Spanish moss.

I'd hang around his office, watch him in the Court Room, and with the other court officers. It is my first introduction to courts.

It's fascinating mostly because the things that happen here really affect people's lives. The courts can stand up for people who are victims. They can also protect us from criminals. Sometimes what the court decides seems fair; sometimes it seems harsh.

Sometimes, when he has time, S.B. takes me on day trips.

We see the shrimp fleet on the Atlantic coast. We saw the Navy ships moth-balled in the St. John's River Harbor. He took me to the Steven Foster home on the Swannee River. We sang some of Foster's songs at home in the evening. I like singing them with Grandma and S.B.

"I dream of Jeanie with the light brown hair, borne like a vapor on the summer air."

Another time we went to see the Greek sponge divers in Tarpon Springs. They have made a Greek community right here in Florida. America is such a wonderful mix of people. I'd like to go to Greece one day. I guess it's all about people living their dreams.

MANHUNTS AND THE PRISON

Some days S.B. doesn't know what to do with me. So I ride with him in his car—wherever he goes. One day he takes me with him and the Sheriff on a man-hunt. I'm not quite sure why the judge is going along with the sheriff. I guess that's how they do it here.

We speed down the highway—several police cars and S.B.'s car.

"Now, when we stop, you stay in the car. Lock the doors!" S.B. calls to me in the back seat.

"I can't hear you," I reply.

The sirens are loud enough to be heard in New York, I think.

"Lock the doors! Don't get out!"

The car pulls onto the grass at the edge of the woods. The men get out. The other car has two men and a dog.

I sit and look out into the woods. It looks kind of swampy. I wait. I wait some more. I hear nothing. About a half hour later they all trudge back with a guy in handcuffs. They pile him into the police cruiser. The sheriff got into the cruiser. S.B. gets into our car. We drive home. No one discussed what's happening with me.

"Have a good day?" S.B. asks my grandma. She doesn't move around a lot. She's sitting on the porch and motions for me to come and sit with her. I do.

"Just another day at work," he replies as he heads off to wash up for dinner.

One day S.B. suggests a unique day trip.

"Carla Lee, do you want to go with me to the State Prison Farm today?" S.B. asks. "I've got some business over there and you can get a tour at the same time."

"Sure."

I've been curious about the State Prison. I've never seen a prison before, and certainly I've never lived near one. I wonder what it's like for people who are sentenced there, for people who work there?

"You have to leave all personal belongings at the front gate," S.B. says. "So don't bring anything with you."

We drive the five miles to the State Prison Farm. This prison is the location for all death row prisoners in all of Florida. It was here that all the electrocutions occur. The chair where people sit to be electrocuted is called "Old Sparky" because it is so old that something is wrong with the wiring and it occasionally shoots sparks when someone is sitting there and the electric power is turned on.

It's mid-day. We go through the formalities to get past the front gate—and then through a second area where we are searched and where all personal belongings are left. We pass more guards and finally we enter the prison grounds and go to the Warden's office.

"How are you S.B.?" My uncle is greeted. "So this is your niece."

I smile and shake hands.

"Well you come with me, young lady." One of the guards says to me. "We'll give you a tour while your uncle is in a meeting here."

I follow the guard. He shows me where people sleep, where they grow their food, where the women's quarters are. The women aren't in individual cells like the men. They are in one big fenced in cell where everyone has a bed and a small night stand. It's like a cage. You can walk all around it. They have no privacy like the men in cells do.

"Most of the men are out on the chain gangs for the day," the guard tells me. "You pass them when you drive down the highway."

"I know," I reply, thinking of the men dressed in black and white striped uniforms and chained together. They cut brush and do other roadside chores. They are guarded by a man with a shot gun.

The State Prison Farm at Raiford is a low-rise modern prison. I think, in 1955, the buildings are fairly new. It doesn't have the tall walls one sees on prisons up north. It has tall barbed wire and occasional watch towers. It has a number of buildings, some larger ones, some smaller.

"Over there is a row of bungalows," I'm told. "Prisoners on good behavior can live in a bungalow." We walk through the prison library and the laundry. "Some prisoners learn the printing trade and publish a magazine—complete with poems and stories written by other prisoners."

"Can I have a copy of their magazine?" I ask.

"Sure. I'll get you one," the guard replies.

We pass the section where Florida auto license plates are manufactured. We pass the kitchen and a dining area.

Now we're at death row.

The guard moves me through the hallway past the cells of death-row inmates. These people, only a few feet from us, will be killed in the weeks and months ahead. I can hear them move in their cells. The cell window is too small to see them. No one talks.

The guard explains, "We have several small rooms here—an anti-room, a place for essential equipment, a spectator area, and the area with the electric chair itself." We walk through each of them.

"This is our electric chair," he says and proceeds to explain how it works.

There's no emotion on the face of the tall young man with the crew cut as he shows me how things work.

I'm looking at this simple wooden chair with a high straight back and wooden arm rests at right angles to the back. It's on a small pedestal. There are leather straps attached to the chair for strapping one's head and chest and arms and legs and ankles. My heart is in my throat. When I shut my eyes, I see one of the people, whose cell we just passed, brought out here, strapped in, and then—when the switch is thrown—he goes limp. He's dead.

"Go ahead, sit down." The guard urges me.

I very gingerly sit on the edge of the chair. The wooden seat is worn, as are the leather straps that fasten a person to the chair. I'm counting the straps—one over the lap, one across the chest, a couple to fasten legs to the wood, a couple more to fasten arms, one to fasten something to the top of a person's head. Ooohhhh, it makes me shiver.

"That's O.K. I think I've sat long enough," I say to the guard. I'm thinking to myself that there's no need to find out how the straps work.

"See, here's the switch. The man who is the executioner works from over here—behind the chair." The guard talks on. He's fascinated with every detail.

"And all these chairs are for the witnesses."

"Witnesses?" I ask.

"Oh, yes. It's a state law that a certain number of people must witness an execution. There's a strict procedure." The guard finishes his lecture on how to electrocute someone. He just does a job; he doesn't make the policy about what to do.

I wonder to myself whether or not "Old Sparky" murders prevent murders?

THINKING ADULT THOUGHTS

We walk quietly back to where I meet my uncle.

"Old Sparky's" malfunctions—shooting flames and sparks instead of only volts of electricity through the person sitting in the chair even made the national news.

Back at Grandma's this evening, I start packing to go back up north. I think about my day. I'm quite certain that I'll be the only girl in my 11th grade class who sat in an electric chair over summer vacation—maybe the only eleventh grader in the U.S.A.

I'll have to think about this. Just one old wooden chair. For some people, it's their job to carry out a task. For some people, it's the end of their lives. For some people, it's supposed to symbolize justice. (That's hard to understand.) For me, it's a vacation experience. There's something sick about this.

Leaving is hard. I love these people and they love me. For Grandma Brooks, I'm all that's left in her memories of her oldest son.

"Would you like to stay here and go to school in Lake Butler? Grandma and S.B. only asked once. They didn't elaborate.

I couldn't quite imagine it; I was really getting to like my school in Syracuse and didn't want to change schools again.

"I think I needed to go back," I said.

It wasn't until years later that I realized how quickly a life changing moment just passed—and I wasn't even focused on the meanings of all those words, for me or for Grandma.

Saying good-bye is always such a mix of bad and good.

I'll be a junior in high school now. Georgianne promises to help grandma send me a box of pecans—straight from the tree.

She keeps her promise—every year for many years. S.B. says he hopes that I'll be a good driver now that I have a license.

"Good-bye. I love you. I had a wonderful summer."

I get on the Greyhound bus for the ride back to New York State.

"Good-bye," Grandma says as she wipes the tear from her eye.

I nibble on pecan praline candy, boiled peanuts, and Georgianne's biscuits all the way north. I marvel at my experiences in the rural south—at the love and warmth so close to the surface in this southern culture. I read some Faulkner in my English class last Spring. I think Faulkner's description of the rural south is true—a place filled with just the "truths of the heart"—"love and honor and pity and pride and compassion and sacrifice."

But I wonder if this isn't true most places; it's just more visible in the way people do things in the South.

I'm glad I have three days on the bus to think about these things. I'm so happy to have spent time with Grandma and S.B., but I don't think I can understand why the memories and hopes brought the tears to grandma's eyes. It's something about history that I don't know. And, it creeps into the present

Chapter Eleven

New Worlds

THE MINISTER'S FAMILY PICNIC

"Oooh." I scramble to swat the mosquito that has just bitten me. Here I stand, at dusk, with fifty Congregationalists in a mountain meadow in North Barnstead, New Hampshire. I'm at a mosquito banquet!

We sing silly songs. "Ninety-nine Bottles of Beer on the Wall." "There's a Rabbit in the Woods." We sing camp songs. "Kum Ba Yah." "Red River Valley." We sing spirituals. "Amazing Grace," "Go Down Moses."

We're just finishing a scrumptious picnic. People sit on the ground surrounded by the tall grass scattered with the yellow and orange blossoms of Indian paintbrush. Every family has brought a home made dish to add to the pot luck. There's potato salad, fried chicken, sliced ham, hamburgers, hot dogs, baked beans, and lemon-aid.

"Save room for the pies," Mrs. McConoghy calls out. "Here they come—lemon meringue, apple, and blueberry from the berries on our mountain."

"We need more ice," the man churning the home-made ice cream says. "I'll get some. Who wants to turn the crank next?"

We take turns. We crank and crank and crank. Making ice cream takes a long time. I've never seen anyone make ice cream like this before. Mother made ice cream in an ice cube tray when I was little. It was really good. She made my favorite, grape-nut ice cream. But *this* is different. Finally it's time to scoop a big blob of ice cream onto the top of the pie.

"Such wonderful ice cream! Makes you forget the mosquitoes—well, almost." I comment to one of the picnickers.

It's nearly dark and time to leave the meadow. We sing again. "Day is dying in the west; heaven is touching earth with rest. Wait and worship while the night sets her evening lamps alight." Rev. Harris leads the group and plays the old pump organ that some men have hauled up onto the meadow from the tiny manse where we are living at the bottom of the hill.

I hope the organ doesn't tip over; it looks a little lopsided perched on the hill.

When the group leaves this evening, summer will end and people will travel back to New York and Connecticut and Massachusetts. I've returned from Raiford just in time to spend this last summer weekend with the Harris's Tomorrow, I go with them back to their house in Syracuse.

My junior year in high school begins in two days.

The reds and purples in the sunset grow intensely. Huge white puffy clouds float in the blue sky; now they turn pink. After some people talk, we sing again. We finish the evening with "For the beauty of the earth; for the glory of the skies; for the love which from our birth over and around us lies." It's true. It is beautiful. It's beyond anything anyone here can create. Nature is amazing. The Spirit here is amazing.

I've never had a weekend quite like this one. I like it because the people care about each other—although I think they may only really care about those who they think are "like" them. But it's a step in the right direction. One small part of me is like them; but I'm fortunate to have also spent time with a lot of people who are not like them. I like people are having fun together; that's always good. It's been a weekend that will be remembered—for most people here. It think that the reason must go past what one saw or did. So what does that mean? I don't know.

Ellie, the Harris's foster daughter, and I both have experienced a lot of situations that aren't as harmonious as things seem here. Have the people here experienced hardship? You wouldn't know it. It seems like they take so much for granted. Or, maybe, everyone's life has hardships and people just don't talk about it. Like my Mother's experiences. Like Doreen's WWII refugee relatives? Hardship in the past must make a difference in how a person looks at the future. Doesn't it?

"Ellie, do you ever feel, when you are here, like Cinderella at the ball. All of a sudden reality will return and Cinderella will be chased away from this all too perfect gathering?" I ask.

"Hmmm." Ellie doesn't say much, but I can tell from when she decides to keep to herself that she has the same feelings I do. I've learned to be a bit wary.

This is Fall, 1955. The Harris's house is the 13th place I've lived in my 15 years of life. The Harris's are the ultimate Dick and Jane family, yet they care about other people.

Where would I be if they hadn't let me live with them, even after I didn't leave at the end of that first weekend?

MISS SEVENTEEN

It's the Harris's oldest daughter, Diane's, senior year. Today the photographers from *Seventeen Magazine* are at our house. They are following Diane's day. She's been selected as a national "Miss Seventeen" winner. One issue of the magazine will feature her, what she wears, and what she likes to do.

"Diane, that's a really pretty dress," I comment as we meet upstairs before she goes down for the photos.

"It is pretty, isn't it? They are loaning me a whole wardrobe to wear today."

"I get to choose one outfit to keep," She says. "Gotta run. I'm supposed to be downstairs." Diane bounces down the stairs to start her memorable day.

I have to admit that it is exciting to see this national magazine bring people here—to my house and my school. But, at the same time, when I look at the magazine, it's just about clothes and how to look. It's not about how to deal with the many things a kid confronts—families, dating, social strata and who's considered O.K. or not, broken families, adults who don't tell kids what's going on, career ideas. It's just puff.

Maybe I'd like puff better if I had learned how to do all the fashion and make-up and social protocol stuff when I was a kid living alone during my first summer as a teenager. Probably it's just me. Probably I'm a 'spoil sport' and I should forget my past and learn 'puff'. To think mostly about 'puff' sure looks like the key to happiness—or at least pretend happiness.

I don't know if I want to like that.

Suzie is standing with me at the top of the stairs. "Look Jim, Diane's boyfriend, is playing the trombone now. His friend Norm is playing the piano."

It's a little early in the morning for the band, but this is the time the magazine set for the photos. Diane is posing in front of the group that is playing Dixieland music.

"The band sounds pretty good," I say. "Good rhythm."

"Hold that pose." *Seventeen's* photographer calls as he flashes pictures of Diane and the band from every angle.

I watch. I wish the magazine would spend more time on Diane's role as an officer of our Student Council. That's where she really is doing some things that make lives better for other kids. But I guess that's hard to picture in zippy photos, and nobody wants too many words.

Time passes. One day Mom Harris brings in the mail with the finished copy of the magazine featuring Diane.

"Look," Ellie says. "They call Diane 'the minister's miniature daughter.'"

Diane is short, small framed and very attractive—especially when dressed in the *Seventeen* wardrobe. The caption fits the situation—and it fits the magazine's image.

DIFFERENT VIEW

Ellie's from a big family that has had problems since she was very little. She and her brothers have been in and out of orphanage living for over a decade. Ellie's really talented. She likes to paint. She sews her own clothes. At school, Ellie is a bit of a loner. She never pledged a sorority. I think she is a victim of the social strata thing; she never had a chance. Ellie sees graduation as the end of education and the beginning of a new and independent working life.

"Don't you want to go on to college?" I ask her one day.

"Why?" She says. "It doesn't get me a better job, and it just costs a lot of money that I don't have." Maybe she's right.

She never talks much about it, but I think everyone around her convinced her that it just isn't practical to go to college. Maybe her view is coupled with a dislike of people who think that they are better because of all their education. The social strata thing magnifies this idea. As an adult she won't have as much problem with this, I hope. Kids in high school can be so cruel to each other.

I think Ellie could be an art professor like my Mother. She'd be good too. Is it too bad that she doesn't see that? I don't know.

I know Ellie looks forward to the time when she isn't anyone's foster child. She's had her fill of welfare bureaucracy. I think she views her time at the Harris's house as one more stop she needs to endure. She thinks the Harris's don't like her brothers. Sadly, she's probably right. Her brothers' life style is pretty different from that of the Harris's. Ellie is practical and is a survivor. She's spunky, to be sure, but she seems to have been taught that she won't win big and that she should abandon her dreams before she's hurt.

While my childhood has similarities to Ellie's, I have totally different expectations for the future. Somewhere along the way I saw the stars, and I decided that I need to catch one to ride on. Why? I've seen people do that and make a difference. So, why not believe it possible? I guess I've just not been shot down as much as Ellie has. Too bad Ellie can't reach for the stars. She deserves the chance. (Maybe she just sees different stars.)

ESCAPING THE FAMILY SERVICES AGENCY

"Carla," Mom Harris calls to me. I've just returned from school. It's late September. "I'd like to meet you after school tomorrow to go to visit a social worker at Family Services. She wants to talk with you."

"Really?"

This is a surprise. No one ever told me that the Harris's and Family Services were talking about me, again. I probably should have guessed that they hadn't planned for me to stay with them another year.

This is a worry to me. I've had enough change.

What's it about? "Why?"

"Oh, we'll discuss it when we get there. I'll pick you up outside the side door of school tomorrow, O.K.?" Mom Harris replies. She moves off into another room.

I hate it when no one tells me what's going on. Don't adults see how inconsiderate this is?

I meet Mom Harris as directed. She and I arrive at the Family Service office after school.

"Come in to my conference room," the social worker says to us.

"Did you have a nice trip last summer?" she asks after we settle ourselves.

"Oh yes," I say, not offering any elaboration. I'm wondering who has been talking with her? How does she know I was away for the summer?

"Now, tell me what your hobbies are, Carla?" she asks.

"I like lots of things," I reply, purposely not answering in more detail. I'm thinking to myself. Who is this woman? Why are we meeting her? What a silly ploy—trying to put me at ease by asking my hobbies.

"Do you like school?"

"Yes."

I think to myself, that there's no reason why I should make this easy for here since nobody's been fair with me by telling me why we're meeting.

Mom Harris just sits quietly. The social worker fills out some forms. We leave. I'm still not sure what this about.

"Family Services just keeps track of kids who have had problems," Mom Harris finally says on the way home.

This really irritates me. Kids who have problems are kids who are delinquents or criminals or kids who are truants or who can't get along with people. I'm not one of those kids; I'm a good student and I have friends and I get awards and I get elected to Student Council. I can't help it if all the adults who were supposed to raise me just disappeared. *I* am not the problem; I'm just trying to live a normal life! The problem is defining "problem kid" as anyone who is not part of a Dick and Jane household. Why do they try to turn me into a problem kid?

I say nothing. I slam the door just hard enough so that Mom Harris knows I've been upset by this Family Service meeting. And I go off to my room.

Time passes. We have a huge Halloween party. I focus on Halloween.

"Ellie, come help me hang these donuts on strings," I call. It's almost time for the next event at our party.

Diane comes over, too. "Our costumes really worked out well," she says.

We had made red and white diamond sleeping shirts with matching night caps. We each carried a lantern in addition to our 'trick-or-treat' bag. Our theme has something to do with Rip Van Winkle—if you have enough imagination to make the connection. Anyway, a half-dozen silly kids running from house to house in the dark is an adventure by itself. The theme is secondary.

"Trick-and-treating is fun," I say. "Look at all the candy everyone spilled out on the table. We'll eat for weeks."

We dunk for apples. We have races to see who can eat the dangling donut fastest—without using their hands. It's one more fun party at the Harris's house.

Sunday morning follows Saturday's parties. This is a regimented routine. Up. Dress. Eat, In the car by 8:30. Church doesn't start until 11:00, but Dad Harris has to get ready for the service, and the choirs need to robe early. Each of us is in a choir. The high school choir wears red robes. The Harris family is always the first to arrive at church and the last to leave. Ellie, Diane and I are caught up in that activity along with everybody else—except when things get boring.

Shhhh. Don't tell anybody, but there have been times when four of us from the high school Sunday School class sneaked off to the Ladies Room to play cards.

I do like singing in the choir. Some of what they talk about in our class makes sense. For example, I like that Jesus, symbolizes a kind of power so very different from the power of kings. If it is in today's English, the point of these stories is powerful. Now we're learning all about all the other religions, Catholics like the boy down the street, Jews like Doreen, Hindus like Mother's student. I'm fascinated because I think that what people believe must influence what they do. Thing is, you have to guess ahead of time what will happen in the Sunday School class, or you get stuck there when it is boring. You can't walk in, then leave to go play cards.

"It's Monday. Today after school, we're going to Family Services again," announces Caroline Harris. "I'll pick you up in the same place. Family Services has someone they want you to meet."

"Who?"

"I don't know their names, but we'll find out this afternoon."

It is all still vague. She picks me up. We ride, silently, to the appointment.

"Hello, Carla Lee," says the social worker. "Come in. Nice to see you again"

I don't reply. Why pretend that it's nice to be here? And, I can't say out loud that it isn't nice to be here.

Mom Harris and I go into her office and sit down.

"There's a lovely couple in the other room. I want you to meet them in a minute. The man is a lawyer downtown. They live in a beautiful home up on Onondaga Hill. They've never been able to have children of their own. They would like you to move into their house, to live with them, to be their daughter. Isn't that wonderful? You'll have a real family, all your own. A good upstanding family at that."

The social worker proudly makes her announcement and sits back like a satisfied matchmaker, ready to close a case.

"Ummm, this is a surprise," I say. "I didn't know I was looking for a family. What if don't like them?"

I wonder about this couple. She says the man's a lawyer; I wonder what the woman does?

"Oh, you'll like them. They are lovely people. Come now, let's get on with it. I'll bring them in," she replies as she walks over to the door to her conference room.

The couple comes in, tall, attractive, prosperous, and hopeful. They are very friendly. We all sit down. They chat. I listen. They have been told that this is a completed transaction. If they like me, I'll go home with them. I don't think it had ever occurred to anyone that the transaction might fall through. It had all been so professionally arranged.

I feel like someone has suddenly thrown me into a prison cell from which I can not escape. What business does this agency have filling out all these forms about me? What business do they have arranging my future? What is going on with the Harris's? Why are they so nice, on the one hand, while arranging to get rid of me, on the other hand? What is happening with this poor couple? They seem nice. Certainly they should be able to have chldren if they want. But, wouldn't it be better if they were matched with someone who needs a family?

"Thank you very much," I struggle to say without bursting into tears. I figure I'd better be polite, but it isn't easy.

"I don't really need a family, you know."

I continue, "You see I know who my daddy is. He just died when I was really little. And I remember my Mother. I don't need a new Mother. I like my own Mother just fine. She just died too. I have a grandma in Rochester, and another one in Florida. No. I don't need a new family."

Silence.

No one seems to know how to respond.

"Well why don't you just go over to their house for dinner?" The social worker is trying desparately to keep her plan together.

"Yes, Carla Lee, please come for dinner," says the nice would-be Mother.

I don't think any of these adults have ever had someone say no to a plan they had developed—certainly not a plan for 'a client', a kid.

I feel badly for the couple who had been promised a daughter. They were nice people. Certainly after they have searched their souls to decide if they can risk taking in *a teenager*, rather than adopting a baby, and after Family Services has processed all their forms, everything should be in order. 'No' doesn't seem to be an option.

Mom Harris is silent. She watches. She never knows what to say at times like these. Besides, if I don't go with the couple as arranged, I'll probably be going home with her again. From the beginning, I'd only been invited 'for a weekend'. She must have initiated the Family Service placement process last Spring, before I went to Raiford. I can see the Harris's deciding that matching me with a good family is the thing to do. It would be best if her family only had the four kids they intended. It would be best for the childless couple. It would be best for me. I'm sure she sees this as 'the Christian thing' to do.

"No," I say. "Thank you for the dinner invitation. I'm sure you are lovely people. I'm sure I'd like your home. I just don't need a family. That's where I stand. There's no sense in your thinking this will work out. It won't."

I think to myself that I simply can't move *again*.

I'm really shaking. I don't know if these people will listen to me. I never said no to an agency before. Can I do that? I have gotten away with saying no to some grown-ups before—miraculously. But what choice do I have? I'm angry. How dare they upset everything again? I've got to not burst into tears.

WHEN AGENCIES ARE GOOD; WHEN THEY ARE NOT

I go home with Mom Harris. The social worker apparently decided that this meeting has done enough damage. Adjourned.

"Whew!" I say. "I hope that's over."

Mom Harris doesn't reply.

"I don't get it," I say. "Everybody at church and at school talks about how important kids are. You always hear adults saying that. Well, if we're important, how come nobody ever talks with us, or asks what we want?"

"The adults work very hard to do what's best for you," Mom Harris says.

She doesn't get it.

The more I think about it, the more I realize how very fortunate I am that the Harris's didn't just put a foot down to say that I couldn't go back to their house after I went to Raiford for the summer. And they haven't made me move out to this Family Services' family either. That's pretty fantastic! I bet most families wouldn't be that nice.

Ellie and her brothers were never given any choice by the welfare agency that 'put' them in an orphanage. They got told where to go, and went. Nobody ever cared what they thought.

Most of the kids at school who weren't allowed to take professional track courses never were asked what they wanted. Someone just 'put' them in a track that would determine their entire adult lives.

When I was little, my friends from Madison never had a chance to go to a better school; the school officials just 'put' them in Madison. Institutions can be dangerous; they can take away someone's hopes and dreams. And a kid is just forced to go. The people in the institutions don't even see how cruel they are, they think they are helping. That's scary!

On the other hand, sometimes institutions can help—if they can stay human. When I was little, the school officials let me go to Thornton rather than Madison—but only because Mother knew how to deal with the school institution. When I started high school some anonymous teacher helped me get into a sorority—the track required for would-be high school leaders. My "Voice of Democracy" contest speech talked all about when a government institution can be good—like when Abraham Lincoln was President. The Student Council is an institution, and we do some things that help the school. So—how can I know if an institution is going to be helpful or if I'm going to feel trapped?

I'm 16 now. I'm definitely more than grown-up. But I am still legally a minor; I have to be very careful to get my way on these important matters. I don't need to change families or houses or schools again. I've done enough of that! Soon I can go to college, have a career and go to Paris. Then I'll be free to not have to find people who will let me live with them.

KID'S RIGHTS

Junior year is moving on. I'm reading textbooks about world history. I'm studying German and third year Latin. We learn what famous people do to make changes in history and in current events.

I wonder if normal people can change things? I think maybe we kids should try. The adults aren't exactly fixing all the things that are wrong. Some don't even try.

"Does it seem like we have to do all the chores here?" I ask Ellie.

"Diane gets to go out with her boyfriend," Ellie observes. "You and I do more chores."

"In school we read all about how things change when people stand up for their rights," I say. "Remember, In our *Weekly Reader,* how we hear that people who want Eisenhower for President work on his campaign to help him win. They don't just watch. Remember when we saw on T.V. what people did to stop the McCarthy Hearings, the witch hunts looking for Communists in Hollywood."

"I remember all that," Ellie says." What does it have to do with us?"

"You gotta stand up for what you care about. Otherwise, no one will ever listen." I announce. "Don't you think we need to tell Mom Harris what we think about distributing the chores so it's fair to all five of us, so the foster kids don't just get most of the work?"

We protest.

"Why do I have to take out the garbage again?" says Ellie. "I did it last week."

"When is some one else going to wash the kitchen floor?" I say. "I did it last week."

"Everyone has to help," says Mom Harris. "Diane is a senior. Jimmy and Suzie are much younger. These things weigh in to deciding what's fair."

That is one point, I guess.

We made our point, too. Time will tell if we made any difference. Mom Harris digs in her heels and can be very firm. But, I think she tries to be fair.

She can be tough, though.

"Where are my shoes?" I can't find them anywhere.

"When I get done with this floor, I need to wear them in order to go to the movies with some kids from school," I complain.

"Your shoes?" Mom Harris asks with a twinkle in her eye.

"Yes."

"Well, they must be in your closet. Surely you would have put them there when you took them off." She says looking at me.

"They're not in the closet."

"Surely, you would have put them away. All I know is that I found some shoes in the middle of the floor near the TV set. I thought they were trash, so I threw them out. They can't be yours, can they?"

"You what?"

I pay for my own shoes from a limited allowance. This simply won't do. I don't have enough allowance money to buy more shoes. I race out of the house and poke through the garbage can until I find them.

Mom Harris won that time. I learned to put my shoes away when I took them off.

We finish the assigned chores. Mom Harris manages to settle these things with a mix of humor and firmness—no fights. No further discussion. Move on.

THE ICE CREAM SHOP

"Really? Are you sure it's OK to eat as much as we want?" I ask my boss, the owner of Marble Farm's Ice Cream Store.

This is my first day at my first job. I work here after school and on weekends. Having a real job is a first step to being really an independent adult.

"Sure. Go ahead," he says for a second time.

"Now I think you know how things work, where to store things, how to wait on customers, how to handle the cash register, and how to lock up at night. If you don't have any more questions, I'm going home now."

Two of us are new employees. The shift manager is still here. He's stayed to watch how we do. It is spring of 1956. I just turned sixteen and I am able to get my working papers.

The weather is warm and the shop is really busy. Scooping ice cream is harder than I had thought it would be.

"Jan, is your wrist getting sore?" I ask.

"Well it wouldn't be so bad if fewer people order strawberry. The strawberry ice cream is really frozen—nearly impossible to scoop." She turns back to the counter to serve one more customer. I take a new customer.

"You want one banana split, a hot fudge sundae, and two double cones—one strawberry and one pistachio?" I say confirming a customer's order. "That will be $3.50, plus $1.25, plus $.60 times two. That's $5.35 plus tax," I say. "Are you planning to take them all out to the car?"

I scurry to fill the order—which was the only thing harder than remembering the order. But I like the variety of orders and I like that new people come in all the time. I can't imagine that I'll ever be bored with this job. Imagine—a real job, and I get paid.

Eventually, the crowd lessens and we have a few minutes to ourselves. "Mr. Marble says we can eat as much as we want," my fellow clerk reminds me.

"Right," I reply. "How many scoops can you put on an ice cream cone? I ask.

That starts the contest. "You've got four," I note. "Let me see if I can get a fifth one on this cone."

"Each scoop is a different flavor," says Jan. "See—no strawberry. I have one chocolate, one fudge ripple, one vanilla, one pistacio, and one grape-nut. Maybe I'll try lemon next. I can try a sixth scoop."

"I have an idea," I say. "It's really hard to keep them from falling over with so many scoops. The cone has more and more balls balancing on it. But, if we decide it is fair to put a piece of wax paper on one side, then we can hold it whenever it starts to tip."

"Hey, let's do that," Jan says. "Let's see if we can get 10 scoops. That's almost one of each flavor."

"Do you think anybody ever buys 10 scoops," I wonder.

"I don't know," Jan replies. "Do you think we can eat 10 scoops?"

"Good thing it's nearly closing time. Maybe nobody else will come in," I say hopefully.

We start eating, and eating, and eating. I love ice cream, but my mouth is getting very cold. After about four scoops—it really seems like enough. I'll never admit it. I eat. Jan eats. We eat and eat—until the last drop is gone.

"I really feel sick," I say.

"Me too," says Jan. "I'm glad it's time to close the shop.

After that day, neither of us ever ate ice cream on the job. It just wasn't appetizing. I guess Mr. Marble knew what he was doing when he told us to eat whatever we wanted to.

BOYS

Springtime of junior year is also the time for a new kind of parties—dancing with boys. The school holds dances on Friday nights. Different classes decorate the gym. One of the teachers with one or two kids handles the record player. They bring the music and take turns changing the records. Sometimes the kids go to a dance with a group of friends. Sometimes we double-date—that is two couples go together.

Elvis Presley is our hero. His style of dancing is something we've never seen before. Everyone tries to copy it.

"Can you jitter-bug?" my friend Cathy asks me.

"I don't think so. Remember the day we tried to jitter-bug at my house. I can't do this in front of other people," I comment.

"Bet you do before tonight is over," Cathy teases.

We're standing by the punch bowl watching the dancers.

Some of our friends are 'going steady.' That's one step short of 'pinned.' These kids twine around each other on the dance floor and sway dreamily back and forth, bodies inseparable, cheeks glued together, eyes closed.

"Look at Tom and Lindy," Cathy says. "You couldn't pry them apart."

"How about Mike and Sue?" I point.

"You want to move more toward the dance floor?" Cathy says. "Then we'll be where people know we're available to dance."

"O.K." I say. "Who's there to dance with?"

I'm in the group who comes with other girls and waits to be asked to dance when the music starts. When we do dance, we never quite know whether we'll have our toes stepped on, or if we're expected to twirl and dip, or if the dance will be like the merger of two tin soldiers in a box step regimen. And, we're very shy about waiting to be asked. It would be easier to just run out and go home; but juniors in high school are supposed to do this.

"That boy is cute," Cathy says.

I look and agree. We whisper and giggle.

"Wanna dance?" A boy named Bill asks me. I go out on the floor with him. Fortunately it's a slow dance.

"I like the lighting," I say. It's very dim. A giant crystal ball rotates in the center of the ceiling. Tiny mirrors reflect the light in a thousand directions.

Bill dances on. I put my head on his shoulder, the way I've seen the other girls do. We share a dreamy three minutes until the music stops. We walk over to the punch bowl.

"Thank you," he says.

"Nice dance," I reply. Then I hurry back to where the girls are because I don't know what else to do. I don't really know how to act around boys. While it might be fun to go steady or be pinned, I need to know more about dating before I get too involved.

Just now, I'm not sure which is worse—having a boy who likes me, or having boys not like me. Later, maybe I'll date.

The boys huddle on one side of the punch table. The girls are on the other side.

"Pretty dress," Cathy tells me.

"Thanks," I say. "It's a *Vogue* pattern. I made it last week. I know you make some dresses too. You can borrow the pattern if you'd like. I like to sew my own clothes."

"Hey, come jitter-bug." Paul, this really cute boy, reaches for my hand.

Here goes, I think to myself. He's too cute to say no to.

"O.K.," I say as we move out toward the dance floor.

"Here, twirl around," Paul says.

I do.

"Let's hold two hands and both go around twice." Paul says. We do.

As the evening passes, both Cathy and I are jitter-bugging as furiously as anyone else with a range of different dance partners. Sometimes we just gather as part of a circle around a couple whose dancing is particularly flashy. We clap to the rhythm of the music. They dance.

It no longer matters if anyone missteps.

TOLGA

Our class has a new member this year–an exchange student. Tolga is from Turkey. He's sponsored by the American Field

Service—the international exchange program. He attends our school for the whole year and lives with a family. The idea is that we learn from him what Turkey is like and he learns from us what America is like.

One day in homeroom, I had a chance to talk with him before class.

"You know so much about history and geography and all these things," I say. "How did you ever learn all these things?"

"Well, you know," he says, "our school at home is much harder than yours is. We have more subjects, harder subjects and longer hours in school. We have to memorize a lot."

"I didn't know that," I say.

"Besides, I live in Europe and we have to know geography because so many countries are close to each other. America has oceans on either side of it, and you don't really need to know that there are other places and other people in the world," Tolga explains.

"My Mother taught at Syracuse University and I was friends with one of her students—a girl from India," I say.

"India is still a long way from Turkey. I guess you could say that Turkey is in between Europe and India." Tolga seems pleased that someone wants to hear about his home. We talk more. He tells me that his school doesn't have the clubs and social activities that we have here. He also tells me that almost everyone at his school speaks more than one language. He tells me that he is Muslim and that Islam has common roots with Judaism and Christianity, but that people practice it differently. They have a call to prayer, sort of like music or chanting. It can be heard all over town from loud speakers—several times a day.

"I'd like to hear that," I say.

"Maybe one day I'll have a recording of it that I can play for you," Tolga adds. "Or, you can go to Turkey."

"I'd like to go there."

"Your English is so good," I say. "I wish I could speak a language that isn't my own. It must be hard to do."

"I'm getting a lot of practice since I arrived in Syracuse. Before I came here this year, I only read English in books."

"One day I want to go to Paris—when I have a career. My Mother did that," I tell him. "I want to learn so many things."

The bell rings. We have to take our seats. I'm day-dreaming about going to far-away places.

AN AMAZING OPPORTUNITY

"Carla Lee," my teacher calls. "The guidance counselor wants to see you—now."

I take my hall pass and head to her office. What can this be about? I don't think I've seen her since that first day over three years ago when we had that disagreement about whether or not I could take college preparatory courses rather than the courses on the secretarial and business track. I hope by now she's realized that I know what I am talking about.

"Come in, Carla Lee. I haven't seen you for a long time," Mrs. Brown says. She motions me to a chair in her office.

"That's right," I say.

"You're more than half way through your junior year already."

"Yes. I'm really busy. My schedule this semester is a good one."

"Let me tell you why I've asked you to come here. Do you know Tolga, our student from Turkey?"

"Yes, I really like talking with him."

"You know that the AFS program works both ways. Central High has a Community Ambassador come here, and we pick someone from our junior class to send abroad," Mrs. Brown says.

"Yes, it's a wonderful program." I add.

"It's time for us to send the applications to New York for the four people the school will recommend as finalists for American Field Service (AFS) ambassador to represent Central High School in Europe this coming summer. The faculty would like you to be one of the four finalists."

"Me?"

"You want *me* to be one of the four applicants?" I really can't believe what's happening.

"Yes. I'd like you to fill out these forms. You need to write an essay about why you think it's important to be a Community Ambassador. You need to return everything to me by a week from today. I'll be sending all four applications to New York together."

"Sure, I'll fill out the forms," I say. "Can you tell me how the program works?"

"Yes. Central participates in the American Field Service Community Ambassador Program every year. AFS headquarters in New York will review our four applications and they make the final choice. One, maybe two, of you will be selected to win this award."

"If I win, what happens? When will we know?"

The more I think about being an AFS student, the more excited I am.

"They place you. You don't have a choice of which country you will live in country or a choice of which family you will live with. While you are in Europe, you will need to write letters back for the local newspaper, and you will have speaking opportunities to tell us all about your trip when you return. While you are abroad, you are a Community Ambassador meeting people and talking with people and explaining what it's like to be a teenager in America." Mrs. Brown seems really happy to explain this.

I pick up the material she has prepared for me. My legs turned into wings. I soar out of her office above the clouds.

I don't tell anyone, because nothing is certain yet. Better not to count on something that won't happen.

I do tell Mom Harris. "That's wonderful, Carla Lee," she says. She tells the other people in the family. Everyone shares in my excitement.

"How do I get a transcript?" I ask. I need one to put with the application.

"Go see the clerk in the school office," Mom Harris says.

"And, I have to have two photos and a doctor's statement saying that I'm healthy. How do I do that?"

"Don't worry. Don't worry. We'll get Virginia from church to examine you and write the doctor's statement. She's on the faculty at the Syracuse University Medical School. Saturday you can go downtown and get the two pictures. I'll tell you where." Mom Harris is an organizer.

I forget about my homework. I spend hours pouring over the application. There are so many questions about interests and viewpoints. The essay requires a lot of thought. I also need to figure out what countries are my first three choices and why. I need to tell them what I can do as a Community Ambassador both in the country abroad and reporting back to the kids here next fall. These are all things I've never thought about before.

"Here it is, Mrs. Brown." I turn in the application. "How long before we hear anything?"

"AFS headquarters will take several weeks to make their choice." Mrs. Brown says. "You need to just go ahead with your regular plans because we won't hear until just before school is out."

"I don't think I can endure the waiting."

BUILDING A CARNIVAL WAGON

I focus on school and working at the ice cream shop. I try to forget about AFS. They probably only choose kids from Dick and Jane families, I'm convinced. They will never let an orphan or a foster child become a Community Ambassador. It's probably not proper.

The next day several of us meet after school to talk about the upcoming Student Council elections.

"If we start a new political party, how can we be sure it will succeed," I ask David, the instigator of this plan. He thinks we need a third party to get some better discussion of important school issues.

"Well, we can't be sure," he replies. "But wouldn't it be fun to do something new in this election. The two parties that exist are very boring. There's not even much interest in the election. Everybody just yawns their way through the whole thing. People should care. They should vote. Council decisions matter. It's our future at stake."

"So, what can we do? We don't want to be some fringe group that everybody thinks is 'kookie,'" I offer.

"We don't want to do this if it splits the vote and the worst of the three candidates wins," I finish.

Jan adds, "It's not a problem. We've got good candidates. The two of you plus Mike and Ellen would all be great. Three of you have been on the Student Council before. You are all clearly leaders in the class and would make good Student Council officers for us when we are seniors. The Council can make such a difference for kids. It set all these policies for the special events, for the assemblies, for getting the freshmen involved. Starting a new political party will liven things up—make people stop and think."

She continues, "Besides, I think all three sets of candidates would be O.K. No one is really horrible. We're just best. And— we *can* win."

"O.K.," Jim joins in. "But, let's think of something that will get everybody's attention. There are twelve hundred kids at Central. Probably a couple hundred won't vote. They didn't last year, or the year before. We've still got to get almost four hundred of them to like us in a three way race. That's a lot. That's more than all our friends added up—even if you add our friend's friends."

"How about some sort of hat that the four of you wear every day?" Jan suggests.

"I don't think they let you wear hats in class," David replies.

We banter ideas back and forth for the next twenty minutes and finally decide to build a carnival wagon—one about six feet tall and six feet long.

"Carla, can you design it? You're good at art." Jan asks.

"I can try. Where do we get the cardboard? They have to be really big pieces." I ask.

"I know a store that has big pieces. I'll get that," Mike offers.

"We can build it and paint it in the Harris's driveway," I suggest. "Then when it's painted, we'll have to walk it to school. I will take several of us to hold it together and lift it up and down curbs."

"No problem," Jan says. David and Ellen agree.

"This will be great," David says. "When it's at school we can park it in the hall and in the cafeteria. It will attract attention to our new party and our candidates. The candidates can stand near the wagon before and after school and at lunch."

"Good idea," Jan says. "If we find enough people to help, we can have one person by the wagon to pass things out to kids going between classes. Of course this all depended on where the administration lets us put it. They probably have all sorts of rules about not blocking stairways and passages. We'll have to propose some visible, yet out of the way places."

"There, we have a plan," Ellen applauds.

"Jim, you go see the Vice-principal to get permission and locations for the wagon. He likes you and you can probably talk him into this plan," David says.

"We need the wagon to really look like a carnival wagon, and to be very colorful," Mike states. "We can use broom stick pieces to make the wheel axles."

"I can make some space in the empty side of our garage. We can work on it in there," I say.

"We'll need a lot of duck tape."

The following week the six of us meet every spare moment at the Harris's garage. I design the wagon and orchestrate the production. One person cut triple thicknesses of three foot diameter circles. We tape three together for each of the four wheels. Another person gets two broomsticks for each of the axles. It took some figuring, but finally we had a plan for fastening everything together.

"Careful," David says. "You can't cut the broomsticks that wide. The wagon won't fit through a door. We've got to be able to get it through the doors at school."

"Good point." Mike says.

"Here, I have six different colors of poster paint and some brushes," Ellen adds.

"Now let's go over these fliers again. You all need to like what we say we'll do for a party platform. There's a mimeograph machine at my church and I arranged to use it after school today to make the fliers," Jan plans.

We work together, debating and finalizing what we stood for and what we would do if elected. We add a short paragraph on why we are running and why a new party is needed. A few days earlier we had each gone through the cafeteria at each of the three lunch periods with questionnaires. We want to get some idea of what kids think about our ideas before we formalize our flier. We want our campaign to be a democracy, just like the real one is supposed to be. Surely if we listen to the kids and say we'll represent their interests, we'll win. We call our new party *The Representative Party.*

"There. That's the last thing to paint," I exclaim as I put the brush down from having written *Representative Party* in big letters on both sides of the wagon. We had already painted the names of all four candidates on all four sides.

The wagon is done. It looks like a cross between the coach they used in England for the recent Queen's coronation, a real carnival wagon, and something parked at the Emerald Castle for The Wizard of Oz. In short, it looks just fine!!

"I hope it doesn't rain the day we need to take it to school." I say. "If it rains, the paint will wash away and the wagon itself will melt into mush on the pavement."

Fortunately the sun is bright. Four of us meet at my house at 6:30 AM—as soon as it is daylight. School is over a mile away, and there's be no way to get the wagon there other than to walk it. Really, we need to sort of carry it. The wheels look great, but they don't really roll.

"Finally," David says. We've just gotten inside the school doors.

"I'm exhausted and I have blisters on my hands," says Ellen.

"Me too," I say. "We're all in the same fix. But we made it!"

It certainly did attract attention. Word got around; go to the hall near the science labs to see the carnival wagon. People came. We passed out our fliers.

TICKET TO THE FUTURE

It's early June—a school assembly day. All the kids shuffled into the auditorium and found our seats with our homeroom teachers.

We stand. "I pledge allegiance to the flag—" Then we sit and listen.

The principal makes some announcements. "There will be a new driver's education course beginning next week right after school. Seniors need to be sure they have ordered their *Yearbook*. The school still needs six more chaperones for next week's dance. Please ask your parents to volunteer. Will Carla Lee Brooks and David Dittman please come up on the stage?"

I had been reading something and not paying much attention. "What's happening?" I whisper to the person next to me.

"I don't know, but you better get up there. He called your name. It was right in the middle of chaperones, year books, driver's ed, or something like that."

My seat mate hadn't paid too much attention either. She's trying to finish a homework assignment. No help. So I start to the long walk to the front of the auditorium. Everyone is watching—except for those whispering, sleeping or doing their homework.

I walk up to the stage. David is coming up another aisle.

The principal has one of us on each side of him. He says, "I'd like to present to you, the students of Central High School, your Community Ambassadors for 1956."

Everyone applauds. We look shocked. At least, I'm sure I do.

He continues. "Carla Lee and David have been chosen by the American Field Service to join the most outstanding high school juniors from across the whole United States to live with families in Europe this summer. Each of them will live in a different community. It will then be their job to report back to the school and to the larger community about their trip and their impressions. We are proud of our two runner-ups, and we are proud of Carla Lee's and David's accomplishments."

"I can't believe it. I don't know what to say." That was all I managed to say. I hope I remembered to say thank you, and I'm honored to be chosen. Wow. After all the horrible things that have happened in the last four years, I just can't believe that something so wonderful is happening. I really do get to be an ambassador of sorts. I'll spend three months in Europe. I'll learn new things, and get started on my career. I'll do things that matter. And it's a scholarship. "I can't believe it. It's totally too amazing!"

I think a lot of the kids are really surprised that I have been selected. They don't think I come from a typical American family. Cathy tells me she heard a couple kids whispering about that. I get along O.K. with the kids after all this time together, although I always feel a little out of place with Dick and Jane kids. But I guess that doesn't matter just now. It doesn't matter what people think or say. Imagine that.

"Too bad," I say to Cathy. "I can't do anything about how they feel. I've already been selected. All I can do is be the best ambassador that I can be, for those kids and for everyone. Maybe that will make it O.K."

"Maybe next time I see them I can suggest that they consider that a good Community Ambassador might be someone who has had lots of different experiences (like you have) rather than someone who is just the same as they are." Cathy offers.

"That's a nice thought. But I doubt if they will understand that. I think that my complicated background might be helpful when I try to understand people who come from cultures not like our own. But, why would those girls understand that? It's not worth having a fuss with them."

"You deserve this," Cathy says.

"Thank you. Thank you so much. Any ideas about what you would like your ambassador to do?" I asked.

AT LAST!

School is out. I'm packed. The Harris's drive me all the way to New York to meet the other AFSers and to catch the ship to Europe. The orientation is over and we're on the dock.

"What a big ship!" I exclaim when I see the 'Arosa Kulm,' our home between today and when we arrive in Europe.

"There's the gang plank," Dad Harris says. "Let's find your cabin."

He and Mom Harris and I lug all my belongings onto the ship and down a million narrow stairs to where my bunk is.

"It's even bigger when we're inside," I remark

"We better go now," Dad Harris says. "You have a splendid summer. Make us all proud that you are our Community Ambassador"

"Bye!" I stand at the rail and wave. "Byeeeee!" The Harrises are moving out of the terminal. They are getting lost in the crowd.

"Where will you stay?" An AFSer from Massachusetts asks me. We're both on deck watching the boat push off from the dock.

"I'm on my way to Germany. I'll be living with a family of a school teacher in a small village about one kilometer from the East German border. It's supposed to be very rural. They have two daughters and a son. Their daughter, Heidi, is close to my age. Most of the family doesn't speak English so I'd have to practice my German," I say.

I can hardly believe what I'm saying.

"I'll be with a family in Denmark," she says. "It's near the German border. Maybe it's near your host family."

"Look, there's the Statue of Liberty and Ellis Island." A boy on deck points to these monuments. The ship is blowing its whistle. The breeze is stiff. Tiny waves slap the side of the ship. "We're leaving the United States. Before long, we won't even see our country. How strange." It's weird to think about all the changes ahead.

"Did you say you are from Chicago?" one boy asks another fellow standing near us.

"Yes, and I'm going to Italy," He replies. "John, here, next to me is from Washington, DC and he'll be in Greece."

"I'm from Ohio and I'm going to Belgium," says the girl on the other side of me.

I look around on the deck. I think about going two stories down where my bunk is—scores of bunks—every one is for a new AFSer. This ship may be leaving America, but several hundred teenagers from most states in the U.S.A. are taking America to Europe with us. We're going to learn all about Europe. How exciting! Everything is new!

How fortunate we are! So few American high school kids get to travel to a different continent in 1956! I'm really overwhelmed by what's happening. I find it amazing that I've been chosen to be part of this.

It's the second day on the ship. We're all assembled on the main deck for a short meeting about our summer schedule.

"You'll be with your families for five weeks. During that time, there may be a couple small gatherings for the six or eight of you who are living in the same town. Otherwise, you won't see any Americans. Then, in mid-August, we'll all meet for a week in Paris. We'll stay in several different hotels there, see the city, travel a bit in the area, and then take buses to Le Harve where we catch our ship home," The AFS Representative in charge of the arrangements announces.

"We'll be in Paris!" I exclaim to the girl sitting next to me.

"That a wonderful surprise," she says.

I simply can't believe what's happening. It's a life long dream come true. I wish I could tell Mother that I'm really on my way to Paris. I have a thousand questions about her time in Paris. Too bad I never thought to ask her before she died.

The trip is more amazing every day.

We've been on the sea now for a week. We're somewhere in the middle of the Atlantic Ocean.

"When I get back, I plan to start visiting colleges," John says. "I plan to be a lawyer. My folks want me to stay in New England, but I'm not sure."

"I'm interested in Penn State," says Mary. "My brother goes there and I went to visit him."

"I'm trying to decide which schools I'll apply to for pre-med. I think maybe Johns Hopkins in Baltimore," adds Ellen.

"I'm not sure what I want to major in, or where I want to go," I say. "My Mother was a university professor. She taught art. I think I'd like to do that. But, I'm also interested in political science and languages like Latin and German. Or maybe I'll take philosophy or religion."

"Sounds interesting," says Paul.

"I think so. I'm new to thinking about colleges. No one at my school has ever talked with me about that yet. So I like to listen to you debate where to go to school. It gives me new ideas."

What a new world I am in.

If all these other kids already know so much about college choices, why don't I?

I just think that neither the Harris's nor the guidance people at Central High really think I'll go to college. Most college kids have parents who pay. Charlie Close said that Mother left some money for me, so I'm not going to worry. Besides, I don't know enough about money to know what to worry about. I'm just going to plan what college I want to attend—and hope I can figure out how to make it happen! Such exciting conversations!

Breakfast is over, and some of the people at my table are practicing for tonight's skit. Every night, different AFSers are in charge of entertainment. Tonight is 'New England Night.'

John has written a song and has all the AFSers from New England singing and dancing .

"And here we go…," he directs the group.

"Up in beautiful New England, we have colleges to burn. The people from the south and west all come up here to learn. We work and work all night and day. So, we can't help it if we play!"

"Again. Let's make the first line a chorus." John says. "Who can invent another verse?"

"Look at that ship," Mary shouts. "Is that the QE II?" It's our thirteenth day at sea. Wasn't the Queen Elizabeth II ship the ship in New York harbor the day we left? Didn't it leave after us?"

"It is. It did leave after us."

"We must be really slow," Tom says. The QE II is passing us for the second time, first going to Europe, and today it's going back to the U.S.A."

"They say our boat has barnacles on it. It's a ship that only carries students—something about flying under a Panamanian flag. I guess it's cheaper that way," offers John.

"Who cares? We're having a very special time," Mary notes.

The QE II sails ahead and eventually disappears from sight. I'm standing alone by the bow of the ship. It's getting stormy and everyone else has gone inside. I need some time alone to think about the kaleidoscope of ideas and experiences I'm encountering. I need to figure out how all this affects what I might want to do and how that can happen. .

There's a stiff salt wind blowing through my hair.

The sea is gray.

The sky is gray.

The clouds are very busy. And there is nothing else—as far as I can see. Just gray.

I watch the spray of water when the waves and the ship collide.

Each drop stands apart—for just a second or two. Some drops are big. Some have an almost rainbow reflection.

The spray from the waves is silver against the gray water. It's delicate and powerful at the same time.

"Am I really here—part of this amazing new adventure?" I say almost out loud.

So many new and exciting discoveries are presenting themselves. The kids I've been talking with have figured out what future direction interests them. It's time I do the same.

The sea is mysterious, a place where one could easily slide overboard and just sink down and die—without notice. People do die. I know that—better than a lot of people. Death is so close to life, so close. But, how sad when people just choose death; they miss so much.

The sea is mysterious for another reason. At the same time that it's possible to see death, it's possible to see life. The sea, while gray, is a shiny surface carrying us through and beyond the horizon—to exciting new worlds, new life.

The gray nothing is like an empty slate to draw upon. To look at the sea is to dream and hope.

I know one thing now. I'll survive growing up. I'm on my way to new frontiers. But, truth be told, I'm only surviving because a lot of people were in the right place at the right time, a few as mentors, others to create hurdles out of their ignorance, others to motivate me to overcome the hurdles. It's as if each year, under the Christmas tree, I have another strange set of gifts. They've not been the usual kid Christmas gifts. Each year, it's a challenge not to be derailed into the "problem kid" people say all orphans are. Each gift, instead of derailing me, has offered new opportunities to learn what goes on in the world and how to keep reaching for the stars.

It's amazing to be here on this ship to Europe. But, I can't let my guard down. I must remember to keep being determined. It's the best way to get past the obstacles—and have an adventure doing it. It is tricky, because you've got to not hurt people. What's rewarding is to learn what others care about and why in order to do things that make everyone's life better. It's got to be more about 'them' than 'me.' That's really hard to control when it's 'me' doing the doing. But, that's the only way there is value in what gets done. There's so much to learn.

I'm ready to follow that gray shiny sea through the horizon and on to the future. I've acquired a spirit, a viewpoint, a way to approach tomorrow as result of surviving all 'my Christmas gifts' and because many people have been at the right place at the right time for me. The future is exciting. It's challenging. It's a little scary. And, God, I hope I get it right.

AUTHOR BIOGRAPHY

Carla Lee Brooks Johnston returned from Europe, earned a B.A. in Religion from the College of Wooster in Ohio, and an M.A. from Andover Newton Theological School in Boston. She was later awarded three post-graduate fellowships at Harvard. She married, raised two children, provided a home for two foster children and a number of international exchange students. Her career combines being a university professor, author of seven books, and a public policy maker (both as head of government agencies and as two term Mayor of Sanibel Florida.) Her focus is strategic planning and management and the role of the media in public policy. She has lectured in 34 countries on 6 continents.

Some of her efforts that she values include: stimulating a new era for Somerville, MA, a city that faced huge problems in the 1960s-1970s; as staff to elected officials, curbing run-away budget of the metropolitan Boston transportation authority in the 1970s; as head of metropolitan planning agency, introducing programs to link planning to actual development in areas where local government jurisdictions crossed and where useful progress could only be realized by integrating previously separate funding (transportation, environmental protection, housing, etc.); in the 2000s, as elected official, negotiating collaboration between biologists, engineers and land use professionals in order to change water release policies that damage SW Florida; and as chair of elected official group, securing vote to return a corrupted $10M federal earmark for a road not wanted to the U.S. Congress.

Her hope is that these efforts contribute to reduced financial burden for families and improved quality of life. 'What a ride,' is how she describes the spirit that drives her to solve these three-dimensional crossword puzzles. 'I'm humbled by the opportunities on my plate.'

www.carlabrooksjohnston.com